THE NOSE K[illegible]

Claudius, having ac[illegible] objective, snarled at the clothes and dug at them furiously with his front paws.

Disgusting, but at least he hadn't lifted his leg. "Stop that!" Annie commanded. "Get away from there!"

He turned and glared at her, head lowered, a menacing growl deep in his powerful throat. When faced with a hostile dog, the books advised one to keep calm and speak cajolingly in a nonthreatening voice. "Come on, boy. Come away from that," she said, trying not to make eye contact with him. She concentrated on his front paws.

A dark red liquid was dripping from them. It looked like blood. . . .

She pulled the leash with everything she had. "Come here! Heel!"

He came like a lamb, leaving wet red prints on the macadam, nudging her leg with his cold nose, whining, telling her something was very wrong with the pile of clothes. . . .

Wolf at the Door

An Annie O'Hara & Claudius Mystery

Ann Campbell

A SIGNET BOOK

SIGNET
Published by New American Library, a division of
Penguin Putnam Inc., 375 Hudson Street,
New York, New York 10014, U.S.A.
Penguin Books Ltd, 27 Wrights Lane,
London W8 5TZ, England
Penguin Books Australia Ltd, Ringwood,
Victoria, Australia
Penguin Books Canada Ltd, 10 Alcorn Avenue,
Toronto, Ontario, Canada M4V 3B2
Penguin Books (N.Z.) Ltd, 182–190 Wairau Road,
Auckland 10, New Zealand

Penguin Books Ltd, Registered Offices:
Harmondsworth, Middlesex, England

First published by Signet, an imprint of New American Library,
a division of Penguin Putnam Inc.

First Printing, May 2000
10 9 8 7 6 5 4 3 2 1

Printed in the United States of America

PUBLISHER'S NOTE
This is a work of fiction. Names, characters, places, and incidents either are the product of the author's imagination or are used fictitiously, and any resemblance to actual persons, living or dead, business establishments, events, or locales is entirely coincidental.

To my dear friend, Gentleman Jim

Chapter One

For the sixth time in the past hour, Claudius, a.k.a. the Hound from Hell, jumped into the front seat and lashed Annie O'Hara in the face with his tail.

"Goddammit!" She took a hand off the wheel of the rented Escort and shoved him away. "Try that again, and I'll stop the car and leave you here." "Here" was Appaloosa, on Route 30, in eastern New Mexico, the land of enchantment. A ribbon of road under the hot summer sun.

Claudius gave her a look of contempt and turned his attention to the passing scene: a sleazy-looking pawn shop, two bars, and a couple of skinny cats slinking around an overflowing dumpster. The outskirts of town flashed by as she pressed down on the accelerator. The houses straggled down to one or two. The overall impression was bleak. Porches rough with flaking paint, screened doors half falling off, and bare, dusty front yards. Then a few stunted trees, empty fields, and one dead scrub oak poking at the sky with jagged black branches.

Seven crows were roosting in it. *Bad luck, Annie.*

Bad luck was something she already had plenty of, thank you very much.

She glanced at Claudius. In the front seat again, he leaned forward, peering through the smeary windshield with an expression that appeared inscrutable, but which, after six weeks of forced togetherness, Annie could easily read. He was bored, looking for something or someone to bark at, to break the monotony of the long car ride. PROUD HOME OF THE APPALOOSA HUSKIES LITTLE

LEAGUE TEAM. COME AGAIN said a rusted sign put up by the Rotarians.

The wind blew her long red hair in her eyes, and she brushed it away. "Maybe they'd take you on as a mascot. What do you think? Want to get out?" The dog grunted. He was no fool, he knew she'd never leave him off here in the middle of nowhere.

Wistfully, Annie reflected on her life as it had been before she'd given Claudius a home. Days and nights of unmitigated boredom, which her mind covered with a sentimental haze. No fifty-pound bags of dog food to be dragged into the house, no one getting into the trash or biting her fingers, no odorous piles littering the backyard. She frowned. Life with Claudius was very difficult.

He was a German shepherd–huskie mix, an alpha dog—that much she'd gleaned from the books she picked up at Barnes and Noble. He viewed their household as a dog pack. He was the leader; her position was well to the rear. Perfectly logical to the canine mentality, and it explained why it was standard practice for him to knock her down stairs every time she attempted to go up first.

Life with him was worse than difficult. It was impossible.

She'd bought a wire crate for the trip, but he'd destroyed that and eaten the blanket she'd lined it with before they'd reached the New York state line. He'd proceeded to throw up for the next fifty miles. So much for the $150 crate. Since then he'd more or less roamed the front and back seat at will.

She pushed his tail out of her face again, and he flattened his ears and snuffled the inside of the windshield, leaving a streak of drool on the glass. He'd been abandoned by Lydia, her sister-in-law—a first-class bitch who'd run off with her lover and left Tom breathing her dust and picking up after her dog. Tom had dumped Claudius on her doorstep with some sound advice. "He's nothing but trouble. The state prison gave up on him—he didn't like being ordered around. Then the Helping Hand Organization gave him a try and kicked him out, so Lydia got him for free. My advice is to get rid of the damn mutt, take him to the pound."

But she couldn't bring herself to do it. For some reason she felt sorry for him. No one in his right mind would adopt Claudius, who looked like a wolf and had the temperament of a first-class fiend. No wonder he was a two-time loser.

She tried to find a place to board him before leaving on vacation and had discovered another problem—he had a well-earned reputation. She'd called every kennel in a thirty-mile radius and had been turned down flat.

Lydia-the-bitch had parked him in one kennel after another on weekends when Tom thought she was working overtime. Unfortunately, Claudius hadn't take kindly to weekend boarding; he'd retaliated with bouts of nonstop barking and kennel wreckage.

Lydia thought his manic behavior was cute, a tribute to his complete devotion to her. She'd taught him a few stupid tricks: he rolled over on command, crawled on his belly, even danced around on his hind legs and begged. Useless, and to Annie's mind, degrading for the dog. But it proved he was willing to learn . . . if he thought you were worth obeying.

So far he didn't seem to think Annie was.

The Escort was running low on gas, and a Mobil station loomed just ahead. She pulled in and got out to fill the tank. The Hound from Hell leered at her through the half-open window, and she glared back.

A man by a pickup truck at the next pump said, "Hey, that's some dog you've got there." Claudius yawned, his teeth snapping together with an audible click, and the man gave a chuckle of disbelief. "Son of a bitch, he's got jaws on him like a shark."

"He's not mine, thank God."

"Shepherd is he?" The man took out a wad of tobacco and tucked it into his cheek. "That kind of dog, you gotta show 'em who's boss."

"No kidding."

He eyed the Escort. "I see by your plates you're from back East. Where you headed?"

"Roswell."

He grinned. "You some kind of UFO nut? We get a lot of 'em, expect to see little green men running around all over the place."

"No kidding."

"Yep. Damn town's overrun with crackpots." He shifted his wad from his left cheek to his right. "Planning on staying long?"

"No, I'm visiting relatives. My aunt's having bunion surgery."

He digested this bit of news. "Your folks know you're bringing your dog along?"

"Not exactly. And he isn't mine. I'm just watching him for a few weeks for my brother."

He spat a wad of tobacco at his feet and grinned. "Better you than me, lady. Good luck, you're gonna need it." Having gotten the last word, he climbed into his truck and roared off in a cloud of exhaust.

Annie finished filling the tank and went inside the station to pay. When she came out a few minutes later, Claudius was barking wildly at a schnauzer in a car that had just pulled up. The schnauzer's owner took one look at Claudius and drove off without getting gas.

She snapped the leash on him and let him out. "Get a move on. I'd like to make Roswell by dark."

If they arrived just after sundown, Uncle Ira and Aunt Hortense wouldn't actually set eyes on Claudius, which would avoid a litany of embarrassing confessions: her brother Tom's failed marriage and the dog's presence as an uninvited guest.

It was like a sauna behind the gas station. The heat and humidity were suffocating—the kind of weather that spawned outbreaks of unaccountable violence, Annie found herself thinking. Nerves frayed in heat like this, people got jumpy, and men shot their wives for no more reason than a burned meatloaf. Although perhaps in New Mexico, they shot one another over burned fajitas.

Distant thunder rumbled and towering black thunderheads were poised over mountains to the west, but it probably wouldn't rain. From the look of the grass underfoot, it hadn't rained here in weeks.

"Listen," she said, eying Claudius at the end of the

leash. "When we get to my aunt's, the plan is for you to stay in the car until I can hustle you upstairs to the guest room. I'll try and sneak you out for one last walk when everyone goes to bed. Understand?"

He gave her an enigmatic look and shook his shaggy black head.

"It's quite simple. My aunt has a pair of Siamese cats. She's crazy about them. You are not, I repeat, *not* to go after them. In fact, you are not even to look at her damn cats. Understand?"

His ears pricked up at the word "cats," but he didn't change expression.

She raised her voice. "Lay a paw on them and you're dead meat. Get it?"

He continued to stare at her, and if she hadn't known better she'd have sworn he was laughing.

Unfortunately, this was no laughing matter. Aunt Hortense had sent numerous postcards, mainly to update Annie about her bunions, referring to them discreetly as her "medical problem," and while occasionally she forgot to mention Uncle Ira, she never failed to mention the cats.

Yes, Claudius had definitely been smirking, Annie thought as he sauntered toward a nearby trash barrel, dragging her with him.

He lifted his leg, and she decided to change tactics. Not only was he smarter than the average dog, he was smarter than she was. Even worse, he knew it. But, hey, he was only a dog. A dog whose habit of jumping from back seat to front was driving her crazy.

The books said that love was the answer to each and every canine problem. There were no bad dogs, only lazy or stupid owners. Which was a matter of opinion.

On the other hand, maybe they were right and a display of affection would help. Forgetting that Claudius refused to accept petting of any sort from her, she reached down to stroke his head, and he jerked away. "Okay, forget it," she told him and turned her thoughts back to the highway and her destination: Roswell, the retirement home of Uncle Ira and Aunt Hortense.

She hadn't seen them in several years, ever since

they'd moved away from New England. But a month ago, Aunt Hortense had called and asked if she would come to Roswell to help her recuperate from foot surgery.

In a weak moment Annie had said yes. Now however, as she mulled over the next few weeks, she found herself wondering why on earth she'd agreed to it. So what if Uncle Ira had a bad back and wasn't supposed to lift anything heavy. Aunt Hortense could have hired a visiting nurse for her bunion problems.

A picture of her life rolled drearily before Annie's eyes. She was the wrong side of thirty, divorced, and self-employed—the owner of a third-rate antique shop in Lee, New Hampshire—hardly anything to crow about. It was located in her home, the old Thurston Tavern, at the junction of Routes 152 and 155. People who notice old houses tended to slow down at the sight of the tavern. It looked like a wedding cake and was a charming example of New Hampshire eighteenth-century country architecture. Two stories of white clapboarded siding topped by a cupola, where travelers two hundred years ago had passed the nights drinking and gambling. Two side wings, a carriage house and barn, a perennial garden always in need of a good weeding, and an old knot garden bordered by a brick path where two drunken patrons had shot each other dead in a duel.

Through the years, travelers passing through southern New Hampshire—everyone from Abraham Lincoln to Madame Blavatsky—had stayed at the tavern. As a home, it was larger than Annie really needed and had begun to show its age, but she had several year-round boarders, and that plus the income from the shop in the carriage house kept the roof over their collective heads. In fact, one of her boarders, Kirk Deitrich, was watching the shop while she was away. A college psychology professor, he knew enough about country antiques to hold down the fort for three weeks; and she'd left her aunt's telephone number if anything came up that couldn't wait until she got back.

Of course, it wasn't the best time to take a vacation. She'd miss several auctions and the Portsmouth and

Deerfield antique shows, but she was in a rut, so maybe a vacation in New Mexico wasn't such a bad idea. A change of scenery certainly was in order.

She glared at Claudius, who so far had done little but sniff his way around the weeds behind the service station. "Hurry up," she ordered. He gave her another one of his patented accusatory stares, and she turned her head away. He had a point. She wouldn't have appreciated his presence in the bathroom, either.

Having won that argument, Claudius advanced purposefully upon a nearby bush and did his business. They got back in the car and headed west, across the Pecos River.

"It won't be long now," she said.

He grunted and stuck his head out the window.

After a minute, he drew his head back inside and grunted again. "You're hungry. Big deal." She was hungry, too. Happily, there were two or three seedy-looking roadside cafes and a McDonald's just ahead. She went through the drive-thru and bought two hamburgers, two fries, and a coke. The cup of water was free.

Claudius lapped up the water and ate his hamburger and fries. He was still hungry, so she gave him her fries. Naturally, he demanded another walk. He had the smallest bladder in dogdom, she decided, snapping the leash on again.

His metal prong collar gleamed dully in the dying sunlight as he ambled from tree to tree. It was the latest of several methods she'd tried to keep him from pulling her arms out of the sockets. It didn't seem to have much of an effect. Probably his thick fur. Maybe one of those harnesses would work . . .

She was mulling this over when a jogger ran by, and Claudius—having retained a modicum of his prison-guard dog training—immediately went bonkers, barking his head off, lunging, and snarling. "It's not an escaped convict!" she shrieked.

But he'd dragged her halfway down the street before she managed to get him under control, and then only because the jogger had taken one terrified look over his shoulder and high-tailed it to safety inside a nearby 7-Eleven.

They went back to the car and resumed the last leg of the trip. Claudius, grim-faced and brooding about the one that got away; Annie, frazzled and making sure the doors were locked and the windows rolled up. An hour later, just as the first star pricked the evening sky, they hit Roswell. She peered through the gloom, looking for Idlewild Circle. Uncle Ira's letter said it was just off Route 30 once she passed the Krispy Chicken, which, unless her eyes deceived her, was just ahead. A short stretch of neon lighting, a motel or two, some package stores, then a thirty-foot high yellow dancing chicken loomed against the indigo night sky. A sign underneath declared the eats to be the best west of the Pecos.

Annie drove by and prayed she wouldn't have the opportunity to find out. The chicken disappeared in the rearview mirror, and she found Idlewild Circle two blocks past the garishly lit Alien Wax Museum, which Claudius seemed to find of considerable interest. "It's a tourist trap," she told him. "They probably won't let you in, anyway."

He flopped on the seat beside her, and five minutes later, having found number 46 Idlewild Circle, she pulled into Uncle Ira's driveway.

At the sound of her car, Uncle Ira came out on the porch and ran down the steps. "Glad to see you, dear." He kissed her cheek and thumped her on the back, then noticed Claudius glowering at him. "Good lord, what's that—some kind of wolf?"

So much for sneaking him into the house.

"He's a shepherd-husky cross," Annie explained. "I sort of inherited him . . . temporarily. His name is Claudius. I hope you don't mind, but I didn't know what else to do with him, and I didn't want to cancel my vacation."

"Well, it's not for me to say. Don't know about your aunt, though. It's her damn cats, Violet and Daisy—she's mighty fond of 'em."

"Er . . . he's a good dog, really." Lying through her teeth with the unpleasant feeling that she wouldn't get away with it for long. "I'll keep him out of the way."

Claudius gave her an insulted look as she put the leash on and let him out of the car.

Uncle Ira took her bags and led the way up the steps and into the house. As Annie followed, she noticed a woman staring at them from a window in the house next door. "Who's that?" she asked her uncle.

"Our weirdo neighbor, Jan Stalker. She's always poking her big nose where it doesn't belong. Pay her no mind."

Aunt Hortense came out of the kitchen in a housedress with an apron with Jesus's face on it. She was holding a box of plastic wrap, which she set down in order to envelop Annie in her plump arms. She smelled like Toll House cookies and had a mass of suspiciously red hair.

"It's good to see you, dear." Aunt Hortense kissed her cheek. "We just got home, ourselves. There was a party over at the church."

"Welcome home party for the assistant pastor," Uncle Ira muttered. "We were better off without him."

"You don't mean that, dear." Suddenly Aunt Hortense noticed Claudius and gave a horrified shriek. "Get that . . . that animal out of the house!"

The Dog from Hell decided to be sociable and leaned against Annie, wagging his tail and baring his teeth in a reasonable facsimile of a canine grin.

"He's a good dog," Annie lied. "Quiet as a mouse. You won't even know he's here."

"I doubt that," her aunt proclaimed with a sniff. "He looks vicious. What if he goes after Violet and Daisy?"

"He won't go near the cats. I'll keep him under control, I promise."

Aunt Hortense frowned. "They have delicate sensibilities. They're very high-strung, and I won't have them upset."

Eventually they got through her aunt's explanations about the cats, their finicky eating habits, their cleverness, their favorite places to nap, how they "spoke" to her, how "the little darlings" woke them every morning by jumping on the bed and clawing at the blankets, and a few more anecdotes about the spoiled felines. Eventually, she ran out of breath, paused, and asked if Annie was absolutely sure the dog could be trusted around her "sweeties."

"Certainly. Claudius likes cats," said Annie, trying to speak in a casual voice to demonstrate how trustworthy he was around cats.

"We'll see." Her aunt eyed the dog for a long moment with deep suspicion. Finally, she made up her mind. "All right. But if there's one single incident, out he goes." The two cats trotted into view, and she hurriedly pushed Annie and Claudius into the living room. "Sit down anywhere." She waved a hand at Ira. "Close the door and for heaven's sake, keep the cats out." Turning back to Annie, who was now seated on a plastic-covered, brown speckled sofa with Claudius at her feet, "Land sakes, dear, you must be tired after a long trip like that."

"Just a little."

"Driving all the way from New England. My, I don't know where you young people find the energy these days. Your Uncle Ira and I always fly everywhere."

"Sure do," Uncle Ira agreed complacently. "It's less tiring, and we make sure we get window seats. They buzz airplanes, you know. Probably curious about our quaint, old-fashioned method of air travel. Of course, they've grown more careful since the crash of that air force plane in the California desert."

Annie nodded, finding the conversation somewhat bewildering.

"Damn fool government's guilty of negligence . . . along with a great deal more," he muttered. "They should have warned everyone right off the bat, but did they? Not on your tintype!" He put on his bifocals and peered through the curtains at the house next door. "That woman's still at it, spying out the window. Damn it, she's got binoculars. I can't take much more of this. Something's got to be done about her."

"Jan Stalker's a menace," confessed Aunt Hortense. "She can't keep her hands off men."

"Is she . . . uh . . . lonely?" Annie asked. The woman hadn't looked like a man-eater. About forty, she'd had short, straight blonde hair and bangs—a menopausal Buster Brown.

"We try not to be prejudiced." Aunt Hortense lowered her voice. "Mrs. Stalker is divorced. Her ex-husband, Chuck, had problems . . . alcohol. We at the church—that's The Neighborhood Church of the Celestial Spheres a few blocks over on Elm Avenue—well, we put up with a great deal from that man. It was just one thing after another. Finally, he was expelled from the congregation. He phoned in a bomb threat."

Annie goggled at her. "A bomb threat?"

"Yes. He definitely had mental problems, but to my mind that's still no excuse for Jan's behavior."

"I don't understand."

"Once Chuck left for California, where doubtless he thought there'd be more scope for his talents," Aunt Hortense gave a vague wave of her hand indicating the godless fleshpots of the West Coast, "Jan had no outlet for . . . sex. She went completely mad. I always thought she wasn't right anyway. You know—in the head."

"Oh."

"Of course, those sorts of goings on don't jibe with the tenets of The Neighborhood Church of the Celestial Spheres," Uncle Ira informed her. "We try to be broad-minded, but we don't hold with that sort of thing."

"Indeed not," Aunt Hortense agreed. "Our church is founded on harmony and love. We try and spread Christ's Word throughout the universe." She frowned. "As for Jan Stalker, that woman is little better than a common strumpet. Nothing but men, morning, noon, and night. To make matters worse, she's tried every church in town. She's even been rebaptized."

"Five times." Uncle Ira grew pensive. "For some reason, it doesn't seem to take."

"She's made a career out of it," sniffed Aunt Hortense. "It's positively disgusting. She rolls out of the baptismal tank, and on the way home eyes the first man she sees and says the church isn't meeting her needs."

"My word."

Aunt Hortense gave Annie a sudden suspicious look. "That's right. You're divorced, too, aren't you?"

"Yes."

"Hmm. Well, I'll go make us some tea." Aunt Hortense went to the hall door, pulling Uncle Ira with her. "You can help." On the way out she muttered in a voice Annie clearly wasn't meant to hear, "We'll have to keep an eye on her, Ira. You never know."

For the moment, Annie found herself left more or less to her own devices. She looked around the room. Her aunt had a thing for brown. Brown and yellow curtains at the windows, a brown rug, a brown plastic-covered recliner in front of a large TV. Brown bookshelves filled with what looked suspiciously like tomes on The Incident, and on a nearby table, an ashtray stolen from the local Holiday Inn in the shape of a UFO.

She sat back on the plastic-covered sofa and contemplated the oil paintings on the wall. Evidently, Uncle Ira had discovered a heretofore unknown talent for the brush. The paintings were signed I. O'Hara. Silver UFO craft swooped dizzily among the clouds at dawn, at sunset, above a wind-swept field, and over a storm-tossed ocean. A man in a boat in the last picture was waving his hand in what Annie assumed was a grateful farewell.

Here and there among the UFO's, Aunt Hortense's thimble collection was displayed in shadow boxes. She had quite a few of them. Presumably, it had taken years to amass them all.

She sighed. Three weeks of this. Good God.

Chapter Two

"I went over to the church a while ago to see Pastor Pennyworth," Aunt Hortense said at the breakfast table next morning. She had shut up the two cats, Daisy and Violet, on the screened porch before sitting down. Now she raised her voice over the faint, indignant yowling. "His office was shut up tight as a drum, but what do you think I saw?"

Uncle Ira had his nose buried in the paper.

Annie slipped Claudius a piece of toast under the table. Making sure all five fingers were still intact, she asked, "What?"

"That Stalker woman, and she was draped all over John Barnard, the church caretaker." Aunt Hortense's lips pursed in disgust.

Uncle Ira turned to the sports section. "What's he doing over at the church? I thought he went down to Albuquerque to pick up a shipment of hymnals."

"I know what I saw!" Aunt Hortense's voice rose in annoyance. "The old fool's over at the church right now, randy as all get out. They were downstairs in the kitchen by the pizza oven, going at it hot and heavy. She had his pants pulled down around his ankles. He doesn't even wear underwear!"

Uncle Ira lowered the paper. "Really?"

"The man ought to be fired, drummed out of the congregation," she said indignantly. "Half the time he doesn't do his job, and now this? The idea of such goings on in the church!"

"Are you sure about all this?"

"Are you going deaf? That's what I said, didn't I?" She turned to Annie. "Believe me, heads are going to roll! And that's just what I'm going to tell the pastor when I see him. Now dear, what about some sightseeing? We could take a run over to the crash site. It's a bit of a cross-country trek, but if you wear sensible shoes you'll be all right."

"Unfortunately, all I've got are sneakers." A nudge from under the table, and Claudius helped himself to another piece of buttered toast topped with congealed egg.

"Hiking boots would be better." Aunt Hortense eyed the sneakers. "But those will do in a pinch I suppose."

"What about your bunions?"

"I'll be all right. I'll wear thick socks. If my bunions act up, I'll find a rock and sit down."

Uncle Ira folded the paper and put it by his plate. "Well, if we're going, I'd better get my boots. The weather's supposed to be clear, a nice day for a hike."

"If it's any trouble, I don't have to go," Annie protested.

"Nonsense." He smiled. "I'm in the mood for some brisk exercise. It'll do me good."

"How about another egg, dear?" Aunt Hortense suggested, glancing at Annie's now empty plate.

"I'm fine. One was plenty. Really. And I should be doing more of the cooking and cleaning. Whatever needs doing. You're supposed to rest."

Aunt Hortense chuckled. "Don't worry, I get plenty of rest. Look at you, you're nothing but skin and bones. I'll fry one up in no time." Waving away Annie's objections, she went to the stove and turned on the gas under the pan. "These eggs come from Elvira Stubenville's hens. Right next door, fresh as can be."

Moments later she plunked the plate on the table. "It looks delicious," Annie lied, wondering whether to laugh or cry. With Claudius's help, she'd already eaten twice as much as her usual breakfast. And how in the world was she going to make her aunt rest? Other than knocking her out and dragging her back to bed, there didn't seem to be any polite way to take over. This called for diplomacy. Tact. She brooded while Aunt Hortense bustled back to the stove to pour a second cup of tea.

Uncle Ira got up and left the kitchen, saying he'd get out his hiking boots.

The table levitated an inch or so, and Annie picked up the egg in her napkin and slipped it underneath. A cold nose inspected the offering. Claudius took his sweet time about accepting it until she shook the napkin. Apparently he was full, too.

A snuffling grunt. He wasn't happy, but finally deigned to eat it.

Aunt Hortense came back to the table and sat down. "We're having a potluck supper at the church on Sabbath. The service will be really special. Our assistant pastor has just returned from temporary assignment in St. Louis."

"How nice. Listen, there must be a few errands I can run. Shopping, picking up the dry cleaning. I need to put gas in the Escort, anyway."

"We can find something for you to do, dear." She patted Annie's hand and beamed. "Well, I can see our desert air has picked up your appetite, already. You'll be putting on pounds in no time. Now Reverend Elmer Morris . . . he's a fascinating man. You'll adore him. Everyone does. Blonde hair like an angel and a golden tongue. He's traveled extensively. Why, he's been on every continent at least twice. More important, he's received messages from aliens. Telepathically."

"He's a damn con man, probably been kicked out of every one of them continents," grunted Uncle Ira, returning to the kitchen. "Why would aliens want to talk to him? Morris lies faster than a horse can trot, runs up bills all over town, and worms money out of foolish women. Says he needs four or five women a week, if you please. Last summer he really hit the jackpot. Ruth Ann Henderson bought him clothes, gave him $1300, a color TV, and her credit card."

"It's not all Reverend Morris's fault," protested Aunt Hortense. "Ruth Ann's crazy about him. He has quite a way with women. His last wife—the one in South Carolina—gave him a house and a car. Then she found out about his debts and kicked him out."

Uncle Ira laughed. "It's typical of the church conference to bring in a dog-and-pony show to cover up their own shortcomings. They pull a boner over that damn satellite dish and think the church members are gonna forget it with the assistant pastor returning. Well, it's not going to work. Morris is nothing but a flimflam artist. I called last week's meeting of the elders to deal with that"—looking meaningfully at Aunt Hortense—"and a few other things."

She raised her eyebrows. "You mean whether or not to sell those—"

"Yes, the . . . artifacts."

"What artifacts?" asked Annie curiously. "Like saint's bones?"

He shrugged. "Something like that."

"Anyway," Aunt Hortense said, going back to her original line of thought, "the assistant reverend is a marvelous speaker. You've no idea how many converts he's brought into the church."

Uncle Ira laughed. "If you mean that bunch of freeloaders who showed up last month, then—"

"Why are you always so negative?" Aunt Hortense glared at him. "Landsakes, there's no fool like an old fool!"

"You can say that again. What I'd like to know is why women always fall for creeps like Morris. He's going bald, and women still can't get enough of him. It's gotta be some damn menopausal thing."

Aunt Hortense's formidable chest puffed up like a pouter pigeon. "What are you hinting at, Ira? That I made eyes at the reverend at the party last night?"

Annie cleared her throat. "Er . . . I should fill up my car if we're going to do any sightseeing."

"Go and do that, dear," Aunt Hortense snapped. "Your uncle and I have a few things to hash out anyway."

"Darn right we do," Uncle Ira grumbled as Annie got to her feet and beat a hasty retreat.

Ten minutes later she was in McDonald's, downing hot coffee. She'd have driven right on by, but Claudius had recognized the golden arches and barked incessantly until she stopped. The coffee was a little strong, but she was in no mood to complain.

A pair of black canine eyes stared at her from across the parking lot. She turned her back to the window. But it was no use, so she ordered a hamburger and large fries and took them outside where Claudius devoured everything but the pickle.

Briefly, Annie reflected on the dog's former life with Lydia-the-bitch. If it could be characterized as a life. Used and abandoned—as Tom had been—Claudius, like Tom, had given a full measure of love and devotion to a woman who didn't deserve it.

If it came to a choice between what was between the ears or below the belt, men generally chose the latter. That old devil sex—in other words a basic commitment to stupidity—to which Tom wasn't immune. A sucker to the end, he'd have taken Lydia back in a minute. And now, a good six weeks later, Annie suspected he still hadn't smartened up.

To give Lydia her due, she was good at what interested her. She'd memorized the Khama Sutra forward and backward by the time she hit puberty, and after she left, Tom said wistfully that her lover was probably getting the best sex he'd ever had.

Well, if that was love, Annie wanted none of it. In her case, once up the aisle had been more than enough. Three months of marriage to Lenny Crandall had been an eternity. In court that last day, Lenny the cheapskate had balked at paying a thirty-six-dollar light bill. Enraged, she'd almost walked away from the agreement, but her lawyer brought her to her senses. Did she want to get on with her life or endure an endless round of bickering over pennies? In the end she gritted her teeth and anteed up the thirty-six dollars. She hadn't seen Lenny since, although he sent her occasional postcards from glamorous places. In winter, they invariably came postmarked Barbados or Bimini. Summers, they tended to originate from somewhere in Europe. Lots of cramped writing, indicating he was doing very well, thank you. Wine, women, and song. He was a louse.

It crossed her mind, and not for the first time, that

divorce was a marvelous institution. Life was much better being single. It might be lonely at times, but at least you knew where you were . . . not living with someone who wouldn't recognize truth and honesty if it walked up and bit him on the ankle.

Deep in reverie and having forgotten her place in the canine scheme of things, Annie started the car and absently reached over to pet Claudius. He jerked his head out of reach and eyed her with derisive scorn. What did she think she was doing—taking liberties again?

"Okay, forget it," she told him. "Sorry, I thought we could be friends."

He grunted, which she took as a grudging acceptance of her apology.

They couldn't stay away from Idlewild Circle forever, so after driving around for a while, she headed back past the dreary outskirts of western Roswell, past the Pristine Cleaners, Jiffy Lube, and the Wayside Carwash, almost to the dubious delights of the Krispy Chicken eatery and the Alien Wax Museum, vintage 1956, entry to which cost $5 by the painted sign out front.

Not much traffic on the streets. It was not quite eleven, but already the sun was pouring down heat from a deep blue sky. A few clouds formed on the horizon, but seemed to dissolve over the mountains to the west. Vaguely annoyed and reluctant to rejoin Aunt Hortense and Uncle Ira just yet, she turned down Elm Street, one up from Idlewild Circle.

It was the lack of green in the scenery, she realized suddenly. She was used to small New England towns with gracious old wooden houses built in the 1700s, narrow, winding roads, and green everywhere. New Mexico, and Roswell in particular, seemed to be mostly shades of brown. Broad dusty streets, beige stucco buildings, everything commercialized and nothing older than 1900. The town made every effort to be welcoming and gracious, but didn't have much to work with.

Just then something white caught her eye. There, a half a block ahead, stood The Neighborhood Church of the Celestial Spheres. It was a white-steepled building that sprouted various additions and extended sideways toward a fenced parking area. Trees shaded the church, which had a sturdy, artless purity and looked well-tended. An old graveyard stood behind the church. The grass between the headstones was clipped smooth and green—evidently the caretaker found time for a few mundane chores between sexual encounters with Jan Stalker.

Curious in spite of herself, Annie pulled over and got out. The parking lot was practically deserted, with only a small dark blue Toyota parked in front of a trash dumpster. The license plate said Missouri, the Show-me State. Tomorrow was Sabbath, so she deduced that the car belonged to the fabled Reverend Morris.

Claudius, bless his soul, had to go again, so she clipped the leash on and let him pull her determinedly through the fence and across the parking lot to the nearest tree.

Apparently nothing doing. They went to the next tree and the next, Claudius charging forward like a fiend, ignoring her determined commands to heel.

"Do you have to christen every tree in Roswell?"

He headed toward the Toyota, where he stood on his hind legs to inspect the back seat. She hauled him down and he whined loudly and dragged her around the back of the dumpster. About fifteen feet away was a pile of old clothes and what looked like a discarded shoe. Claudius, his ruff stiffening and his nose quivering, caught sight of the clothes, barked, and took off like a shot.

Peeing on old clothes—doubtless leftovers from the church clothing drive—wasn't kosher, so Annie dug in her heels and hung onto the leash with all her might. "Heel! Heel, dammit!" But the dog was past the stage of obeying, and she was all but airborne on the end of the leash. When she came down, she grabbed the lid of the dumpster to keep from falling on her face.

Claudius, having achieved his objective, snarled at the clothes and dug at them furiously with his front paws.

Disgusting, but at least he hadn't lifted his leg. "Stop that! Get away from there!"

He turned and glared at her, head lowered, a menacing growl deep in his powerful throat. His white teeth gleamed—she had a vision of slavering jaws. Her heart skipped a frightened beat. There was something truly terrifying about his expression. His glittering eyes and stiff-legged stance suggested imminent attack, as if he'd suddenly reverted to his wolf ancestry.

When faced with a hostile dog, the books advised one to keep calm and speak cajolingly in a nonthreatening voice. Don't stare straight at them—that was taboo. Her legs were shaking. She swallowed, conscious that he sensed her fear but unable to hide it. "Come on, boy. Come away from that," she said, trying not to make eye contact with him. She concentrated on his front paws.

A dark red liquid was dripping from them. It looked like blood—which was ridiculous. She'd seen no sign of broken glass. What would blood be doing . . .

She pulled the leash with everything she had. "Come here! Heel!"

He came like a lamb, leaving wet red prints on the macadam, nudging her leg with his cold nose, whining, telling her something was very wrong with the clothes.

Apprehensively, she moved forward. Claudius, she realized with a burst of shock, was right about the clothes. There was something wrong with them. The suit was blue serge, and there was a man inside it. His hair, what there was of it, was blonde, and he wore only one shoe, a tassled loafer. His left leg was twisted under him, as if he'd fallen awkwardly, and his left shoe had come off. He wore socks with little red hearts on the cuffs. His blue eyes were wide open and staring, and he had a terrible wound on his throat. There was a lot of blood by his head. It was congealing now, darkening in the hot sun.

She took a deep breath and looked away. She couldn't help looking again. Dead, he was certainly dead. She knew perfectly well that the dead don't move, so she almost screamed when a sudden gust of wind fluttered his tousled golden locks, almost as if he were waking up.

It had to be the famed Reverend Elmer Morris, his golden tongue silenced forever.

The women of the parish would be devastated, she thought hysterically. *She* was devastated, and she didn't even know the man. Claudius, on the other hand, looked smug and matter-of-fact about the whole thing. A quid pro quo was in order here. He expected a reward for his astute, grisly canine discovery . . . another serving of hamburger and large fries, no doubt.

With some difficulty, she managed to pull him away from the dumpster and ran to the church. A side door was open, and she raced up the steps. "Hello? Anyone here?"

From downstairs somewhere came a giggle and a scurry of footsteps. Moments later, the woman who'd been watching Uncle Ira's house the night before came up the steps, straightening the collar of her dress. Her blonde hair was rumpled and her lipstick smeared.

This is no time for niceties. Annie grabbed Jan Stalker's arm and stopped her in her tracks. "Something terrible's happened. There's a man in the parking lot. He's terribly hurt." There was no point in saying he was dead. The woman would find out soon enough. "Call an ambulance and the police."

Jan Stalker edged as far away from Claudius as she could, all the while eying Annie nervously. "Who's hurt?"

"I don't know. Don't waste time. Where's the phone?"

Jan Stalker drew herself up and said haughtily, "Downstairs."

Annie left her and raced down the steps to a long, narrow hallway. Claudius's nails clicked on the linoleum as he ran ahead of her. A man was coming out of the last room on the left. He buttoned his cuffs and eyed her up and down with suspicion. "Hey, no dogs allowed in here."

"He goes with me everywhere." She wished she'd thought to put the Helping Hand cape on him. "He's a guide dog."

"Is that so?" John Barnard's voice was hushed and respectful. "Does he bite?"

"If he doesn't like your looks . . . Never mind him. There's a man lying injured in the parking lot. Call an ambulance!"

Jan Stalker came back downstairs, looking shocked.

"It's Reverend Morris! He's up in the parking lot, dead as a doornail! Blood all over the place. It looks like a wild animal tore out his throat!" She spotted Claudius and ran behind the caretaker, shrieking, "That dog must have done it! He's a killer!"

Chapter Three

Twenty minutes later, one of Roswell's finest was glaring down at Claudius, who glared right back. "You don't think this dog could have done it? Someone or something just about took that man's head off."

Lt. Rhodes pointed to the dumpster across the parking lot where the police photographer was taking pictures and the medical examiner and his assistant were busy with rubber gloves and a body bag. "A dog could have done it. A big one with jaws like his."

"He couldn't have done it," Annie protested. "For one thing, he hasn't been out of my sight the whole time I've been here. He's not a killer—"

"Hold it right there, lady. I don't know you or your dog from Adam, and so far, I don't like what I see."

The fat, dark-haired lieutenant had arrived soon after Jan Stalker's hysterical phone call to the station. He'd taken one look at Claudius and jumped to the conclusion that a bird in hand was worth two in the bush. Why waste time running around looking for some crazed killer when he could pin it on a big, black dog.

Having put up with fifteen minutes of badgering, Annie finally lost her temper. "I don't care what you think, *sir*. My dog's been with me all morning. We went to McDonald's."

"Just you and the dog?" Lt. Rhodes jotted that down on his notepad. "Unless someone at McDonald's can corroborate your story, you have no alibi."

"I bought two orders. One for him, one for me, and I have a receipt. I couldn't possibly have eaten all of it myself."

"Maybe, maybe not. What made you stop at McDonald's? You said you were staying with relatives. What's the matter, can't they cook?"

"Claudius wanted fries and a Big Mac. He barks when he sees the golden arches."

"I see. And he's a Helping Hand guide dog?"

"Well . . . he was." She left out the fact that he'd been kicked out of the organization for his rebellious nature. That wouldn't win any points with Lt. Rhodes.

"Dog like that costs quite a bit." He gave Claudius the once over again. "He's a lot of animal."

"My sister-in-law got him for free. He's half husky, half German shepherd, really a wonderful dog." She'd told that lie so often by now, she almost believed it. Happily, the Lieutenant didn't know that and it was for a good cause. She didn't want Claudius's death on her conscience.

"Is that so." He eyed her up and down, obviously wondering if she was nuts. "A piece of advice, Miss. If you care about the dog, keep him leashed. The chief will probably order him shot on sight if he's found running loose."

"He can't do that, it's illegal!"

"Out here, the chief decides what's legal and what's not. Until we know for sure what killed Reverend Morris, everyone's suspect—even Rin Tin Tin here."

He was dead serious.

She tried speaking slower, emphasizing each word. "Claudius isn't a killer. He found the body, and neither one of us ever saw Reverend Morris before."

"Don't leave town, Miss."

"I wasn't planning on going anywhere."

"Good."

She watched as he turned back to the bodily remains of the Reverend Elmer Morris. The photographer was taking the last photos, and two policemen were stringing up day-glo yellow plastic tape along the perimeter of the church parking lot. The coroner's meat wagon stood nearby, back door open, awaiting its lifeless cargo. It was all very depressing, and she shivered a little and rubbed her forearms.

Claudius cocked his head at her and whined as if he

wondered why she was standing there doing nothing. She wondered, too.

Just then, Jan Stalker came out of the church. She stared over at the knot of activity around the dumpster. There was an odd look on her face, a combination of controlled excitement and fear. Annie had heard her tell the police she'd arrived at the church early, to work on the computer figures for the budget.

Which was a bare-faced lie. According to Aunt Hortense, Jan Stalker had spent the morning indulging in hanky panky with John Barnard in the kitchen by the pizza oven. Hardly the usual place for a romantic tryst, and John Barnard wasn't exactly Mel Gibson. But then Jan Stalker wasn't too particular. With her it was quantity, not quality.

Annie sighed. Perhaps it was too easy to criticize Jan Stalker's overactive libido. At least she had a love life.

Suddenly, Jan noticed Annie watching her. At once, her face took on a secretive expression, and she all but ran down the steps, disappearing around the side of the church. Whatever she knew about Reverend Morris's untimely demise, she was keeping to herself.

John Barnard had joined Lt. Rhodes near the dumpster, and unlike Jan Stalker, seemed to have a great deal to say to the police—complaining loudly about the fuss and scandal visited upon the church. Tongues would wag for sure, and the congregation would suffer. He knew his rights and wasn't about to take any Gestapo police tactics lying down.

He turned angrily and stomped back into the church just as Pastor Pennyworth rode up on a motorcycle. Although he wore a gold helmet, boots, and pants, Annie recognized him by his clerical collar and the look of shock on his face as he saw what had happened in his church parking lot while he'd been off communing with God or whatever. He jumped off of his bike and rushed over to the knot of police by the dumpster.

"The good pastor looks somewhat flabbergasted," Annie told Claudius. "I wonder where he's been all morning."

Claudius yawned, which she took to mean Who cares? Or maybe, Baloney. Either way, he was bored stiff.

She wondered what her aunt and uncle would say about the macabre discovery behind the dumpster. On the bright side, maybe they'd skip the hike out at the ranch for a day or two, until the murder was solved. Because that's what it was—murder. Either Reverend Morris had committed suicide by tearing out his own throat, or someone had done it for him. But who and why?

Questions she had no answers for.

She decided she couldn't stand looking at the dumpster anymore and dragged Claudius, who was by now barking his head off at a squirrel in a nearby tree, back to the Escort. It was a wrestling match, but she managed to get him in the passenger seat and slammed the door.

He glared at her through the open window and barked again.

Half-deafened, she yelled, "For God's sake, shut up!" There was no point in arguing with him. Not about the squirrel, not about Reverend Morris's murder, not about how long it took him to find a particular bush, not about *anything*. She slid behind the wheel and found a classical station on the car radio. The Berlin Philharmonic playing Mozart's Overture to *Figaro* . . . sheer delight.

He stopped barking.

She turned the volume up as he let out a loud groan. He liked country and western, Lydia's favorite.

"Too bad," she told him with malice. "Lydia's two thousand miles away. You'll have to learn to put up with classical."

He shot her a look that said, In your dreams, and turned his back.

By now the sun was high, and the front seat felt like a sauna. The Escort's a.c. was on the fritz, so she cranked the window down all the way and breathed in facefuls of hot, dusty air all the way back to Idlewild Circle.

As she pulled into the driveway, she noticed Aunt Hortense hanging clothes in the backyard. There was no sign of Uncle Ira's car, so she assumed that he'd gone off on an errand. She shut off the engine, got out, and followed the path around the side of the garage. Naturally, Claudius had to be dragged past the garbage cans and recycling bins. Then by the potting shed, he got busy sniffing Uncle Ira's rakes, edgers, overturned flower pots, and every bush and blade of grass he could reach.

She pushed open the gate to the backyard and stared in astonishment. It was a sight to behold. Every inch of space had been utilized. Uncle Ira's pride and joy, the vegetable garden, was meticulously laid out in straight rows of broccoli, beans, peas, and peppers. Beds of frilly red lettuce, onions, Swiss chard, peppers, and cabbages grew in front, with tomatoes trained on six-foot-tall bamboo tepees in the center. A scarecrow in overalls, flannel shirt, and straw hat, was propped against the largest tepee.

Uncle Ira liked bright colors, so yellow and orange marigolds and nasturtiums bloomed along the edge of the metal-framed strawberry cage, and here and there green mounds of thyme and basil surrounded lush stands of poppies and flowering rue. Nearby, a patio table and chairs were set beneath a large shade tree.

Annie pulled Claudius past a raised bed of chives and mint without incident, and wondering how to broach the subject of Reverend Morris's untimely demise, managed to steer the dog away from the laundry basket at her aunt's feet. "Hi, not quite noon and it's already getting hot. Why don't you sit in the shade and let me do that?"

"This will only take a minute, dear." Aunt Hortense took a white nightgown from the basket and secured it to the line. "Elvira had better keep her hands off this one. I'll kill her if she doesn't."

Annie sighed and handed her a pair of Uncle Ira's shorts. "What did she do to get you so mad?"

"Elvira has a thing about my laundry. A week ago she cut up a pair of my underpants. Frilly pink ones. Cut them to ribbons, then had the gall to tell me she'd seen a blackbird do it. What did she think? That I didn't have eyes in my head? I saw her scuttle back over the fence with a pair of scissors in her fat hands. And it's not the first time she's ruined my underclothes. Last month she slashed my black nightgown down the front, and when I confronted her she said it was indecent, that I'd go straight to hell!"

"That's terrible!"

Aunt Hortense pinned the shorts to the line. "I'm not made of money. I can't afford to replace my underwear just because she doesn't like it—which is what I told her."

"What did she say to that?"

"She said she was sorry and promised to sew up the nightgown."

"At least she tried to make amends."

"Don't be ridiculous. She short sheeted it. I couldn't even pull the damn thing on. I had to throw it out."

"What's wrong with her? Is she crazy?"

"Elvira's got more than a few screws loose. Sometimes I think she's in the first stages of Alzheimer's. She does the damnedest things. She forgets where she's going when she goes out, and the other day she pulled up all my pansies. She said they were past it, but they were blooming their heads off. I suspect she destroys my underwear because she's afraid her husband, Roger, will get turned on if he sees it on the line."

"Oh."

"I hope the old boy's watching." She picked a cotton bra, size 40, double D from the basket and hooked it on the line. "This will give him a thrill."

Annie looked around. "Where's Uncle Ira?"

"He had a few errands to run. I know you're anxious to go out to the site, but he won't be gone long."

"I happened to go by the church a short while ago and stopped to walk Claudius."

"Did you, dear?"

"Yes, and something terrible happened." Annie paused as her aunt turned with a puzzled look. "I found a body behind the dumpster in the parking lot. It was Reverend Morris." Her aunt's face went white with shock, and she put an arm around her shoulder. "I'm sorry I had to tell you like this. I didn't know how else to break the news."

"Reverend Morris dead. I can't believe it." Her aunt

groped for a chair and sat down. "What happened? Was it his heart? Last night at the party, I told him to pay more attention to his diet. He had a terrible sweet tooth. Too many triglycerides and high blood pressure can kill quicker than a wink. One minute you're here, next, you're a goner."

"It wasn't his diet." Annie sat down in the other chair. There was no point in beating about the bush. Sooner or later, her aunt was bound to learn the grisly details. "The police said it was murder. Someone ripped his throat out."

Aunt Hortense took out a handkerchief and wiped her eyes. "I don't believe it. Who would have done such a thing? Why, he didn't have an enemy in the world."

"He had one," Annie said gently. "One was all he needed."

"It must have been a thief looking for church funds. A mugger." She paused, then said, "But the reverend didn't have access to our bank accounts. He was killed for nothing."

As they sat and discussed the reverend's untimely death, Violet and Daisy appeared in the garden near the strawberry cage. Claudius, lying at Annie's feet, stiffened. He watched the cats' progress as they sauntered past the peppers and broccoli, sniffing the cabbages. They hadn't realized he was there.

Annie wound the leash around her wrist twice. "Try it, and I guarantee you'll regret it to the end of your days. Which won't be too much longer."

He gave her a look expressing his disgust and put his head on his paws.

"Oh, my darling Daisy," Aunt Hortense cried, getting up to clasp the struggling Siamese to her considerable bosom as Violet disappeared to the far side of the garden. "Have we been a naughty kitty, chewing Ira's cabbages? Mustn't do that, darling." The cat wriggled impatiently, black tail twitching, and her claws came out. "No, no, no! Naughty girl!" Aunt Hortense put her down and turned back to Annie. "Maybe you're wrong, dear. Maybe it was his heart. Although he was still quite young, not more than thirty-eight or -nine, and certainly it isn't a normal age for heart attacks or a stroke, for that matter. Oh my, I can't believe someone would kill Reverend Morris. All the good he did, so many conversions to the faith." Her voice broke, and she got out the handkerchief again.

Annie led her back to the chair. "Just sit here for a few minutes. I'll go in and get you a glass of water."

"Yes, dear, that would be nice."

Taking Claudius with her, Annie hurried into the house and ran the water in the kitchen sink while she opened cupboards, looking for a glass. Platters, dishes, pots, and pans, but no glasses. She yanked open the doors over the sink and found it full of Pyrex bakeware.

The cats' dishes were on the floor by the stove. Since Annie wasn't watching, Claudius polished off the cat food in short order. He was still licking his chops when the front doorbell rang. He began barking at the top of his lungs.

She yanked on the leash hard. "Stop that, shut up!" Still frowning, she went down the hall and opened the door. "Yes?"

A gray-haired man in overalls and glasses stood on the front step. A look of surprise crossed his face. "Is Ira here? I'm Roger Stubenville from next door. I heard something he ought to know."

"He's not home." She was about to suggest that he come back later, when her uncle's car pulled into the driveway.

He got out of the car and hurried up the front walk, looking upset. "Hello, Roger. I suppose you heard about the murder."

Roger Stubenville's eyes gleamed with curiosity. "That's why I came over. Just heard about it on the radio. I wondered if it was a mistake."

"No mistake. Morris is dead as a mackerel. Somebody cut his throat."

"An angry husband, perhaps?" Roger pushed his glasses up his bony nose. "Sorry, I shouldn't have said that. But hell, he was a damn fool. There must have been dozens of irate husbands who wanted him dead."

Uncle Ira nodded. "You could be right about that.

Poor Elmer. How many times was he married? At least twice, so two wives could have been enraged and come looking for back alimony."

"They'll never get it now," Annie pointed out. "By the way, where do you put the glasses? I told Aunt Hortense I'd bring her some water."

"Never mind, I'll do it." He led them inside, took a glass from the one kitchen cupboard Annie hadn't searched, and filled it with water from the sink. "Annie, this is Roger Stubenville. He lives next door and goes to our church. Annie's my niece from back East."

"Welcome to Roswell," said Roger, smiling. "Don't let the murder give you the wrong idea. We're really pretty average out here. Not much excitement usually. I own a hardware store downtown."

"Really. How interesting."

He nodded. "We carry a lot more than hardware these days. All kinds of goods. Fans, housewares, gardening tools. I hope you stop in while you're here."

"I'll make a point of it," she promised.

Uncle Ira opened the refrigerator. "There's some coffee cake, Annie. How about bringing some out to the backyard. I'll take a jug of ice tea and we'll have a spot of refreshment."

"Okay." She found a tray and plates as the two men went outside to join her aunt. The coffee cake was fresh, cinnamon and raisin with pecans. She slid it out of the box and gave Claudius a small piece. "If you've got a brain in your head, you'll keep your big mouth shut and behave. If the police get their way, they'll hang a murder charge around your neck and shoot you."

He stared at her, his tail wagging. Obviously, he assumed she'd make it her business to put a stop to any heavy-handed police tactics. After all, this entire mess was her fault. She was the one who'd stopped by the church and let him out to piddle.

Annie thought about that for a moment, then muttered, "It looks like we don't have a choice. We've got to find out who really killed the good reverend."

He nodded encouragingly. She wasn't quite as stupid as he thought.

She picked up the tray and opened the back door. By now quite a crowd had gathered under the big tree in the garden. Aunt Hortense was still dabbing her eyes, and Uncle Ira, sitting beside her, looking troubled but observant. Roger Stubenville was wandering between the vegetable garden and the tree, nervously wiping his brow.

Aunt Hortense waved her handkerchief as she saw Annie and Claudius standing on the back porch. "We'll have to fetch more chairs from the garage. Elvira's coming over along with Pastor Pennyworth, Jan Stalker, and several others from the church. They'll be here any minute."

Uncle Ira nodded. "The elders will all come, except Wallace Hapgood. You know how he is lately. Too busy to budge from his office down at the bank."

"I don't know what's wrong with that man," Aunt Hortense added with a shrug, "You'd think he'd be over it by now."

"Over what?" Annie asked.

"Just one of those things. He's hard to get hold of these days." Uncle Ira headed for the garage with Roger Stubenville following to lend a hand.

After the chairs were set about the table under the shade tree and plates of coffee cake and glasses of ice tea handed around, Uncle Ira announced, "We need to discuss what to do, how to handle the publicity."

Pastor Pennyworth appeared at the garden gate and unlatched it with a hand that trembled. His gold shirt highlighted the pallor of his weak, somewhat boyish face. He looked devastated. With him was an elder of the church, George Digby, who kept mopping his face with his handkerchief, and seemed to be in a state of shock. But he'd just come from identifying the body.

"I didn't know Reverend Morris, but I'm sorry this tragedy's happened," Annie said quietly, putting the tray with coffee cake on the table. All but unnoticed, she sat down in the shade nearby. Claudius curled up beside her.

"Whoever did this terrible thing, it wasn't a member of the congregation," declared Pastor Pennyworth. The others fell strangely silent, and he stared at them, troubled. "I know what you're thinking, and it's ridiculous! Certainly, we've all had disagreements at one time or another, but nothing ever serious. This must have been a random act of street violence."

Uncle Ira cleared his throat. "Doesn't make any sense. Morris's death was particularly brutal. Why wasn't he killed with a gun? A thief would've used a gun. No, there's something . . . personal about his death. Whoever killed him was angry and grabbed what was at hand."

"Someone he knew?" Jan Stalker said witheringly. "I'll never believe it. He was a good man." Her brown eyes softened in remembrance. "He always had time for me."

Elvira Stubenville snapped, "The Good Book is quite clear about the seventh commandment."

Jan's face reddened and she sank down on a low bench and sat looking straight ahead at the line of flapping laundry as if she were about to throw up.

"Poor Reverend Morris. All I can think of is how dreadful it is," Aunt Hortense said in a faint voice. "So sudden, such a shock. He was so happy at the party last night. Who could have predicted his death?"

"It's my fault," said Pastor Pennyworth quietly. "I asked him to return. If he'd stayed in St. Louis, he'd still be alive."

Aunt Hortense gazed at him wide-eyed. Her lip trembled.

"For heaven's sake, try and be more considerate," Uncle Ira retorted. "This is getting us nowhere. You're only upsetting everyone."

"What are we supposed to do? Say 'that's life' and forget what's happened?" George Digby's cheeks puffed out in indignation. "The police won't forget."

"George!"

Pastor Pennyworth muttered, "He's right. The police will look under every rock and they'll stir things up. People will be hurt."

"Elmer Morris wasn't perfect, but he wouldn't have hurt a fly," put in Aunt Hortense. "Not deliberately, anyway. And here we sit, worried about how his death will affect us. We're acting like hypocrites."

George Digby shrugged. "It's only natural to worry about it. There's no sin in that. All the negative publicity is bound to have unpleasant repercussions."

Aunt Hortense whispered to Annie, "Poor George Digby. He's a dentist. His wife left him last year. It's terribly sad."

Annie hissed back, "That's too bad."

"The last days are upon us! This is the judgment of the Great Whore," began Elvira, staring at them all, her high, light voice cutting through the airy garden.

"Stop it." Roger patted her hand. "Mustn't say such things now, my dear."

She looked at him with blazing eyes. " 'Wherefore if I come, I will remember his deeds which he doeth, prating against us with malicious words; and not content therewith, neither doth he himself receive the brethren, and forbiddeth them that would, and casteth them out of the church'!"

There was a shocked silence, broken by Pastor Pennyworth. "Third Epistle of John, of course. Elvira knows her Scripture." He sighed. "At any rate, we all may be getting hysterical over nothing—"

"Elmer Morris is dead. I wouldn't call that nothing," said Roger Stubenville.

George Digby cleared his throat. "Morris liked a drink as well as any man. It could have been an accident . . . if he had a skinful and fell on something sharp behind the dumpster. You might say he sort of did himself in, kind of got what he deserved."

Aunt Hortense shot him a furious look. "Don't say such cruel things about the dead. It's un-Christian!"

"Nothing can hurt Morris now," said Roger Stubenville. "We're the ones you should worry about."

"The autopsy will show if he was drunk." Uncle Ira gazed at them with a question in his pale blue eyes. "Or if he was murdered."

"It was the dog," Jan Stalker burst out. She pointed at Claudius who was licking his tail. "He's a vicious killer! He should be put down!"

"This dog hasn't been out of my sight since I arrived in Roswell yesterday. *He didn't do it.*"

"We only have your word for that, and we don't know you from a hole in the ground," Jan Stalker sneered. "You could be lying."

"Well, I'm not."

At that moment, a police car pulled into the driveway and two policemen got out. A patrolman and Lt. Rhodes, who came up the walk with a purposeful tread. "Sorry to interrupt," the lieutenant said from the gate. He got out his notebook and pen. "Rather than chase all over town, we thought we'd get a list of names—all of you who were in any way involved with Reverend Morris's arrival."

His no-nonsense manner was cleverly calculated. Even Aunt Hortense gulped back a sniffle and paid attention. The others, Annie noticed, had stiffened and gone quiet. Each was nervously estimating his position. Roger Stubenville stopped pacing up and down, and George Digby's hands went still. His cold gray eyes remained alert and suspicious.

"These are just the preliminaries," Lt. Rhodes told them, flipping his notepad to a clean page. "Let's go over what happened last night. Where you all were, what you were doing. If someone was with you to corroborate your story, that would be helpful." He eyed Uncle Ira. "Mr. O'Hara?"

"We had a welcome home party for the reverend last night. Sometime during the evening, he left. That's the last I saw of him. The party was breaking up by then anyway. Then I came home and my niece arrived. We talked a while, then I went up to bed."

"You stayed there the rest of the night?"

"Well, I got up once to go to the bathroom—"

"Okay," Lt. Rhodes interrupted, scribbling a line or two. He turned to Aunt Hortense and raised his eyebrows.

Somewhat flushed in the face, she nodded. "Yes, we went to the party, then came home and were in bed about eleven, before the news. We don't watch that anymore. All those shootings and street crime. Not like the old days, when you could turn on the TV, and there'd be something cheerful to watch, like a local spelling bee or someone getting married. I like that show about shopping, though . . . Supermarket Sweep, but that's on earlier."

"Fine." He glanced at Annie. "You found the body."

"I told you all I know at the church."

"I'll be the judge of that." He bared his teeth in what passed for a smile. "You want to add anything to your story?"

"No."

"Suit yourself." He looked at Roger Stubenville and waited.

"Yes . . . I . . . Roger Stubenville. I own the hardware store downtown. My wife and I were at the party for a while, then went home and went to bed. Right, dear?" He squeezed Elvira's hand.

"Indeed." She narrowed her eyes at the lieutenant. "Reverend Morris is dead, and you're wasting taxpayers' money questioning us while his murderer walks the streets!"

"Did I mention anything about murder?" His voice was sly. "Maybe we're investigating an accidental death."

Annie laughed, a derisory snort. "Not unless he tore his throat out with his bare hands."

"That's enough out of you." Lt. Rhodes glowered, then turned to George Digby. "And you are?"

"I'm a dentist. George Digby. I don't have anyone . . . that is, after the party, I went home. I was alone. Er . . . except for my dog."

"No alibi." He smiled, made a check mark by Digby's name, and glanced at Jan Stalker. "I talked to you at the church earlier. Got anything to add?"

"No." She swallowed nervously and shifted in her chair. "After the party, I went downtown to the Art Theatre. They had a midnight showing of one of my favorites, *Dial M for Murder.* I got home around two and went straight to bed."

"I see. The old George Brent and Madeline Carroll

classic." He wrote this down as if they were finally getting somewhere.

An obvious trap, which Jan saw through at once. Her voice was dry as she retorted, "George Brent wasn't in it. Neither was Madeline Carroll. Ray Milland tried to kill his wife, Grace Kelly."

"Oh, yeah, that one." He glanced at the pastor, whose face showed his displeasure.

"I spoke to you at the church. I want to go on record as objecting to this line of questioning. You're getting nowhere. We're innocent. Reverend Morris died at the hands of some poor deranged person, possibly an indigent. We may never find out who did it. Furthermore, I demand that the state police be put in charge of the investigation."

Lt. Rhodes sat back with a sigh. "I was waiting for this. Believe me, pastor, I'm a pussycat compared to the state cops. They'll take you downtown and use the rubber hose."

"They wouldn't dare!"

"Would you like to find out?"

"No."

"At least we agree on that much." The lieutenant perused his notes, while they sat in an awkward silence broken only by the sound he made flipping the pages of his notepad. Finally, he looked up. "So no one here had any reason to want the good reverend dead?"

This had to be a rhetorical question, Annie thought. No one in his right mind would contradict the lieutenant, not in front of the others anyway. In private though, it'd be a different story. She had no illusions about her aunt and uncle's ability to keep their mouths shut, and the rest of the church elders appeared to be little better. If he grilled them, one by one, he'd get a great deal of information in the form of gossip, all of it damaging and most of it probably false. Two questions occurred to her: Did Lt. Rhodes have the intelligence to recognize and disregard petty gossip when he heard it? And the murder weapon. Why had the murderer removed it from the scene of the crime? Perhaps it incriminated him in some way. But what did that tell her about the killer's identity?

While she was mulling this over and coming to no firm conclusion, Lt. Rhodes gathered a list of church elders and board members not present. He looked around to see if he'd missed questioning anyone, then closed his notebook.

"Thank you all very much for your cooperation. I understand that it's a difficult time for you and your congregation, Pastor Pennyworth. Putting aside the possibility of a homicidal indigent, can you think of anyone who might have had a grudge against the deceased?" No one spoke, and he went on, "Did any of you happen to see Reverend Morris after the party?"

"I was over at the church early this morning." Aunt Hortense slid a quick glance at Jan Stalker, who stared right back. "I didn't see Reverend Morris—"

"What about his car, a blue Toyota. It was found parked in front of the dumpster in the church parking lot."

Aunt Hortense shook her head, trying to remember. "I . . . I didn't notice the car, but it could have been there. I did see John Barnard, the caretaker—"

"Of course!" George Digby cried, looking about in an almost jovial fashion. "Barnard could have done it. His wife had an affair with Morris last summer. Er . . . no offense, ladies, but you've got to admit, it looks damn suspicious."

"We talked to Barnard. He's got an alibi for most of the morning. We won't know the exact time of death until the autopsy. It may turn out Reverend Morris died last night."

Jan Stalker reddened. "Er . . . yes, we, that is I was over at the church this morning working on the budget. The computer crashed. John helped me reboot it."

"Indeed," sniffed Aunt Hortense.

"Yes. We had a devil of a time getting it to work," Jan went on quickly. "We really need a new computer in the office. The one we've got now is slow and has practically no available memory."

"We'll take up the matter of a new computer at the

next budget meeting," Pastor Pennyworth said in his smooth voice.

Annie watched him, a cynical smile curving her lips. Raising ready cash was always touchy, even with a gullible congregation who had deep pockets. It sounded as if The Neighborhood Church of the Celestial Spheres had the same financial difficulties as many other religious organizations. Perhaps spreading The Word beyond the stars wasn't all it was cracked up to be.

"Haven't you got any idea when Reverend Morris was killed?" asked Uncle Ira.

Lt. Rhodes hesitated. "Sometime after the party. Which broke up when?"

"Nine or nine-thirty," said George Digby. "I spoke to him around eight, about the time the party started. He wasn't himself. He seemed upset about something."

"That's odd," replied the pastor thoughtfully.

"He died in the night with his throat torn out—like Dracula!" Jan Stalker shuddered. "God, how creepy!"

"This puts an entirely new aspect on things," muttered Uncle Ira. "Some sort of Satanic ritual? You read about that sort of goings on in the newspaper now and then. Usually Minnesota or Wisconsin. They have a lot of cows—"

George Digby sighed. "Nobody said anything about Satanic rituals or cows."

"Nobody who knows us could believe we'd . . . anyway, what could be the motive?" asked Uncle Ira. "Someone wanted to drink his blood?"

"Oh, Ira, that's appalling! How could you!" Aunt Hortense gave him a disapproving look over her spectacles.

"As far as we know, nobody drank the good reverend's blood," Lt. Rhodes informed them in an annoyed tone.

Annie wondered idly about church doctrine. Other than her aunt's vague remark that they believed in spreading Christ's message among the stars, she really hadn't a clue as to what went on during their service. Was it based loosely on the Last Supper? Or something more modern and up to date? Not vampirism, though . . .

"In other words, we're back to square one, and you have no idea who or what killed Reverend Morris," said George Digby.

Lt. Rhodes gave him a cold smile. "I didn't say that."

"You didn't have to," the dentist retorted. He rose and faced the policeman. "It's typical of the bumbling police. You have no hope of actually solving Morris's murder, if indeed that's what it is. No, you're content to smear our church's good name with insinuations of moral turpitude and vampirism. Well, I, for one, have no intention of sitting here, watching you ride roughshod over my rights or those of the other members of the congregation. I refuse to answer another question without talking to my lawyer."

"To set the record straight, I never indicated there was evidence of vampirism, and I agree with you. Your morals are your own business. Break the law, then it's my business. Who is your lawyer?"

"Fred Carrado," George Digby blustered.

"Well, now, I believe he's a corporate lawyer. You'll have to find one specializing in criminal matters. A good one." Lt. Rhodes put away his notepad. "If I were you, I'd do that right away."

Chapter Four

Monday, Reverend Morris's funeral got under way at The Neighborhood Church of the Celestial Spheres. The church was packed. Surprisingly, the reverend drew an even larger crowd dead than he had alive.

The funeral was long on symbolic trappings. Organ music filled the sanctuary, tall vases of flowers stood on either side of the simple altar and at the foot of the opulent satin-lined mahogany coffin. The cosmetician had had a difficult time covering up the terrible wound in the deceased's throat, but a carefully folded white scarf had done the trick. The late Reverend Morris looked quite peaceful lying on a heart-shaped satin pillow with his thinning blonde hair tidily coiffed and his hands folded over his chest in final prayer.

Pastor Pennyworth went on and on in fulsome eulogy about the late Reverend Morris's mission on earth, the lives he'd touched, the many conversions. The choir sang several rousing hymns and the ladies of the congregation wept copious tears while the other assistant pastor, Bruce Wolf, ran the new video camera. They'd replay the funeral all week on the church TV channel for home consumption and for those unlucky enough to have missed the real thing.

Police photographers and the local press took pictures of the crowd out at Bellwood Cemetery, on county road 102. The graveside service went on for half an hour.

Pretending interest in the surrounding gravestones, Annie looked around, recognizing some of the faces: the pastor, wearing his collar and a suitably funereal expression, and a slender blonde woman who must be his wife, Melinda. Roger Stubenville and his wife, Elvira. George

Digby, the dentist, even the caretaker, John Barnard, in a blue suit and a clean shirt. In the back row she saw Mrs. Fielding and a thin woman Aunt Hortense identified as Mrs. Hapgood, the banker's wife. Of the banker, himself, there was no sign. Aunt Hortense said with a sniff that he'd become rather reclusive. Oh, he hadn't always been that way. He'd gone through a bad patch eighteen months ago—she declined to identify the nature of his unhappiness, but her disgusted expression spoke volumes—and he'd become almost a hermit. Wallace Hapgood went to work and straight home again. The bank tellers saw more of him than his own wife did. Definitely peculiar.

In fact, the congregation seemed to be full of sinister secrets. She shook herself out of her reverie and realized that neither of the reverend's ex-wives had shown up. But there was Jan Stalker, seated under the canopy, her metal folding chair nearest the coffin. Annie hardly recognized her. She wore a large black hat with a veil and a black tailored suit.

During the final hymn, Jan stood up, knelt by the coffin for a moment, then placed a white rose on the lid while cameras snapped. Then the crowd dispersed, most heading back to the church for a remembrance meal for the dear departed. The mourners made little noise walking over the thick grass as they headed toward the cemetery gates.

Annie, having left Claudius locked in the Escort in the parking lot in a shady spot, walked beside Jan Stalker. A group of curious onlookers gawked at them from the other side of the rusting wrought-iron fence.

Jan took out a lacy handkerchief and dabbed her eyes, and Annie frowned. "Are you sure you're okay?"

"Yeah, I enjoy a good funeral, even Elmer's. Maybe I'll go home and tie one on. He'd understand."

They stopped among the gravestones, and Annie noticed that her eyes were dry behind the veil. "I didn't know Reverend Morris, but from all I've heard he was . . . universally loved."

"He had what you'd call charisma, and he was a good friend." Jan gave her girdle an absent tug. "I haven't known too many real good friends, not since my husband left."

"Oh."

"Well, he left kind of sudden like. Maybe you heard . . . he had a problem with drink and made all kinds of trouble. Finally, the church kicked him out of town."

"That's too bad."

"It sure made a hell of a difference as far as my life went. I get kind of lonely. Elmer understood."

A uniformed policeman pushed the crowd aside as Jan walked through the gate. Annie followed and went across the parking lot to the red Escort. She'd left the front windows half open, and Claudius glowered at her through the driver's side.

"Move over, you," she told him and opened the door. She got in, managing to swat his tail out of her face just in time. She put the key in the ignition but didn't turn it. The air smelled like a flower from long ago. Her mother's voice saying, "Rue for regret. Never waste time on regrets."

Annie felt lonely and knew why. Reverend Morris at least had mourners at his funeral. Who would miss her? Her brother, Tom, maybe—certainly not Lenny. He was busy living high off the hog. He had a swinging social life. Well, she didn't. In fact, she had none at all. Normally, it didn't bother her much, but the reverend's funeral brought with it a sense of mortality she couldn't ignore.

She glanced back up the hill. They were already shoveling dirt on the coffin. She shivered a little. Her mother would say it was a goose walking over her grave. A silly superstition, but then her mother was Irish and believed in omens. She didn't approve of Annie's current lifestyle. No daughter of hers could be happy, running a seedy antique shop and taking in boarders in that godforsaken town in New Hampshire. If Annie had an ounce of common sense, she'd move to Florida and settle down with a nice dentist or doctor with a solid income and a Mercedes. And she'd get pregnant.

Her mother called from Florida every week or two

and between pointed remarks about ticking biological clocks, asked two things: Was she going to church and was she seeing anyone special? The answer to both, of course, was "no," and her mother's comeback was that Annie was going straight to hell. Presumably, marriage to a nice Catholic dentist would save her. Not.

Life was too short to waste living according to her mother's dictates—or anyone else's, for that matter. People never thought they were going to die, but sometimes death came calling—an unexpected, unwanted guest.

The hot breeze shook the tree leaves overhead, and she glanced back at the gravesite again. Claudius growled suddenly, and for a horrible second she relived that moment by the parking lot dumpster, finding the reverend's body lying on the hot asphalt, and the dog's fearsome, snarling presence, his bared teeth. More than anything, she realized suddenly, she longed to get away from here, to go home to New Hampshire. Yet she knew it was impossible.

The police had warned her not to leave. If they couldn't find Reverend Morris's real killer—and hard evidence be damned—they'd settle for Claudius, who, as a prime suspect, possessed two obvious advantages: a set of slavering fangs and a wolflike appearance. He was remarkably photogenic. His arrest—or maybe they'd simply shoot him, saying he'd "resisted arrest"—would sell papers at a brisk pace. Everyone would be happy: the police basking in public euphoria, having rid the town of a homicidal killer dog, the good citizens of Roswell—thinking they were safe—and, of course, the real murderer.

She glanced at Claudius stretched beside her on the front seat. Busy leading a dog's life, he was oblivious to this entire mess, and there was no one else to protect him. She had to do it.

The line of cars leaving the cemetery thinned out. Among the last were the police, one or two patrol cars, and a dark blue Taurus driven by Roswell's resident Sherlock Holmes: Lt. Rhodes, himself. He flashed her a nasty grin as he roared by.

She repressed the urge to flip him the finger.

Annie had her share of faults. Impatient and stubborn to the point of pigheadedness, she had a hot temper, which she managed to control most of the time. But she didn't like to be bossed around, especially by someone like Lt. Rhodes, who barely bothered to be civil. He was a big man, with a belly that sagged over his tight belt. His face was pale and rubbery, his eyes an icy blue, and his smile a sneer. She suspected he didn't have the intelligence to notice the impression he made, or maybe he didn't care. He probably sat around all day, eating donuts and scratching his crotch, thinking up ways to avoid real work. One thing was certain—he didn't like women, especially stubborn, lippy women who didn't know their place.

Annie's face took on an implacable expression. If there was one thing she knew, it was that she didn't know her place.

They had a good turnout at the church remembrance dinner, more than a hundred and fifty hungry souls. Lacking one of the late Reverend Morris's rousing speeches—which customarily had lasted an hour or more and had them on their feet, yelling and screaming with religious fervor—they could relax, eat their fill, and indulge in the latest juicy gossip: the identity of the reverend's killer.

Annie was in the kitchen getting serving dishes from a cupboard above the pizza oven. A TV in the dining room replayed the funeral, first pious hymns, then Pastor Pennyworth's eulogy. Somewhere on another plane of consciousness, Reverend Morris was leading a new throng of the faithful with his magnetic personality and famous charm.

Grimly she laid out a stack of styrofoam plates for the faithful on this plane. Only half the potluck committee had shown up. Aunt Hortense and Uncle Ira were hard at work, but Melinda Pennyworth, the pastor's wife, seemed content to order everyone else about while she tossed her blonde mane back and inspected her manicure, looking for nonexistent hangnails.

Uncle Ira rubbed his hands with satisfaction. "Mmm, mmm! Chicken's almost done. Smells good."

"It should be," Aunt Hortense retorted. "It's been cooking for the better part of an hour and a half. I told you to cook it last night, but you knew better. 'Wait until morning,' you said. Well, look at the trouble the delay has caused. We need that oven for lasagna, and you know how cantankerous it is. I don't know if we'll get everything cooked in time." Though wearing slippers, she had an expression of acute agony on her face as she washed several heads of lettuce for the salad. Her bunions were acting up, but she insisted on doing everything herself. In her opinion—stated loudly and often—the rest of the potluck dinner committee was worse than useless.

Melinda Pennyworth had made a pot of beef stew. It was liberally laced with wine, but there didn't appear to be much meat in it. In fact, it looked a bit like gruel. She turned on the gas under the pot and said, "I'm sure it will feed several dozen."

"It would thicken if we added flour," Annie suggested.

"Certainly not!" Melinda eyed her coldly. "It's fine just the way it is. In fact, it's my husband's favorite."

Annie raised her eyebrows. "Really." The stew wasn't fit to eat. Pale and watery, with a few miserable potatoes, a lump or two of fatty meat, and an onion. Melinda was either a dreadful cook, notoriously stingy, or both. Since she'd waltzed into the kitchen bearing the stew pot and a loaf of burned banana bread, she'd done little but stand around and get in the way, issuing impractical orders that everyone ignored. They had no time to waste on place cards or handing out individual salads along with a special prayer as the congregation charged the dining room like a herd of water buffalo.

Uncle Ira looked around with a frown. "Hey, where's the salt?"

"Forget salt," ordered Aunt Hortense. "You don't need it. There's plenty on the chicken already. Did you go down to the bank and deposit those checks like I told you to yesterday?"

But he had only one thing on his mind, and it wasn't checks. "I tasted it. Needs salt. That's the trouble with you, you never put in enough salt."

"It doesn't, and I know what I'm talking about! I've cooked more chickens than you can count, Ira O'Hara, and don't you forget it!"

"There's little chance of that, dear. You never let me forget anything. Sweetheart."

"If that's an apology, don't bother. And if you forgot to deposit those checks, I'd better not find out about it." She turned the water off and began tearing the lettuce apart. Green bits flew everywhere.

At this rate, they'd end up with a very small salad, indeed. While Uncle Ira muttered that of course he'd deposited the checks, what did she think he was, an old fool, Annie handed her aunt a roll of paper towels and wisely refrained from comment.

Jan Stalker rushed in, still dressed in black, looking rather drunk. "I decided to come over to the dinner. I ran out of booze, and it was too dreary at home, watching the funeral over and over again." She shuddered. "God, that mob out there's pushing and shoving like you wouldn't believe. Two people had the gall to demand dessert now and plates to take home for relatives they said were too sick to come to church. Huh. They just want a free meal for later on tonight." She grabbed a loaf of bread and dumped it on a plate.

"Don't put that bread out. Mrs. Fielding brought it, and you know how she is," warned Aunt Hortense. "Brings us stuff you wouldn't feed a sick cat. It's moldy. Just throw it out. Honestly, why do people think they can foist off spoiled food on the potluck dinner?"

"They're just trying to save a buck." Jan helped herself to a sizable serving of lasagna. She piled several rolls on top.

"What do you think you're doing?" cried Aunt Hortense "Put that back. None of us have eaten yet."

Jan added three pats of butter and a dollop of strawberry jam to her loaded plate. "If I wait until everyone's served, there'll be none left." She picked up a knife and fork and dug in with gusto. After several bites, she muttered, "S'a damn shame, Morris dyin' like that. But I'll get even, you see if I won't. I know secrets, plenty of 'em, things people'd pay plenty to hide." She giggled. "Right there in plain sight, that's the best place."

Annie gave her a puzzled glance, wondering what the woman was mumbling about. Probably the booze talking.

"Funny," Jan muttered as she helped herself to another roll, "funerals always give me an appetite."

"I don't give two hoots about your appetite. Half the congregation's convinced we eat the best food and serve them leftovers." Aunt Hortense stumped over to the table. She swept the plate from under Jan's nose and put it on a high shelf. "You can eat later."

"But I'm hungry."

Aunt Hortense was implacable. "We're all hungry. Get up off your rump and make the punch before those idiots out there decide to come in and take it by force."

"Oh, very well." Jan heaved an annoyed sigh and began slopping ginger ale and strawberry soda into a huge steel pot. She added ice and ladled portions into paper cups on a tray, in the process spilling half of it.

Annie mopped up the mess while Jan took the tray out to the dining room. As the door swung open, a woman outside waved imperiously and yelled, "Hey, fix me two dinners with pot roast and salads. Thousand island dressing and no macaroni and cheese or baked beans. Wallace is allergic."

"It's Peg Hapgood, the banker's wife," said Aunt Hortense. "Dreadful woman. Pay no attention, Annie. She's incredibly rude. All she does is grab, grab, grab."

The door swung shut as Uncle Ira drew two envelopes from his jacket pocket with an air of utter disbelief. "Oh, no! I can't believe it, I was sure I'd deposited this yesterday!"

"For heaven's sake, you'd forget your head if it wasn't attached," snapped Aunt Hortense. "You'll have to do it after the potluck is over."

"It'll be too late then. I need to deposit them now. I . . . uh, paid a few bills."

"You mean they'll bounce?" Her voice was deceptively calm.

A nervous silence from Uncle Ira, then, "Well, they

might." He headed for the door, and she grabbed his arm.

"You're not going anywhere, Ira O'Hara. We need help right here in this kitchen. This meal won't cook itself."

"I know, but—"

"No 'buts.' We don't have time for that. The checks need to be deposited right now. Annie can do it. Give her the checks and the card."

Knowing what was good for him, he handed over the endorsed checks and his bank card without further argument. "Go downtown to South Sherman. The bank's right near Hondo Park. Workman's Credit Union. When you're done, you can put my card and the receipt in the hall table at home."

Delighted with the turn of events—if she played her cards right, maybe she could catch a glimpse of the mysteriously shy bank manager, Wallace Hapgood, and who knew where that might lead—Annie untied her apron and tossed it over the hook on the back of the door. "Okay, I'll be back in a jiffy."

About fifteen minutes later, she was standing in line before the teller's cage at Workman's Credit Union. The bank was a square, solid brick building with fake white columns and an eagle over the front door. The original idea, halfhearted at best, had been to make the outside of the bank resemble an early American colonial mansion, on the theory that people would feel comfortable depositing their money. Inside, they'd dispensed with the niceties. Tellers' cages were protected by bullet-proof glass. The ceiling bristled with all-seeing cameras that swiveled to follow every movement, and customers tended to huddle together under the eye of the armed guard by the door.

Only two people were ahead of her. A man and a woman who shuffled up to the counter, conducted their business in short order, and left.

Now it was her turn. She put on a look of worry, fumbled with her purse, and managed to drop the envelope twice before hurrying up to the teller. "Goodness, I don't know why I'm so clumsy today. I'm not usually like this." The teller, a blonde woman of forty or so in a peachy-pink dress, gave her a thin smile and a penetrating stare.

"May I help you?"

"Oh, of course." Annie laughed and handed over the envelope and bank card. "I'd like to deposit this in my uncle's account. Ira . . . O'Malley. No, wait a second . . . I didn't mean O'Malley. It's . . . O'Hara. Yes, that's it. O'Hara." The teller raised her eyebrows.

"And you are?"

"His niece, Ann O'Hara. He . . . uh . . . asked me to deposit it for him." She made a big production of swallowing nervously, whereupon the teller gave her another hard look and promptly pushed a button under the counter.

"Wait just a minute, please."

Annie didn't have to wait long. A few seconds later, Wallace Hapgood emerged from his office door, right beside the vault. He was a short, fat man with a cherubic expression. He exchanged glances with the teller and motioned her away. Coming around the side of the cage, he eyed Annie up and down, then said, "There's a small problem with your transaction. Would you come back to my office, please?" The "please" was an afterthought.

Annie followed him meekly down a short hallway to a door labeled, WALLACE HAPGOOD, MANAGER. He ushered her in, then walked around behind his expansive rosewood desk and sat down.

"Do you have a driver's license?"

Annie rummaged in her purse and produced it. He examined her photo, then her face. "Hmm, your name is O'Hara, all right. So you're Ira O'Hara's niece. I suppose there's a family resemblance. The red hair—not that your uncle has much of his left." He shifted some papers on his desk and gave her back the license. "We're a small-town bank here, Ms. O'Hara. Everyone knows every else. That's why the teller buzzed me about your transaction. We like to be thorough, and naturally, we need to make sure things are on the up and up. You could have gotten your uncle's checks by nefarious means."

"I understand. Perhaps I should have come in and explained first. But since I was only depositing the checks and not making a withdrawal, I didn't think it would matter."

He sat back in his well-padded swivel chair. "You're from back East. Maybe banks in New Hampshire are a bit sloppy about IDs, but I assure you we're not." Pausing, to admire his choice of words. "Well, let me suggest a few helpful hints guaranteed to make your life hassle-free: Dot the i's and cross the t's, even when you don't think it's necessary. For instance, you should have brought a note from your uncle."

Her smile became a stiff line across her face.

He struck her as both rude and overbearing. Casually dressed. No starched collar and businesslike blue serge suit. His dark hair, what was left of it, had a touch of gray at the temples, and he was a good forty pounds overweight. He wore expensive linen pants and an open-neck gray shirt with a scarf tied at the neck. There was a soft brown cashmere jacket tossed casually on a chair. Having made his point, he decided on a change of tactics and held out a pack of Kool's.

"Cigarette?"

"Thank you no. I don't smoke."

"Well, take a seat," he said, lighting up and inhaling greedily. "My wife won't let me smoke, so I spend a fortune on mints and mouthwash and try to confine my smoking to my office. How about some coffee? I'd hate to leave you with the impression that we're unfriendly out here."

Annie wasn't in the mood for this nonsense. She didn't like Wallace Hapgood, and she didn't appreciate his glance slithering over her body. Every time he did it, she felt a surge of temper rising in her like nausea.

She perched on the edge of a chair while Wallace Hapgood eyed at the silver-framed photograph on his desk. His wife's face simpered back at him. He looked away, his expression pained.

"I believe I saw your wife over at the church a little while ago."

"Yes, Peg said she was going to the memorial supper."

His eyes slid across Annie's breasts, and he said, "I'll have to miss it. No offense, but I've never been one for those potluck suppers. Too much chili. Gives me gas. Of course, Reverend Morris's unexpected death is a terrible thing."

"He was murdered."

"Quite right. I believe you found . . . the body. It must have been a shock." He stubbed out his cigarette and glanced at his watch. The interview was about to be closed, and just when Annie thought they might be getting somewhere.

There was something fishy about those rapidly blinking eyes. He knew something, she was sure of it. He might just take a nibble if she dangled a fat worm. She cleared her throat. "I heard that Reverend Morris had a few enemies. Looks like one of them decided to get even."

Wallace Hapgood shrugged, his face impassive. "I wouldn't know. I barely knew the man, haven't seen him in months."

"I see. Then he didn't do his banking here?"

"Well, yes, Morris was one of our customers. But I didn't know him personally."

"That's surprising, considering that you belong to the same church. It's such a small congregation, too. The poor man. It was really awful." She leaned forward, confidential now, just between the two of them. "He wasn't quite dead when I found him. He was still breathing. In fact, he didn't die until just as the ambulance and the police arrived."

Annie studied his reaction. He looked as if he'd had a terrible shock. The color drained from his face and he didn't speak for several moments. He stared at her. "Did . . . he say anything before he died?"

"You mean, did he tell me who had hit him?"

His eyes didn't leave her face. "Er . . . yes."

"Well, that's something the police told me not to discuss with anyone."

He frowned. "I see. Well, I don't like to talk about my personal affairs, but I wouldn't like you to get the wrong impression—"

"Yes?"

"My wife and I were having problems a few years ago, and she turned to Reverend Morris for . . . consolation." His face glistened with sweat as he went on, "She's been . . . distant with me ever since. She's a cruel woman. The truth is, we hardly speak to each other; these days my job here as bank manager is really all I've got. She didn't bother to be discreet about their affair, so everyone knew. I became a public laughingstock."

Oddly enough, Annie felt a sneaking sense of sympathy. She knew something about unpleasant spouses, and Wallace Hapgood looked miserable. "It sounds like a recipe for disaster . . . living with someone you don't love. But perhaps your wife didn't realize that people knew."

"Oh, she knew all right. That was part of the fun. With my luck, the police know all about it. But I didn't kill Morris. I went to bed early—I ate something at the party that made me sick and spent half the night in the bathroom with my head in the toilet." He gave her a thoughtful look. "It seems to me that committing murder is ten percent motivation and ninety percent opportunity. I couldn't have killed Morris if I'd wanted to, which I assure you I didn't."

She rose with a smile and held out her hand. He shook it. She saw the glitter of dislike in his hard stare.

She drew a deep breath when she got out into the corridor. She'd baited a trap and now wondered if she'd catch a minnow or a whale. Wallace Hapgood had plenty of reason to dislike Reverend Morris, but enough to kill him? Annie didn't know, and worse, she was beginning to regret her fiendishly clever remark that the reverend hadn't been dead when she found him, that he'd stayed alive until the ambulance and police arrived. As a ploy to frighten him into a revelation of some sort, it had more or less fizzled. Furthermore, she didn't like the look she had seen on his face as she'd left his office. He regretted revealing his private affairs, and his cold eyes had promised revenge.

When she got back to the house, Claudius was where she'd left him an hour ago, tied up under the shade tree. As she unhooked the garden gate, he started barking.

Where had she been all this time? He wasn't accustomed to being tied up for hours on end like a pet goat, and he let her know it.

"Shut up," she told him. She untied his leash and brought him into the house where—having disdained the water bowl she'd left for him under the tree—he drank a quart of water before sitting on his haunches and giving her a gimlet-eyed stare. She handed over several biscuits. Bribery, and she hated herself for giving in. But what choice did she have? Claudius kept a meticulous list of accounts. It was really quite simple. If she didn't fork over a few treats from time to time, he'd get even in spades. Perhaps a pillow torn to shreds or a shelf of books with the covers chewed off. He'd pick his time and place, and the sooner the better. He believed revenge a dish best served hot.

In spite of wondering how to explain such outlandish behavior to her aunt and uncle, she had put all the books up out of reach. He was only a dog, for God's sake. Here she was, turning her entire life, not to mention that of her relatives, upside down in order to accommodate his bad temper. Was she out of her mind?

She put Uncle Ira's bank card in the desk drawer in the hall where it would be safe. As she was closing it, the phone rang. "Hello?"

Low laughter and a muffled male voice whispered, "Hi baby. I got somethin' for you. How about takin' off your clothes and lyin' down right there on the floor? That'd really turn me on."

"Too bad it wouldn't do anything for me."

Silence, then, "Uh . . . sorry, wrong number." The receiver went down with a bang.

Annie stood there a moment, listening to the dead phone. Finally she hung up, wondering who the man was and who the lucky lady was he'd called. He hadn't sounded like Einstein, but then the nuances of his conversation hadn't lent themselves to high-flown talk. He could have been anyone with a poor vocabulary and a mind to match.

She dismissed him from her mind and decided to call New Hampshire. Kirk Deitrich was watching the antique shop. Maybe he'd sold half the inventory. Maybe she was dreaming.

He answered, sounding reassuringly normal. Everything was fine. He'd sold a few things. Not the big maple armoire, unfortunately—the profit from which would have been enough to have the tavern repainted—but he hadn't done badly. Six side chairs and that old trellis. Oh, and some coin silver. Spoons.

"So how's Roswell, New Mexico?"

"Fine," she lied. She didn't have the heart to tell him the truth. They talked a few minutes more, and she hung up wondering why she'd ever left home. Granted, life was dull back in Lee, New Hampshire. But dull was definitely preferable to murder.

She was hungry. The prospect of returning to the church and downing Melinda Pennyworth's beef vegetable stew held little appeal. Maybe a buttered roll. That would be quick and filling.

Claudius watched with keen interest as she got out the bag of rolls and butter. She selected a knife from a drawer, and he shifted his body a fraction of an inch so he could keep an eye on the rolls and the tub of butter at the same time.

The morning paper lay on the counter. Headlines two inches high screamed that a local minister had been killed, his throat torn out. By a wild animal or something more sinister.

Frowning, she put down the roll and picked up the paper. Her name was mentioned prominently, along with the fact that she'd found the corpse. The reporter, Bob Colfax, waxed eloquent about Claudius, a big, black dog who looked like a wolf and could have killed the reverend, although it was rumored that the dog was with her all morning. The police hoped someone in the vicinity of the church had heard the reverend cry out. Coyotes roamed the prairie, preying on herds of sheep, but the police did not think it likely that one had killed the Reverend Morris.

The story continued on page three.

She groped for the roll. It was gone, and Claudius was licking his chops, a look of satisfaction on his face.

"Hey, that was mine! You had two biscuits!"

He shot her a look that indicated she could starve for all he cared, then yawned and lay down on the rag rug in front of the stove. She stood there and fumed. Yet if she was stupid enough to leave food lying around on the counter, he'd do what any sensible dog would do—eat it. Why waste good food?

"God knows why I let Tom talk me into taking you in. I must have been out of my mind. You've done nothing but wreck my life. You eat my lunch, my pillows, my books." She counted to ten.

He yawned again to show her he wasn't interested in her ranting and raving, then, as an insulting afterthought, started licking his hindquarters.

She had to laugh. It was either that or scream. "You're disgusting, do you hear? Absolutely disgusting!" Seething, she buttered another roll and ate it. "This time, I'll make sure you don't get any!" Popping the last bite in her mouth. It tasted as good as it looked, and she wouldn't have to eat anything weird at the church.

After putting the butter away, she eyed the dog reluctantly. He raised his head. His eyes were bright, his body tense, and his tail wagged. She had no doubt what he wanted and after a brief mental battle, she gave in. "Okay, you can come back to the church with me. If I left you here you'd figure out how to get the refrigerator door open. Aunt Hortense would love that."

Exactly. He went and got his leash and stood by the back door, his eyes glowing.

"It must be very gratifying to know you're always right." She snapped the leash on his collar. "Naturally, you won again."

With a grunt of satisfaction, he dragged her outside and down the street toward the church.

As they passed the Stubenville house, Elvira hurried down the front steps. She was carrying a Pyrex casserole dish wrapped in a checkered towel. "Oh, Ms. O'Hara, are you going over to the church?"

"Yes." Annie wrapped the leash around her hand and stood her ground.

Claudius, raring to go, tugged on the leash. Let's get the show on the road, ladies. Time's awasting. But Annie figured she didn't need any more enemies. The game plan was to cultivate good will and innocent trust among the natives, at least until these ridiculous suspicions about Claudius died down.

Elvira's lips compressed, and her eyes narrowed. "Surely, you don't intend to take that animal to the church. He's dangerous!"

"Not at all. He's a Helping Hand guide dog, a boon to mankind."

"Is that so. Well, I read the morning paper from front to back. It didn't say anything about his being a guide dog."

"It didn't say he wasn't."

"In any case, that's a side issue. The precise point is, did he kill Reverend Morris. If he did, it's your fault because you didn't keep him under control. You could go to prison for that!"

By now Annie was walking down the sidewalk at a pretty good clip. Claudius made sure of that. Looking over her shoulder, she informed Elvira, "He was with me all last night, and he was never off the leash. For heaven's sake, I never even met Reverend Morris. Do you seriously think I'd kill a man I don't even know?"

Elvira was huffing and puffing as she tried to keep up. "Don't worry. I put you on one of my prayer lists."

"What?"

"Several prayer lists, actually. I have one for nonbelievers, one for those who commit sins of the flesh, that is sluts, fornicators, and adulterers. And one for aliens, of course." Elvira sighed. "Now I'll have to start one for murderers."

"What about one for women who steal underwear off other people's lines?"

"Whatever are you talking about?"

Annie told herself to stay on track with her original resolution. "Sorry," she muttered, trying for sincerity.

"Women who cover their nakedness with immoral garments are a temptation to men. Whores, all of them. It's no secret what they want."

"You're probably right," Annie agreed, adopting her sweetest manner. She tried to look as if she thought Elvira's destruction of lacy underwear was not only sensible, but even commendable. Immorality should be rooted out and destroyed wherever one discovered it.

They reached the end of Idlewild Circle and headed down Elm toward the church.

"You may not know this," said Elvira, "but I met Betty and Barney Hill. They came out West in the seventies on a fact-finding mission. They were the first to be abducted."

"Abduc—"

"By aliens."

"Oh." Somehow Annie kept a straight face.

"I met them. Some years later, naturally."

"Naturally."

"They were taken up to the spaceship. Tests were performed, and hours later they were returned. It's a very famous case."

"No doubt."

"Actually," confided Elvira, "I've listened to alien broadcasts since last May when I had a root canal done. The wires the dentist used are attuned to alien frequencies. Naturally, I have to turn my head in the right direction to cut down on static."

Annie made a vague wave of the hand, a gesture meaning, whatever makes you happy.

"Perhaps this is all confusing to you. Do you go to church?"

"No." Short and sweet. No need to go into chapter and verse about her differences with established religion. Furthermore, it was none of Elvira's business.

"I see. Well." A pregnant pause, then Elvira gave a superior smile and went smoothly into a detailed account of the wages of sin and the indisputable fact that Armageddon was right around the corner. Hellfire and damnation awaited all but the favored few. There was still time to save her eternal soul, but the aliens had informed her that Jesus was coming soon. If Annie planned to change her ways, she'd better get started.

"On the other hand," Annie put in when Elvira

paused for a much needed breath, "every generation thinks Armageddon's right around the corner."

"Nonsense. The end is near. The signs are all there if one knows what to look for. Earthquakes, tidal waves, hideous plagues mankind can't cure—AIDS and ebola—even that red heifer they found in Israel."

"That was unusual, wasn't it?" Annie smiled, hoping to change the subject. "As a matter of fact, I've always been interested in archaeology. Did you happen to hear about the discovery of human fossils in Turkey? They were more than eight hundred thousand years old!"

Elvira burst out laughing. "Don't tell me you believe that!"

"They used carbon dating. It's incredibly accurate."

"Poppycock." She surveyed Annie with a look of pity. "Everyone knows mankind has only been on the earth a few thousand years, just since the Garden of Eden."

"Oh." Annie had her own ideas about the Garden of Eden. And of fanatics who took every word in the Bible literally and tried to foist their beliefs on everyone else.

"Actually, it's a comfort, knowing my time on this planet is so short. Just before He comes, it will be dreadful. The government will make everyone worship heathen idols, and there will be hundreds of false prophets."

"Oh, Revelations," said Annie, getting interested in spite of herself.

"That's right."

"How do you tell the real Jesus from the fakes?"

"His feet won't touch the ground, and he'll throw the fake prophets into a lake of burning fire."

"That ought to do it." She smiled and a second later wished she hadn't.

Elvira wagged an admonishing finger. "Go ahead, laugh. You'd do well to heed my warnings. This will all come to pass, and sooner than you think. Only the righteous will be saved, so there's no use joining some other church. Our Friends from beyond the stars have already been in contact with me concerning the Savior."

"Really?"

"Yes, indeed. We hold weekly meetings at the church . . . well, I call them Celestial Thought sessions.

We gather in the Sanctuary and pray for heathens in distant galaxies. We've already been visited."

"So I gather."

"More than fifty years ago. A great day for mankind."

Annie frowned. "But wouldn't you think that after coming all this way, they'd find a better spot to land than the middle of the desert? Why not land on the White House lawn or at the United Nations?"

"Never fear, Our Friends know what they're doing. All will be made clear when the time comes."

"Come on, Mrs. Stubenville. Do you really believe this stuff?"

"*Believe it?* Of course," said Elvira, smiling in a superior manner. "Money is the root of all evil. There are some who would like to profit from Our Friends. When the time comes, they will burn in eternal hellfire. Like you, I'm afraid, dear."

Annie went into the church with a distinct sense of relief. Even Melinda Pennyworth's stew would be an improvement over Elvira's company.

Chapter Five

Sitting at one of the long tables in the church dining room more than an hour later, Annie was fully occupied with eating what purported to be an oriental salad. Strips of shoe leather and peanuts on a bed of lettuce and dried noodles. The dressing was mustard and congealed honey with globs of what looked like marshmallow. A glass of lemonade, a plate of ravioli, and a bowl of Melinda Pennyworth's stew sat cooling at her elbow. Claudius, masquerading as a blue ribbon guide dog, was under the table devouring whatever came his way. Annie passed the salad to him and looked around the room. Tables filled with people eating standard potluck fare: green molded Jell-o salad with nuts and pineapple bits, runny macaroni and cheese, overcooked ravioli. And at the table in the near corner, a woman weighing at least four hundred pounds with enough food in front of her to choke an elephant.

She shuddered and caught sight of her aunt and uncle talking to Elvira Stubenville across the room. No doubt, Elvira was launching into a lengthy harangue about her religious shortcomings. Wonderful. Two weeks of unmitigated hell was sure to follow, with prayer lists and Bible lectures forced down her throat at every turn. She tried to sip her lukewarm lemonade and almost gagged.

A tall, dark-haired man about thirty-five came in, looked over the crowd, and headed in her direction.

Smiling, he sat down across the table. "You look refreshingly normal, therefore you must be Annie O'Hara from New Hampshire. I'm Bob Colfax, reporter for the *Roswell Post*. I'd like to talk to you about your finding Reverend Morris's body."

"I don't want to be interviewed." She sat up straight and looked him firmly in the eye. "Go away."

He smiled again, and his eyes crinkled at the corners. "Hey, just doing my job. How about helping a guy out? It'd only take a minute."

"Go away."

Claudius growled, and Bob looked under the table. "Aha, the prime suspect, I presume."

"Yeah, so what."

Taking a flask from his pocket, he unscrewed the cap. "I hope you don't have any religious scruples about vodka. No smell, and it makes even The Church of Celestial Spheres bearable."

She ought to tell him to disappear and take his vodka with him. On the other hand, The Neighborhood Church of the Celestial Spheres really did require a little anesthesia.

"Thanks." She passed her glass of watery lemonade and he dumped in two fingers, then poured some in a glass for himself.

"Hair of the dog," he said, his brown eyes twinkling merrily.

"Yeah." Annie took an experimental swig and then another. Her ramrod posture began to relax.

"So," he said. "What was your impression of the good pastor's sermon this morning?"

"I didn't pay much attention."

"Lucky you. It was twenty minutes of baloney followed by ten minutes of piously malicious references to the late reverend's present whereabouts." He grinned. "I do believe Pastor Pennyworth has a mean streak under that shiny gold helmet of his. Reading between the lines, I heard him mention something to the effect that Morris got what he deserved. As you sow, so shall you reap and all that."

"Interesting." She smiled, batted her eyelashes at him, and decided that Bob Colfax had a beguiling charm. His face was thin and bony, and that smile of his was irrepressible. Pure Michael Palin, she thought and felt a spark of interest zing through her body. Or maybe it was the vodka. Whatever. She passed the stew under the table and took another drink. "Tell me more."

"The problem is you can't trust religious types," Bob Colfax confided as he sipped from his cup. "They read portents in everything, and I don't just mean tea leaves. My career is going down the tubes as it is."

"How awful." Annie blinked and wondered if her voice had slurred. By now she was feeling slightly sloshed.

Bob didn't seem to have noticed. "You know how it is in Roswell. Alien spaceships coming out of the woodwork all year long. Area fifty-one, black helicopters, scorch marks in the desert. That stuff practically writes itself. Morris's death is the first hard news we've had in months, and I want to sink my teeth into it."

A puzzled look floated briefly over Annie's face. "What's stopping you?"

"It's not that simple. Nobody wants to talk to the press, plus reporters from KRVA-TV managed to lock up most of the church bigwigs. I haven't been able to get even one lousy interview."

"I don't understand. You had most of the facts right in the story."

"Shucks, m'am. Anyone could have done it." His brown eyes crinkled up at the corners again.

She found herself smiling back.

"So how about that interview?" he said, sipping his vodka again.

"I suppose a few questions wouldn't hurt." Then she remembered the obscene phone call and quickly added, "Don't mention my aunt and uncle. They don't need, well, notoriety."

He whipped out a small tape recorder, turned it on, and got out a pen and notepad. "You're out here on a visit, right?"

"Yes."

"Ever been to New Mexico before?"

"No."

Chairs scraped as several church members sat down at the far end of the table. They glanced over at Annie. It was obvious they knew who she was and that she'd found the body. Whatever else it did, murder spiced up a dull summer, and they had another topic of conversation besides aliens and a supposed government coverup.

They noticed the tape recorder, and the man nearest Bob Colfax broke in chattily, "Hey, you a reporter? We usually go to the Methodist church, but the wife wouldn't rest until we came down to pay our respects. Reverend Morris used to give real Biblical sermons if you know what I mean. You went home with somethin' to chew on the rest of the week."

"Yeah." Bob shifted in the chair until he turned his back to him. He smiled at Annie. "Where were we?"

"I don't think this is such a good idea." She wished he wasn't desperate for a juicy story. That she'd never found the damned reverend . . . she wished a lot of things.

He gave her an exasperated look and switched the recorder off. "Getting cold feet?"

"Maybe." He had nice hands and she noticed he wasn't wearing a wedding ring—which meant nothing in this day and age. Lenny the jerk hadn't worn a ring. He'd said he was worried about getting electrocuted. The worst part was that she'd believed him. She sighed.

"Okay, no tape recorder. We just talk."

Did he think she was a total idiot?

"I don't want to discuss Reverend Morris's death. I don't know anything, so there's nothing to talk about."

"Okay, let's talk about your dog," he suggested. "I could write a story about him. People love dogs."

"They wouldn't love Claudius. Nobody loves him except my sister-in-law, about whom the less said, the better."

"She's not one of your favorite people?"

"She's a damn slut, if that answers your question." Annie took another sip of the vodka. "And you can quote me on that."

Bob grinned. "Getting back to Fido here. You don't think he's capable of killing someone?"

"I suppose he could if he felt threatened. But he didn't kill anyone." She drained her glass. "I said I didn't want to talk about Reverend Morris."

"No problem. I'm just collecting information. " He took a look under the table. "That's some collar he's wearing. What is it? Spikes?"

"Yes. I've tried every collar on the market, and he still does as he pleases. His fur is so thick he doesn't feel anything."

"He doesn't seem vicious."

"Not vicious." She struggled to explain. "Just stubborn and smart."

"You sound as if you don't like him."

"He's not crazy about me, either."

"Too bad, he's a handsome dog. What's the problem? Wrong chemistry, or are you just not a dog person?"

"You might say that."

"Then why bring him along on your vacation?"

"It's a long, boring story. Let's just say we're stuck with each other for the time being." She hiccupped.

Claudius nudged her leg, and she tossed him a buttered roll. He swallowed it whole and gave her another bump.

"Hold your horses." Without a twinge of conscience, she passed him the ravioli. "Don't say I didn't warn you. It tastes like cardboard."

He gave her a barely concealed sneer, sniffed the ravioli, and gulped it down.

Bob laughed. "I'm impressed. He's got a hell of an appetite."

"With my luck he'll probably get diarrhea."

"There's a vet on the corner of Main and Oak Streets. He's supposed to be good."

"Thanks, I'll keep it in mind."

"Glad to help." He gazed at her for a second, then said, "I probably shouldn't tell you this, but the cops are more or less certain Reverend Morris was killed with some kind of gardening tool. One of those claw diggers. I got an advance look at the autopsy report. Seems they found traces of manure and fertilizer in the wound. They're planning to ask everyone if they're missing a small garden digger."

Annie drew a sharp breath. "Then Claudius is definitely off the hook?"

"Unless he's got manure breath I'd say he's in the clear. Listen, you could really be a big help. You're in the inside, you can talk to church members without arousing suspicion. Keep your ear to the ground—you've no idea how much you might learn."

"Maybe, but why should I?"

He leaned across the table. "I've got the outlines of the murder clear enough, and with someone like you as a source, I can fill in the details. Not just who, but when and why. If I solve this crime, it could be a gold mine. Coast to coast publicity, interviews on *Today* and *Good Morning America.* I could write my own ticket, you name it. The sky's the limit. A book deal, even a movie option."

Annie, who'd found herself slowly relaxing in Bob Colfax's company, suddenly frowned. Why did she feel such a sense of disappointment? Most men played the angles. He was no different, and as long as she kept that pertinent fact clearly in mind, she wouldn't be disappointed.

She opened her mouth and shut it again.

"What were you going to say?"

"It wasn't important."

"Say," the man at the end of the table called to Annie, "ain't you the gal from back East who found Reverend Morris?"

She let out a sigh. "No."

"Funny, I could have sworn you was the one." He gave her another long look. "On TV they said she was a redhead."

Bob nudged her. "See what I mean? With a little encouragement they'd talk to you."

"Too bad. Find yourself another source and write the article. Someone's bound to talk eventually. You'll get all the information you need."

"I've already tried that. The pastor was willing to give me an interview until I brought out the recorder. Then he clammed up tight as a drum. But you could keep your eyes and ears open, and with any luck I'd come up roses."

Claudius bumped her leg with a cold nose, and she handed him the jello salad.

Bob laughed. "He's even eating that stuff. Is there anything he won't touch?"

"Not that I know of." It occurred to her that Bob's ambitions were more or less on the same plane as Claudius's gluttony. He made no bones about wanting to make a name for himself. Perhaps he wasn't as nice as he seemed at first. He saw people not as individuals but as objects to be used for his advantage. In other words, he was as selfish as the next person. It was no good thinking his character matched his handsome face.

But he had such a nice smile and really interesting hands. He should play the piano, she thought. Long fingers and strong wrists. Athletic but not muscle-bound. She decided to reserve judgment. If he turned out to be a louse, then what was good for the goose was good for the gander. If he was hell-bent on using her, she'd make sure she used him first.

Her aunt and uncle came over with loaded trays and sat down. "Where's your dinner, Annie?" her aunt said, forking up ravioli and looking around with a frown. "You couldn't have finished already."

"I wasn't all that hungry," she replied cunningly, kicking the dishes farther under the table. "Not after that big breakfast we had this morning."

Claudius grumbled a bit, but lay down again when no more food came his way.

She introduced Bob to her aunt and uncle. They smiled and chatted in a congenial fashion, and she noticed that their mood had changed from an hour ago. Evidently they'd made up in the kitchen.

"So." Uncle Ira gave Bob the once-over. "Are you a friend of Annie's from back East?"

"Actually, I'm a reporter for the *Roswell Post.*"

There was a dead silence, then Aunt Hortense put her fork down and announced, "If you're planning to write sleazy trash about Reverend Morris, young man, you can think again. We've nothing to say."

"No, ma'am. I have no plans to write anything but the

truth. The public needs to know why he was murdered. Everyone's in danger as long as the killer's loose."

"Maybe so," Unce Ira huffed. "But that doesn't mean we'd allow our names to be splashed all over the front page. It'd put us in danger."

"Why? You have nothing to hide surely."

"Of course not. I never said such a thing."

"We had nothing to do with the reverend's death," Aunt Hortense protested. "He was a fine man, a great loss to the congregation. Why in the world would we want to kill him?"

Bob grinned toothily. "If you gave me an interview, you could make that point perfectly clear. There'd be no doubt about your innocence."

He sat back in his chair with a look of satisfaction. And why not, Annie thought. Apply a bit of pressure, scare their pants off, and he had them right where he wanted.

She put a hand on her aunt's arm. "You don't owe him anything. Let him get his story from somebody else." Bob kicked her under the table. She smiled at him. "You should be digging for news, not pestering innocent people."

"That's right," her uncle declared, realizing belatedly that he'd been bamboozled. "We don't know why Reverend Morris died and we have nothing to say."

Bob shrugged. "Okay, but you knew him. Did he have any enemies? What about debts?"

"How would we know?" Uncle Ira retorted. "He was the assistant pastor. We'd just thrown a welcome home party for him, and someone killed him. Fini. End of story. You want a list of enemies, go talk to people who really knew him."

"Okay, maybe I'll do just that." Bob rose to his feet and nodded. "Nice meeting you folks."

He walked off, and Annie gazed after him, worriedly. No doubt he'd think up some other underhanded way to get what he wanted. He was smart and determined if not particularly ethical. These days in journalistic circles, two out of three wasn't bad, she supposed.

Uncle Ira took out his handkerchief and wiped his

glasses. "Jeez, that was close. If we hadn't been careful, we'd have ended up on page one."

Her uncle was in total denial, they still might get chewed up by the Fourth Estate, Annie thought with a sigh. She rubbed her temple where a small headache was starting and mentally added cheap vodka to Bob's list of sins. "I'm afraid he's still up to something. He gave up too easily."

Bewildered, Aunt Hortense protested, "What do you mean?"

"Bob Colfax wants this story so bad he can taste it. He'll try again. Whatever works."

"Huh," huffed Uncle Ira. "We'll be ready for him next time. He won't get a word out of us."

Aunt Hortense looked dubious. "But he made sense. We don't know why Reverend Morris was murdered. Oh dear, what if it's one of those serial killers? Maybe he's left a trail of victims across the country."

"We've got enough trouble without worrying about another Ted Bundy running around loose." Uncle Ira ate some of the jello salad and put his spoon down with a look of disgust.

"Ted Bundy's dead." Aunt Hortense thought for a moment, then added, "Anyway, he only killed women with long dark hair."

"I know that," he retorted. "It was merely an expression."

Annie could see another one of their arguments brewing and cleared her throat. "It didn't look like a serial killing to me." Not that she was an expert on serial murders, but it would have been front page news by now if several people had had their throats torn out.

"Serial killers are everywhere," Aunt Hortense said with a knowledgeable air. "That young man in Atlanta and that awful woman in Florida. She killed six or seven men. They made a TV movie about her. Women usually aren't serial killers."

Looking somewhat fed up, Uncle Ira pushed back his chair and got to his feet. He piled his dishes on his tray. "I'm going back to the house to water the garden. You two coming?"

"Good grief, there's Mrs. Fielding." Aunt Hortense frowned as a stout woman bore down on them. A vision in red and white stripes that resembled a circus tent, she carried a tray with enough food to feed an army. "I cannot abide her," muttered Aunt Hortense. "Gossip's her middle name. Give her the opportunity, and she'll talk your ear off. Come on, Annie, let's go."

Hurriedly, Annie picked up the dishes under the table, piled them on her tray, and hauled Claudius out. He gave her a look of withering contempt. She shrugged. "So it wasn't steak tartare. No one told you to eat it."

After putting their trays in the kitchen, they left the church and started across the parking lot. With Claudius safely leashed, Annie trailed along in her aunt and uncle's wake. A few yards ahead, the pastor and John Barnard were putting up a new sign—much bigger than the old one. The name of the church and the street number were carved in white and gold. Floodlit from the front and backed by a bed of shrubs, it was about six feet by twelve, with the pastor's name prominently displayed. SENIOR PASTOR MICHAEL PENNYWORTH. It was already set in cement. The old sign, with REVEREND MORRIS, ASSISTANT PASTOR beneath that of the pastor's, lay on the grass by a toolbox and sledgehammer. Pastor Pennyworth's name wasn't as prominent on the old sign. Progress marches on, she thought. Onward and upward in gold letters five inches high. Morris was dead. Long live Pastor Pennyworth.

Aunt Hortense crossed her arms over her plump breast, took a step back, and eyed the shining new sign. "It's not straight."

"What are you talking about?" retorted the pastor. "Of course it's straight. Do you think we'd go ahead and set it in cement without checking to see if it was level?"

"Yes."

He cocked his head at the sign. "Looks perfectly straight to me. What do you think, John, straight as an arrow—right?"

"Well, we checked it first," the caretaker agreed, shrugging. "But it could've moved some when we was sinkin' the posts. Maybe she's right."

"It's slightly on a slant," Uncle Ira chipped in. "But not much. It's almost straight."

"How much did it cost?" Aunt Hortense demanded.

"Around seven hundred." The pastor's neck was getting red. "And don't tell me the finance committee's going to complain. I already know that. We needed a new sign. The old one looked stupid with Reverend Morris still listed as assistant pastor."

Aunt Hortense cut to the heart of the matter. "Why do we need a new sign? The fact that Reverend Morris is dead doesn't mean the old one couldn't have been repainted. It would have worked just as well—even better, as a matter of fact, because it would have saved us seven hundred dollars we can't afford to waste on nonsense like this. And it was *straight.*"

Annie agreed with her aunt's assessment of the matter, but the pastor did not. His face went beet-red, his mouth curled unpleasantly, and in one swift movement, he picked up the sledgehammer and smashed the old sign to bits. "I think that pretty well settles the matter."

John Barnard and Uncle Ira both looked stunned.

"Well!" Aunt Hortense drew an affronted breath. "Go ahead, smash things like a spoiled two-year-old, Michael Pennyworth, but it doesn't change a thing! That ridiculous sign is still crooked, and it's not a matter of degree. It's like being pregnant. Either you are or you aren't, and that sign is crooked as a corkscrew!"

Muttering something about once a jackass, always a jackass, she marched off down the street toward home. Uncle Ira swore under his breath and hurried after her, and Annie followed along with Claudius. She was thinking about the smashed sign and the sledgehammer. Hitherto, the pastor had seemed a quiet sort—more or less rational, even-tempered—not at all the type to grab a thirty pound sledgehammer and beat a wooden sign to bits. Yet, as sure as God made little green apples, Pastor Pennyworth had been seized by an urge for sudden, violent behavior.

She tried to picture him doing something similar to Reverend Morris, only using a garden hand fork, and she had no trouble at all. What if the pastor had been overcome with jealousy? According to Aunt Hortense, the pastor's sermons were usually a litany of his own achievements, few and far between though they were. He liked to sing and did so at every opportunity, loudly and off-key. Despite a penchant for having himself videotaped while giving his all in the pulpit every Sabbath, Oral Roberts and Jimmy Swaggart had little to fear from him. His career was going nowhere.

The late Reverend Morris, on the other hand, had been a rising star in the church, a fine speaker who'd brought in many converts, which meant big bucks for the church coffers. Unfortunately, he was rumored to have ignored the commandment about not coveting his neighbor's wife, which, not surprisingly, had angered a good many people in town. He'd done his fair share of traveling too, doubtless indulging in sexual peccadilloes when and where his fancy took him, so his enemies were bound to be numerous and far-flung. But opportunity had to be the key here. Someone who knew he'd be at the church that night. Someone here in town . . . and probably a member of the church.

Annie's brain whirred busily as she walked down the shady street toward Uncle Ira's. At first glance, the method of killing seemed to rule out a woman as murderer. It wouldn't take that much strength, she supposed. But it was such a grisly way to kill someone. Blood and gore spattered everywhere. Somehow, it didn't feel like a woman's crime, which left only men. And if you didn't count the odd tramp or lunatic overcome by a sudden homicidal impulse, it had to be someone she knew. Pastor Pennyworth, Roger Stubenville, George Digby, John Barnard, or the banker, Wallace Hapgood.

Maybe Reverend Morris had discovered Hapgood was an embezzler—a classic setup for blackmail. Hapgood said he was sick the night of the murder, but that wasn't much of an alibi. If it meant keeping her opulent lifestyle, his wife would lie through her teeth for him. That made five suspects, not counting Uncle Ira, now hurrying down the street after Aunt Hortense, his arms full of potluck dishes, pots, and pans. Uncle Ira was out, he wouldn't kill a flea.

So five suspects remained.

Well, it wasn't really her problem . . . the police were hard at work, questioning everyone and checking alibis. For some reason, though, this wasn't terribly reassuring. She had a sneaking suspicion the police would be satisfied with anyone who fit the profile of number-one suspect. Never mind that he was innocent. A quick arrest meant big headlines, and that translated into political power. Heady stuff, indeed. Look at what had happened to Sam Sheppard. It had taken years and the discovery of DNA to clear him, long after his death.

She swallowed hard. Maybe it was her problem, after all.

The garden was in dire need of water. Cabbage leaves hung limp, and the tomato plants drooped in the hot sun. While Aunt Hortense went into the house to make iced tea, Uncle Ira fiddled with a complicated system of hoses and sprinklers, and in no time a fine spray of water was soaking the ground beneath the plants.

"I should weed a bit, I suppose," he said. "I'll get a hoe from the potting shed."

Annie led Claudius to a tree where he began digging a hole. She pulled him away from his excavation. "Cut that out." Immediately, he turned and headed for the shed, dragging her with him, and she yelled to her uncle, "We'll get the hoe."

The shed was overhung with luxuriant ivy and dutchman's pipe vine. Hummingbirds darted here and there, and red blossoms nodded in the hot breeze as she pulled the door open and stepped inside.

The interior of the shed was meticulously kept. Tools and hoses hung from wall pegs, and shovels, spades, rakes, and gardening forks were stored in a barrel of oiled sand by the window. Terra-cotta pots and baskets of varying sizes were neatly piled on wooden shelves. Jackets were hung from wall hooks. Beneath them stood boots and brooms in an orderly row. The floor was brick and the air was cool. Annie wandered around, peering into pots of seedlings set out on an old table. Cucumbers, by the look of them. She frowned. It was late in the season to be putting them in. They'd hardly have time to ripen before frost.

But planting times here in New Mexico were bound to be different from New England.

She glanced at the trowels, hand forks, and dibbers on the wall. Her uncle's name was painted on the handles in blue paint, and he'd hung them in order of size. Biggest on the left down to the smallest on the right.

A hook in the middle was empty.

Claudius was snuffling about by a barrel labelled POTTING MIX.

She switched hands holding the leash and then everything seemed to happen in a blur: One of the cats walked in, saw Claudius, and shot out again. Annie's arm was all but jerked out of the socket as he let out a bark and whipped past her out the door. She grabbed the edge of the door and hung on to the leash as it caught the edge of the seedbox, knocking it off the table. The seedbox hit the brick floor and smashed to bits. Dirt and cucumber seedlings flew everywhere.

Annie smiled at Claudius who was all but cross-eyed, choking on the other end of the leash. She wound the leash around her wrist again. "I told you not to chase the cats and I meant it."

He lifted his lip in a barely concealed sneer, then it was gone as he gazed at her, his expression perfectly plain. He'd never agreed to her stupid rules. She could lecture until her face turned blue, and it wouldn't change the fact that cats were meant to be chased and had been since the beginning of time. It wasn't his fault she was a blithering idiot.

Ignoring him as he flopped on the bricks and continued to glared at her, she found a broom and swept up the spilled dirt. Pieces of the broken seedbox were lodged behind the barrel. She pulled them out and felt something else in the shadowy darkness, something hard and metal.

She bent down and got it out with the broom. It was the missing hand fork. Her uncle's name was painted on the handle, it was dirty. She felt pretty sure her uncle wouldn't have left it behind the barrel in that condition. He would have wiped it clean and hung it back on the hook.

The fork had been hidden on the floor behind the barrel. There were reddish stains on the steel tines.

Chapter Six

Uncle Ira didn't take the news about his garden fork very well. His face turned red and the veins stood out on his neck like cords as he stared at it on the potting table. "Damn it, someone broke in here! I never would've left my fork dirty like this, and for sure I wouldn't leave it behind the barrel. I respect my tools. When I'm done with them, I scrub them clean and put them away without fail. Dammit, someone used a key to get in." He peered at his keys, each neatly labeled and attached to a keychain in the shape of a flying saucer. "Thank God, mine are all here."

Annie examined the door. "You don't have a lock on the door. All somebody had to do was walk in and take it."

"Oh, yeah, I keep meaning to put a lock on. Well, the door was shut tight, and some son of a bitch got in and took my garden fork."

"The stains look like dried blood. We should call the police. After all, it could be the murder weapon."

"I don't care," he snapped. "I'm not getting involved. Reverend Morris wasn't exactly a friend of mine, and I made no effort to hide how I felt. He was a creep, a louse."

"But you can't conceal evidence in a murder case."

"You don't think so? I'll clean it, hang it back on the hook, and no one's the wiser." He picked up an oily rag and reached for the fork.

Annie grabbed it first. "I'm calling the police, Uncle Ira. You're too upset to think clearly."

"What the hell. They'll probably arrest me."

"For heaven's sake, everyone who knows you knows you're not capable of killing anyone."

He gave a hollow laugh. "That's what half the prison population says."

"Oh, come on."

"They'd be delighted to pin Morris's murder on me. I had motive and opportunity. The fact that I'm innocent won't matter a hill of beans. The truth is, I've had one or two run-ins with the police. That idiot Jan Stalker plays her TV too loud at all hours. Generally I just call and complain, but she started leaving the phone off the hook. So one night I went over and banged on her front door and she called the cops. They don't like me."

"That's ridiculous. If you're arrested, which is highly unlikely, we'll hire a lawyer and get you released."

"Your aunt's going to take this very badly. She's having her feet done in a few days. You'll have to keep an eye on her if they arrest me."

"Nothing's going to happen. Aunt Hortense will be just fine. The police will analyze the stains on the fork, and if it's not blood—"

He shrugged. "Then I'm a monkey's uncle. Let's stop kidding ourselves. It's blood, and it's probably Morris's, damn his sanctimonious hide. I'll bet he's sitting in hell laughing his fool head off. He didn't like me, either."

It was an hour before Lt. Rhodes arrived. An hour during which Aunt Hortense went into hysterics, and Uncle Ira paced helplessly. "Maybe they won't arrest me," he said without much conviction. "After all, I didn't kill Morris. I was asleep in bed when he died."

Aunt Hortense blew her nose and tried to compose herself. "I have a terrible confession to make. This is all my fault! I took your fork over to the church last week. I was planting some bulbs for fall bloom in that bed by the annex. I . . . I must have forgotten it. I thought I picked it up along with the empty bag of bulbs, but you know how bad my memory has been lately. I'd forget my head if it wasn't attached. Oh, Ira, what if that fork turns out to be the murder weapon? They'll think you did it and hid it in the shed."

Annie stared at her as the full implication of her

aunt's confession set in. The fork had lain, forgotten, in the grass for several days. The killer had grabbed it because it was there at hand. He'd murdered the reverend, then he'd hidden the fork in the shed. Uncle Ira's name had been right there on the handle. The perfect patsy.

Maybe not. "Uncle Ira, if you'd left the house that night, Claudius would have barked like crazy and he only barked once when he heard something getting in the trash. That's proof you're telling the truth."

He shook his head. "They won't believe me."

The doorbell rang, and Annie, feeling decidedly guilty for having called them in the first place, went to let the police in.

This morning, Lt. Rhodes wore the latest in sunglasses with slim black frames. His blue suit was rumpled, and his dark hair was combed straight back in a wet look that he must have thought made him look like Robert DeNiro. He took a last drag on a cigarette, tossed the butt away, and got right to the point. "Okay, where is it?"

"Out back in the potting shed."

A second policeman got out of the squad car. Lt. Rhodes yelled, "George, keep an eye on the front of the house and see that no one tries to leave while I check this out." He turned back to Annie. "Who found the fork?"

"I did."

"Aren't you the busy little bee. First you find the body, now the fork. Well, I suggest you show me the shed."

Her aunt and uncle eyed them nervously from the dining room window as she led Lt. Rhodes around the side of the house.

Jan Stalker's kitchen faced this end of the backyard. As Annie opened the garden gate, she could see her at the sink, washing dishes. The damn woman didn't miss a trick.

"So where were you when you found it?" Lt. Rhodes stood in the shed doorway and cast an appraising eye around at the neatly kept shelves.

She pointed toward the corner. "Over there."

He gave her a sour look and pulled on a pair of latex gloves. "You've probably ruined any chance of prints."

"Well, I didn't think—"

"Exactly," he muttered, glancing over his shoulder. "Where's that damn dog?"

"In the house."

"Good. See that he stays there." He held the garden fork up to the window, then frowned and bagged it. "Where was it?"

"Under the potting table."

"What were you doing when you found it?" he said, as if the mere fact of her being in the shed marked her guilty as sin.

"Sweeping the floor."

He eyed the empty space on the pegboard. "Your uncle's thorough, I'll say that for him. He's painted his name on all his tools." He glanced at the bottles and boxes on a nearby shelf. "Ah, the latest in weed killers."

"Uncle Ira is really into gardening." That smacked of expertise in poisons. She tried again. "Actually, he's an incredible gardener. You should taste his lettuce."

"Your uncle's just lucky the reverend's throat was cut. If this were a poisoning case, we wouldn't think twice about charging him. He's got enough stuff in this shed to wipe out half the state."

"He didn't kill anyone."

"Let me get him downtown for half an hour, and he'll sing a different tune. I'll get his confession, then we'll apply for a search warrant and probably turn up all kinds of evidence."

It was like banging her head against a stone wall. She cleared her throat. "As a matter of fact, it turns out my aunt left the fork over at the church annex last week when she was planting bulbs. She forgot all about it. Obviously, the murderer found it and used it to kill Reverend Morris."

Lt. Rhodes raised his eyebrows. "You're saying your aunt had a convenient lapse of memory?"

"She's an old lady. It was an innocent mistake."

"Well, we'll talk to her and get to the truth." He smirked. "That story of hers doesn't explain how the fork ended up here, and it didn't just walk back on its own."

"The killer had to have planted it. He knew it belonged to my uncle. You can't miss his name on the handle."

He jerked his head toward the door. "Let's go have a little talk with both of them."

"Look, my aunt's rather upset. She's having surgery in a few days. It'd be best if you were . . . gentle with your questions." Annie winced. That sounded lame, even to her ears.

"Let me make myself perfectly clear . . . just in case you share your aunt's faulty memory. Reverend Morris is dead. This is a murder investigation, and that fork is very likely what killed him. Your uncle's name is on the fork. It goes without saying that he's a suspect in the investigation."

A few minutes later, they were in the kitchen.

Claudius was lying asleep on the rug by the sink, dead to the world.

Lt. Rhodes sat down and placed the bagged garden fork on the table.

The murder weapon retained an eerie quality of menace. Blood stains and ragged bits of skin were visible through the clear plastic. Annie drew a sharp breath and looked away.

A faint spark of cunning lit the detective's eyes as he watched Uncle Ira, who hadn't taken his eyes off the plastic bag. There was a terrible quiet in the kitchen. "Do you admit this fork is yours?"

"Yes." Then Uncle Ira muttered something that to Annie's horror, sounded like, "I'm not sorry he's dead. I'd be a damned hypocrite if I said I was."

"Don't answer any more questions, dear," cried Aunt Hortense. "They'll arrest you. They'll put handcuffs on you and throw you in jail. I just know it."

Ignoring her outburst, the lieutenant took out his notebook and pen and made a few notes. "Mrs. O'Hara, your niece says you left the fork by the annex sometime last week. Is that true?"

She nodded. "I was planting fall blooming crocuses. I

ordered some lovely purple ones by mail. They'll make a lovely show by the annex door. That bed has always been a problem. Not enough sunshine. And thrips. You wouldn't believe the infestation—"

"Never mind that stuff. Let's get this straight. You're saying the fork was lying there in the grass for several days?"

"Yes, I'm so sorry. The murder is all my fault. Reverend Morris would probably still be alive if I'd remembered to bring it home."

"I doubt it. The killer would have used some other weapon. The fact is, he wanted Morris dead. Now, Mr. O'Hara, you admit you knew Reverend Morris?"

"Yes."

"I see. What was the reverend like?"

"Gregarious, a good talker. He got along well with most people. Women liked him . . ." Uncle Ira faltered to a stop. "Do you want the truth?"

"That would be helpful."

"He was a goddamn jerk, a royal pain in the ass."

"Oh, Ira, no!" Aunt Hortense wailed.

Claudius lifted his head and stared at Aunt Hortense as her face crumpled and she mopped her tears.

Annie put a comforting arm around her. "Don't worry. Everything's going to be all right."

Lt. Rhodes spared Annie a sour look that amounted to hostility. "So, Mr. O'Hara, you admit you didn't like Reverend Morris?"

"Couldn't stand the goddamn son of a bitch."

"I'm glad you decided to be honest. It's really the best course in the long run."

"Nobody liked him. Women though, they fell for him like a ton of bricks. For the life of me I can't figure it out. Morris was a total sleaze, a nymphomaniac." He frowned. "Are men nymphomaniacs or only women?"

Lt. Rhodes looked annoyed. "Where were you Wednesday night after the party?"

"In bed with my wife, sleeping."

"If that's your alibi, Mr. O'Hara, then you have a big problem."

Uncle Ira opened his mouth and then shut it again.

"You were going to say something?" Lt. Rhodes asked.

"No . . . nothing."

"I don't understand," Annie put in. "My uncle is incapable of killing anyone."

"That's right. He wouldn't hurt a fly." Aunt Hortense stared at the detective in outraged disbelief. "He was with me all night. My niece was here in the house, and she'll swear he didn't leave the bedroom."

"Your niece will say any damn thing you tell her to," Lt. Rhodes retorted.

Annie glared at him. "That's a cruel thing to say."

"Murder is a cruel business."

Uncle Ira's shoulders sagged. "What have I done to be treated like this?"

"That's a good question," said Annie hotly. She took one look at her uncle's miserable face and bit back the rest of what she'd been about to say. It wouldn't do him any good if she told Lt. Rhodes where to get off. She managed an apologetic smile. "It's true. My uncle never left the house. Claudius would have barked his head off, and he didn't. Look, it's common knowledge that a lot of people were mad at Reverend Morris. He had debts all over town. He had two ex-wives and was way behind on his alimony payments."

Lt. Rhodes raised a negligent eyebrow. "Maybe so. But unlike your uncle, both the ex's have iron-clad alibis. One was in Vegas, the other was looking after her sister's kids."

The kettle on the stove whistled, and Annie told her aunt to sit and rest her feet. She'd make the tea. She took down the mugs and spoons, mulling over a variety of things to say that would prove her uncle's innocence beyond a shadow of a doubt. Unfortunately, none of them sounded even remotely sensible.

She plopped tea bags in the mugs while the detective told her uncle that if the forensics panned out the way he expected, they'd probably throw him in jail and toss away the key. So why not spare everyone a lot of pain and expense and confess right up front? She stiffened with resentment. Lt. Rhodes was condescending, sarcastic, and rude. He was truly detestable.

After pouring boiling water in the mugs, Annie plunked one down in front of Lt. Rhodes. Hot water splashed over the rim, scalding his hand.

He jerked it away. "Damn it!"

His ruff stiffening, Claudius growled and stood up. Lt. Rhodes shot Annie an angry look.

"Sorry," she said, grabbing the dog's collar and shoving him under the table.

"Okay. Where were we? Oh, yes." Eyeing the dog warily, he picked up the plastic bag containing the fork. "Mr. O'Hara, let me tell you where you stand. The only reason I'm not taking you in right now is that there's one chance in a hundred you're telling the truth. People generally don't kill unless they've got a good reason or at least one that makes sense. I haven't figured out a reason yet that would make sense to you."

"What if the killer's a nut?" Annie suggested. "A psycho?"

"Then all bets are off. But somehow I don't think your uncle here is a psycho. He's as sane as I am. I think he quarreled with Reverend Morris after the party and killed him in the parking lot behind that dumpster." Giving Claudius a wide berth, the lieutenant walked across the kitchen and opened the door. "One more thing, Mr. O'Hara. Don't leave town."

The door closed with a decided bang. Claudius flung himself against it, barking vociferously, and Annie muttered, "I hate that man. He's a fool."

Uncle Ira looked aghast at her lack of respect for Roswell's finest, then he shook his head. "He actually believes I killed Morris. My God, what am I going to do."

Aunt Hortense's fingers tore at her handkerchief. "Oh, Ira, this is terrible!"

Just then shouts erupted outside. Claudius, who had stopped barking, started up all over again. Annie shouted at the top of her lungs at him to be quiet and jerked the door open to find Elvira Stubenville in the middle of the path glaring at Lt. Rhodes. She was holding a cup in one hand and pushing him away with the other.

"There's no need to blaspheme, young man! I merely stopped by to borrow some sugar."

"Sure, lady. Just remember curiosity killed the cat." He shook her hand off and stalked on down the path to the driveway, yelling to his partner out front, "Wake up, George. Let's get the show on the road."

Elvira came bustling up the back steps. "Thank God that dreadful police detective's gone. What happened? Are they going to arrest anyone?"

"It's nothing that concerns you," Uncle Ira said sourly.

"Police crawling all over the neighborhood, and I'm not supposed to be concerned? That'll be the day!" She sat down at the kitchen table and looked around with a smile. "My, my, Hortense, your kitchen is so cozy. Homey. I've always said you had a talent for making a house really homey."

Aunt Hortense glared at her as if wondering whether to throw her out. Finally, she gave in with a sigh of disgust. "Have a cup of tea."

"Thanks, I don't mind if I do. Decaf if you've got it. I never touch caffeine. It's against my principles." Morris's death and the subsequent uproar had Elvira at the top of her Bible-thumping form. Her mouth set in a firm slash and her eyes gleamed. "Didn't I say it'd be like this near the end? The aliens broadcast terrible warnings. I hear them almost every day. Plagues and violence everywhere. The police can't stop it. Global warming and glaciers melting. Tornadoes and earthquakes. Soon the seas will rise and wipe out the entire East Coast, that is if China doesn't bomb us all to smithereens first. I'm just glad I don't live in New York!"

Uncle Ira gave Annie a meaningful look. "About that book you wanted to read. I've got a copy in the living room."

What book? Annie frowned at him.

He nodded toward the hall. He wanted to talk to her in private. Well, she had a few things to say to him, too. "Oh . . . right, that book."

From Aunt Hortense's outraged expression, it was clear she wasn't fooled, but was too busy dealing with Elvira, the aliens, and the Second Coming to protest.

He led the way to the dim little room with the brown plastic-covered sofa and the ashtray shaped like a spaceship. There was a loud whooshing noise as Annie sat on the plastic cushions. "Okay, what's up?"

He strode up and down on the carpet. "It's your aunt. I'm worried about her. She's a nervous wreck. On top of that business about the garden fork, there's her bunion surgery. She's practically tearing her hair out, and what can I do about it? Nothing. You've no idea how this galls the hell out of me, Annie. I feel so damned useless."

"I know, I feel the same way."

"If I could only figure out how the killer returned the fork to the potting shed without being seen." He frowned thoughtfully. "The shed faces the path by the side of the house. It's not locked. All he had to do was walk in and toss it behind a barrel. I wouldn't have seen it for days, weeks, maybe."

"That's true, but why bother to bring it back? He took a chance. Why didn't he simply throw it away somewhere or leave it by the body? It doesn't make sense."

"Sure it does. The damned bastard wanted to throw suspicion on me. If I'd killed Morris, I'd have been nuts to leave the fork by the body. It had my name on it."

"But if you'd killed him, all you had to do was clean the fork. No one would have suspected you. It looks like someone went to a lot of trouble to frame you. Come on, Uncle Ira, think. Who hates you that much?"

"How the hell should I know? Half the town of Roswell could have killed Morris."

Claudius padded in and sat down. He started scratching energetically.

"Christ, fleas. Your aunt will love that."

"It can't be fleas. He's got a flea collar."

"Sure, for Eastern fleas. Out here in New Mexico, they're probably bigger and meaner, immune to that kind."

"Come on. Flea collars are pretty much the same everywhere."

"You don't have the same bugs in New England," he told her. "Trees are different, climate's different. Stands to reason fleas would be tougher out here."

Giving up the useless task of trying to explain fleas to her uncle, she changed the subject. "A funny thing happened after I came back from depositing your checks at the bank this afternoon."

He turned with a frown. "What?"

"While I was in the kitchen, you got a phone call from some weirdo. Heavy breathing, the whole bit. I told him to buzz off, and he said it was a wrong number and hung up."

Uncle Ira pondered this a moment, then shrugged. "Our number is one away from Pastor Pennyworth's. We get his calls all the time."

"The pastor? It doesn't make sense. Why would some man call him up and tell him to take his clothes off and lie down on the floor?"

"Good grief, maybe there's more to the pastor than meets the eye."

"Maybe it was meant for his wife."

"You took the call. Maybe you have an admirer. That reporter fellow."

She shook her head. "It wasn't Bob Colfax."

Uncle Ira looked as if he were struggling to understand the social life of a divorced woman. "Well, I realize it's a different generation. With different standards."

The plastic stuck to the back of her knees and squeaked loudly as she got up. "Baloney, I don't talk to heavy breathers."

Chapter Seven

It didn't take long for the neighborhood to react to the news that the police had been questioning Uncle Ira again. The paper boy brought the *Roswell Post* right to the door, something heretofore unheard of. Annie opened the door and took a ten out of her wallet to pay him.

"You owe six bucks for last week," the boy said, handing her the paper and digging in his pocket. "Wait a sec. I think I got change."

Aunt Hortense called from the kitchen, "Who is it, dear?"

"Just the paperboy."

He fished four dollars from his grubby pocket and darted her a sharp glance. "Ain't you scared, lady? I wouldn't stay here for a million bucks. You couldn't pay me enough money to live with a murderer!"

Aunt Hortense's expression of pinched disapproval as she hurried to the door indicated that she'd heard that last remark. She dragged Annie inside and slammed the door in the boy's face. "Of all the nerve! I taught that boy in Sabbath School. I'll have a talk with his mother, and don't think I won't!"

Annie unfolded the paper. The headline read: Reverend's Killer Still on the Loose. The byline was Bob Colfax's, but she didn't see her name anywhere on the front page, which she took as a sign that he wasn't quite the louse she'd thought he was.

"I'll never read that dreadful ragsheet again," Aunt Hortense snapped. "In fact, I'm canceling our subscription. What does it say . . . that your uncle is a murderer?"

Annie ran her eyes down the page. "No, just that the police are still investigating a number of leads and that they expect an arrest soon."

"I'll bet," her aunt grumbled. She peered out the window. "That squad car drives by the house practically every hour. The way they act you'd think your uncle and I were Bonnie and Clyde. Here, give me that." She grabbed the paper and stomped off to the kitchen. "I'll line the garbage pail with it before Ira sees it."

Claudius walked to the door and sat down facing it. He wanted to go out.

"You went out ten minutes ago," Annie reminded him sourly. "How about a biscuit? Let's get one from the kitchen."

Cheap bribery? He didn't move.

Finally, she admitted defeat, got his leash down, and they went for a walk. They passed the Stubenville house and trudged all the way to the corner before he found a tree that met his exacting standards.

Bored out of her mind, Annie gazed across the street toward the church parking lot and shivered slightly. The yellow police tape and the body were gone, but the dumpster was still there.

John Barnard, the handyman, was starting the mower in the old graveyard near the fence. He was wearing filthy jeans and a black T-shirt with a silver spaceship on the back.

The mower engine sputtered and died. "Shit." He gave it an angry kick. "Ain't nothin' but a piece of junk. Hell, they expect a man to work with a friggin' piece of junk." He aimed another resounding kick at the engine, and a bit of metal snapped off, which he picked up and tossed negligently over his shoulder.

Claudius, by now hot on the scent of something interesting—and dead, no doubt—had his nose to the ground and was snuffling madly across the street to the parking lot and the dumpster. Annie followed at a dead run. Her appearance did not go unnoticed by the handyman, who stopped trashing the lawn mower and frowned.

"Hi there," she called, giving him a wide smile.

"Nuts," he snarled. "What the hell do you want?"

"Nothing, I just wondered how things were going."

He gestured contemptuously at what was left of the mower. "What's it look like? A man tries to do an honest day's work and gets saddled with crap like this."

Claudius sniffed the mower and was rewarded with a kick from Barnard that landed in thin air. The dog danced away, his hackles and the fur along his back rigid. He growled, baring his teeth, and Annie grabbed him by the collar and held on tight.

"Damned mutt! Get him away from me!"

"Don't you kick him!"

"Nobody asked you to bring that stinkin' mutt around here." Barnard pushed the mower to the edge of the graveyard path, the wheels bumping on the gravel. Obviously he was about to put the mower away in the tool shed.

In Annie's considered opinion, if anyone knew the ins and outs of church politics and the latest gossip, it would be John Barnard. He was a church fixture, always around the building, practically part of the wallpaper. People forgot he was there; they'd talk in front of him.

She followed him to the shed, determined to get him to tell what he knew about the reverend's murder.

Things did not go well.

He shoved the mower inside with such force it crashed into the wall. The resulting clatter hinted of a wheel detaching. He slammed the door shut, fumbled with the padlock, and said heavily, "What do you want, lady?"

"Maybe you haven't heard, but the police think they've got the murder weapon."

"What the hell's that got to do with me?" He hitched up his pants. "You can't prove nothin'. I didn't kill nobody."

"No one said you did." She eyed the sparse hedges and weedy flower beds with an insincere smile. "You do a really nice job, Mr. Barnard. The church grounds are beautiful."

"I don't get a lot of help," he growled, somewhat mollified. "The elders won't authorize a damn thing. Stingy as hell. That damn mower's nothin' but a piece of friggin' junk."

"That's too bad."

"Damn right." His heavy-lidded eyes were full of angry self-pity. "The stupid church board don't know when they've got it lucky. No one in their right mind would put up with working conditions like this."

"I'm sure you're right."

"If that's a crack about the fact I ain't got no college education, forget it. A man don't need no friggin' college degree to wax floors and run a friggin' mower. Besides, I ain't had a raise in two years. How's a man supposed to live? Everything's goin' up—food, taxes, and they don't want to pay me half what the job's worth—well, they can damn well shove it."

"No doubt they will."

He lit a cigarette and pointed down the street to a tall, dignified, Victorian house painted white with blue shutters. "See that? It's mine. The mortgage is paid off, and I don't owe a dime to nobody. That's the way I live. People don't like it, they kin drop dead for all I care." He glared at Claudius who was sniffing his shoes. "I told you, keep that damn dog away from me unless you wanna get sued."

A bit of diplomacy seemed in order. She pulled Claudius a short distance away and said conversationally, "The police think the murder weapon was a garden hand fork."

"I told you, whatever the hell it is, it ain't mine. I don't use no fork."

"As a matter of fact, it's my uncle's. A few days ago, my aunt left it by the flower bed. The killer used it, then returned it to my uncle's potting shed."

"No kiddin'." He bared his nicotine-stained teeth in a nasty grin. "Tell you one thing, lady. I ain't stupid and I didn't leave no weapon around your uncle's shed for the cops to find."

Succinctly put and unfortunately, Annie tended to believe him. He was no fool and knew which side his bread was buttered on. Killing the church's assistant pastor and getting caught would certainly put an end to his present position. But if he was that smart, wouldn't he be clever enough to use someone else's hand fork for the murder? Especially when it was lying around in plain sight.

She thought hard, mulling over a possible motive for John Barnard. Jealousy over his wife's affair with Reverend Morris? Uncle Ira had said the reverend had boasted of having four or five women a week. What if he'd been having an affair with Jan Stalker, too. Her aunt had seen Barnard and Jan Stalker together the morning of the murder. Maybe he'd killed the reverend in a fit of jealousy over Jan.

Or maybe he'd loaned money to Reverend Morris and got tired of being stiffed. Once Morris was dead, the loan was a dead issue. Of course, he'd never get repaid; but then maybe Barnard had decided murder was payment in full.

He dropped his cigarette and ground it flat with his boot. "Anything else you wanna know? I gotta get back to work."

"Guess not. Sorry I bothered you."

"I'll bet," he sneered.

This was getting her nowhere. She decided on a direct attack. "You spend a lot of time around the church, Mr. Barnard. Did the Reverend Morris seem worried about anything the last time you talked to him?"

"Who said I talked to him?" He lit another cigarette and gazed at her through the smoke.

She ignored that. "Can you think of any reason someone would have to kill him? I mean other than the fact that he—"

"Was a friggin' asshole?" He grinned.

"Well, yes. But that's not a very good motive for murder."

"Somebody sure thought so. Anyway, it ain't no secret what I thought. I told him to his face the last time I seen him. Thursday night at the party. We had a big turn out, and I was bringing in extra chairs."

"What happened then?"

"He said he was gonna sleep in the annex. He arrived in town that afternoon, and the house the conference leased to him wasn't ready. No furniture. I told him what the hell, it wasn't no skin off my nose where he slept. So I gave him the keys and left."

"Did he say anything else?"

"No, the last I saw of him, he was usin' the phone downstairs." Barnard grinned again. "You can't call long distance from that phone. Maybe he had a hot date with someone here in town and couldn't get it up so the lady did him in."

"With a garden fork?"

"Whatever. Some broads like it rough." He picked up a rake and stomped off around the corner of the church in the direction of the graveyard.

Claudius, who'd been sniffing around a hole in the dirt, suddenly jumped backward and barked as a hornet darted around his head. Several more emerged from the hole in the ground and darted at him.

He took off at warp speed, whipping out of the parking lot and down the street in record time, with Annie bringing up the rear. Halfway down the block, she managed to slow him to a walk and grabbed his collar. "What the hell's wrong with you? Did you get stung?"

His muzzle looked swollen and puffy. He was whimpering and rubbing his ears with his forepaws. Obviously, the poor dog had been stung by several hornets.

She thought a moment. Bob Colfax had mentioned a local veterinarian who was supposed to be good. Another worried look at Claudius, whose face seemed worse. She could hardly see his eyes now, they were so swollen. He looked almost like a different breed of dog with fleshy folds sagging from his jaws.

Maybe he was allergic to hornet bites. *God, nothing about this dog was simple.*

She marched him to the end of the block and looked up and down the main drag. Nothing in sight but a building painted to look like a UFO—the Celestial Dry Cleaners . . . "for the cleanest clothes in the universe," and a bank. She looked in the other direction and there it was just down the street: Shepherd's Veterinary Clinic.

Claudius lifted his leg against the fake fire hydrant out front of the clinic, and they went inside. He seemed to realize he needed help and was willing, at least for the present, to let her make the decisions. Every dark cloud has a silver lining, she thought and walked up to the front desk where a dark-haired young receptionist was typing at a computer keyboard.

"Good afternoon," said the woman with a smile. "Can I help you?"

"I don't have an appointment. My dog's been bitten by a hornet, and his face is swollen. He may be allergic."

The girl got up and looked over the counter at Claudius who was shaking his head and whining. "Goodness, he's a mess. You'd better see Dr. Shepherd right away."

For the first time, Claudius's gaze strayed to the posters on the wall. A German shepherd beamed with blinding white teeth, extolling the benefits of dental care. Annie had the impression Claudius didn't find this much comfort as he let out another loud groan.

Several shelves laden with pet food, leashes, toys, and flea powders stood to the left of the counter beside a white blackboard with a message written in red marker: Wouldn't you like a dog who came promptly when called? Who didn't eat pillows and wet the floor? Obedience classes, three nights a week. Sponsored by The Neighborhood Church of the Celestial Spheres, and taught by Pam Hardaway. Sixty-five dollars. Register at desk.

Annie read the notice again. It sounded like paradise, and at the very least it would get her out of the house at night.

A door to one of the examination rooms opened, and the pastor's wife, Melinda Pennyworth, emerged, looking quite upset. She carried a cat carrier from which loud, insulted meows issued. She threw an angry look over her shoulder at the closed door, then walked up to the counter. For a pastor's wife, she looked incredibly well-dressed and seemed to possess, in Annie's opinion, the sort of confidence that comes from having plenty of money. Her face was expertly made up—at least an hour's effort with pink lip gloss, smoke-gray eyeliner, and ivory foundation. A fashionably frizzed hairdo. A forearm laden with silver bangles, and dangling silver earrings still swinging as she took out her checkbook.

Though Annie was sitting ten feet away, Melinda pretended not to see her, so she smiled to herself and loosened her hold on the leash. Immediately, Claudius stood up and stared at the cat carrier. His nose quivered and his whole body stiffened. Silently, he took a step forward, then another. He growled.

Melinda just stood there, the epitome of svelte smartness, going through her leather purse and shuffling about a hundred credit cards. Click, click, jingle, jingle, she went through them at an incredible speed. It was a wonder she kept them all straight.

Enough was enough. Annie got up and picked up the cat carrier. She put it on the counter.

Melinda Pennyworth glared at her. "That's *my* cat! Just what do you think you're doing?"

About to point out the obvious, that she'd saved her darling cat from being eaten alive, Annie opened her mouth, and the receptionist got in first. "Mrs. Pennyworth, this lady was only trying to help."

"The most helpful thing she could do," Melinda muttered, "would be to mind her own business and keep her hands off my cat. Tell Fred I'll call him later."

Claudius, busily sniffing a nearby display of flea products, lifted his leg.

"Stop that!" Annie hauled him to a chair some fifteen feet away and sat down. So much for being at death's door. Her sympathy for him was fast disappearing.

He heaved a sigh of self-pity and flopped on the floor.

It wasn't her fault he'd stuck his big nose in a hornets' nest. He'd done that all by himself. "Idiot," she muttered.

Melinda Pennyworth aimed a look of acute dislike in her direction, and the receptionist, ever alert to disagreements among the clientele, whether four or two-legged, said hurriedly, "The doctor will be with you in a minute."

Melinda must have been over the limit on her cards. She wrote out a check and plunked it down. That done, she glanced at Claudius. "What kind of dog is that, anyway?"

"A German shepherd–huskie mix."

"Oh, a mutt." Her remark dripped with contempt. "Well, he looks quite peculiar. Did he eat something that disagreed with him?"

"He was stung by a hornet."

"Really? He looks terrible."

"You can take him in now." The receptionist indicated the examination room beyond the shelves of dog and cat food.

Annie got up and hauled a reluctant Claudius behind the counter to the open door. She hadn't been in a vet's office in a long time, not since she'd had her cat put down three years ago. Not a happy occasion, and one she'd tried hard to forget.

This examination room was depressingly bare. All traces of previous patients had been removed. A metal table stood in the center; there was a chair in one corner and a stool and cabinet in another. A couple of university diplomas on the wall written in elaborate script proclaimed that Frederick Shepherd had graduated magna cum laude from Tufts School of Veterinary Medicine, along with a cross-stitched prayer by St. Thomas Aquinas and a poster of dog breeds of the world. Tiny dogs standing at attention with a numbered legend underneath headed by the information that the swift and graceful greyhound had been known on every continent of the world since before 800 B.C.

Claudius wanted out right now. He headed for the door. He was having second thoughts about allowing any stranger to lay hands on him.

"Keep your pants on. The vet will be here any minute."

At that, he made another lunge for freedom, which she dealt with by manhandling him back to the table. "Besides, you don't want to look like this forever. Your face would stop a clock." Not exactly diplomatic, but she was mad.

He grumbled and stared at the shiny metal leg of the table, examining his reflection. It was clear that he didn't like what he saw, because he turned his head away and refused to look at the table leg again. Annie sat down in the chair, and after another few minutes, the door opened, and the vet came in. He was rather good-looking, dark-haired, in his early thirties. There was a quiet competence about him, a sense of kindness—animals had nothing to fear at his hands.

Claudius, however, was immune to the vet's finer qualities and remained, glowering, behind the table. This was war.

Obviously, she'd have to think up some way to get him to cooperate. Annie got to her feet as the vet smiled. "I'm Dr. Shepherd. What seems to be wrong with your dog?"

It took forever to haul Claudius out from underneath the table, but eventually he stood stiff-legged in front of the vet, looking like a belligerent fathead. Panting and out of breath, she explained, "He's been stung in the face by several hornets."

"Let's take a look. Hmm, he's a nice dog. What's his name?" The vet held the back of his hand out to Claudius, who unbent sufficiently to give it a suspicious sniff.

"Claudius." She wondered whether to tell him that the dog was arrogant and stubborn as a mule, that he didn't take kindly to strangers—or to herself, either, for that matter—and lastly, that, if provoked, he'd probably bite.

Maybe that wasn't such a good idea. For one thing, she didn't want to give Claudius any ideas, and he understood every word he heard. It was like dealing with a difficult adolescent. Doubtless the vet was used to dealing with recalcitrant patients, she thought. Very few animals who came through the door were deliriously happy about shots and other painful, invasive procedures. He probably dealt with dogs of Claudius's stripe all the time.

She decided half a loaf was better than none. "He's not mine. I'm just taking care of him temporarily."

"I see. Is he up to date with his rabies vaccination and other shots?"

"I believe so. He's my brother's dog. All his papers are back in New Hampshire, but he's got a current rabies tag."

The vet glanced at the tag and wrote some information on a white card. "Okay, so all we have to worry about are the hornet stings. I'll give him a shot to take the swelling down."

Claudius moved decisively toward the door and let out a low growl.

"If you'll just hold his head," the vet suggested to Annie, "I'll give him the shot."

A young woman in a blue apron came in to help, and presenting a united front, they moved around the table toward Claudius, who opened his jaws wide and made a sound reminiscent of Godzilla about to attack Tokyo.

"Stop it!" Grabbing his collar, Annie attempted, with a noticeable lack of success, to hold him still. "Nobody's going to hurt you. You've had shots before."

He growled and tossed his head. She almost fell on her face.

"It's just a little shot, no big deal."

He ignored that bald-faced lie and hauled everyone around the table three times before the vet's aide gasped, "Do you think I should get the gauntlets?"

Dr. Shepherd stood up with a frown. "Get me a dog biscuit. Maybe that'll do the trick."

"He's trying to help you," Annie told Claudius, gazing into the dog's mutinous face and trying a bit of friendly persuasion. "Come on, be a good boy and stand still a minute. It won't take long. Please."

He grunted, and his big black ears twitched as he fixed her with a grim stare. They'd get one chance. If they blew it, too bad. They wouldn't get another.

The attendant disappeared in search of a biscuit. When she came back, she handed it to Dr. Shepherd who held it out to Claudius, who remained obdurate. Staring straight ahead, scorn, rejection, and contempt written all over his bulbous-looking face. He would not be bought with a paltry biscuit. He turned his head away, but stood very still.

"So much for that idea," sighed the vet. He picked up the hypo. "Does he bite?"

"I don't know. Maybe he'll let you give him the shot if it's quick."

"Okay, boy, this will only take a minute. Hold his head, please." Dr. Shepherd gently slipped the needle in. "Good boy, that's it." He patted Claudius. "There we are, fella. That wasn't so bad, was it?"

The attendant scratched Claudius's ears. "You're a sweetie, aren't you, boy?"

Enough was enough. He shrugged her hand away and headed straight for the door.

Annie grabbed her purse and followed. It was quiet in the reception area, pleasantly peaceful after the tense atmosphere of the examination room. She began to relax and waited at the counter while the attendant made out the bill. Claudius sat beside Annie and sulked.

Just then the outer door opened and a man came in with a chocolate retriever who spotted what was clearly a big, black wolf and began barking his head off, leaping and jerking at his leash as if possessed.

Claudius stiffened but didn't growl.

Annie read him like a book. The retriever was beneath contempt, a wimp, a panty waist, a total loser.

Shutting the door behind him, the man muttered, "Shut up, Pokey."

"Pokey?" Out of the corner of her eye, Annie saw Claudius's lip curl.

The man dragged his dog behind a plastic ficus tree and sat down, while Pokey growled and didn't take his eyes off the huge, vicious black monster on the other side of the room.

All they needed was someone to show up with a cat. She forked over thirty-five dollars for the allergy shot, and wondering why the vet hadn't divided the waiting room into one area for dogs and another for cats, stuffed her wallet back in her purse. It would still be easy enough to do, she thought. A simple dividing wall. A day's work for any competent carpenter, and trouble would be averted.

Claudius was busy staring out the window so no one would think he was concerned in the least by the antics of that stupid retriever.

Time to hit the road. She untangled the leash, grabbing it tight, and they left the office and walked out into the sunlit afternoon again. She was deep in thought, wondering how long it would take for the swelling to go down. Claudius's head was high and he moved in an aggressive swagger. He wanted to explore the vet's parking lot.

Annie wanted to cut things short, but naturally lost the battle of wills. They did the perimeter in fifteen minutes, and he managed to examine every bush and blade of grass of the sizeable lawn area before he agreed to head back to her uncle's house. While she seethed with impatience, he sauntered along the sidewalk, sniffing every pebble and stopping at each telephone pole. Halfway home, she inspected his face. Close up, he looked less and less like a shar-pei, one of those dogs from China with all the skin hanging down in folds. "Swelling's going down."

He tossed his head and, eyes glittering with arrogance, padded down the street, lunging at the end of the leash.

She wondered which was worse, Claudius hale and hearty and baring his teeth in a fearsome leer, or Claudius off his feed, grumpy and grim. Either way, he made sure his needs were met before anyone else's. Much to her annoyance, he barked at a passing car in a booming woof that well nigh pierced her eardrums and terrified the driver half out of his wits.

The car hurtled down the street and out of sight, and he resumed his progress down the center of the sidewalk, scattering pedestrians left and right. With every passing minute she could see that he was looking and feeling more like himself. Handsome, clever, the epitome of canine perfection. Taken up with a feeling of bonhomie, he spared a glance at Annie, sizing her up and down. She had no trouble reading his expression. A spark of kindness lurked in his dark eye. He was considering going easy on her. A temporary truce, until Lydia came back for him.

Just about then, a black BMW passed with a blonde woman at the wheel. Melinda Pennyworth. She was smiling behind dark glasses as she headed downtown.

Annie wrestled with a snarl of tangled leash and dragged Claudius away from a potted topiary in front of a fancy clothing store. Understandably, she wasn't in the best of moods. She'd had a bad day what with the hornet sting and the subsequent trip to the vet's. The afternoon had barely started, and things weren't likely to improve.

While Reverend Morris's murder remained unsolved, Uncle Ira was the prime suspect. She hadn't been consciously thinking of Melinda, but seeing her drive by made Annie wonder about her relationship with the handsome veterinarian, Fred Shepherd. The way she looked when she came out of the examination room certainly had had nothing to do with getting her cat its shots—unless they'd argued about where to give the damn things.

Still, it was none of her business, Annie decided as Claudius turned the corner and stampeded down Elm Street, dragging her along in his wake. She had enough problems without worrying about what the pastor's wife was up to. Bob Colfax, for instance. He definitely had something up his sleeve where her aunt and uncle were concerned. He was ambitious and wanted the inside story of Reverend Morris's death so badly he could taste it. There wasn't much he wouldn't stoop to in order to get it.

But of primary concern was Uncle Ira, and the strong likelihood that before long the police might arrest him for murder. The consequences of that didn't bear thinking about. Aunt Hortense in raving hysterics, the neighborhood grapevine revving into high gear with the phone ringing off the hook, Jan Stalker and that wretched Stubenville woman peeking in the windows every chance they got.

Changing the leash from one hand to the other—her right hand was going numb—Claudius took advantage of the temporary slack to make for the church parking lot and the dumpster where he'd found the dead man. He broke into a businesslike trot, snuffling through the weeds near the fence. A few yards away, a piece of day-glo yellow police tape flapped in the wind. Immediately, he picked up the pace. The dumpster was in sight, the odors stronger now, wafting on the afternoon breeze.

He put his muzzle down and snuffled around near the base of the dumpster. A couple of neighborhood dogs and a few cats had been snooping around. He lifted his leg.

Meanwhile, Annie—trying to be tactful—turned her back and gazed around the parking lot. The body was gone, but the chalk outline was faintly discernible. Not that she needed that. She still had a mental picture: Morris sprawled on the pavement, surrounded by junk and weeds. And later on, the coroner crouched by the corpse, going about his grisly business, black bag by his side. Taking body temperature, checking for rigor. She shivered a little, wondering what Claudius had sensed about the corpse. Had he caught a lingering smell of fear, even after death? Or had he caught the faint scent of the killer's fear and rage. If he could speak, would he be able to tell her who the killer was?

There was nothing here but a parking lot and a dumpster. So why did she feel as if her skin was crawling? She yanked him away from the dumpster. "Let's go!"

He shot her an annoyed look, and they walked back to Uncle Ira's house in silence. They'd just reached the driveway when a car roared by. She turned and stared. It was Melinda Pennyworth in her BMW, again. This time, though, the pastor's wife didn't looked at all pleased with life. In fact, her face was set and angry.

Annie was intrigued and curious. Without thinking how silly it was to follow a woman she barely knew, she decided to do just that. Shoving Claudius in the Escort, she jumped behind the wheel. In moments, they were speeding east down the road after the fast-disappearing BMW. The sun was still fairly high, and the glare off the windshield unbelievable. She shoved a pair of sunglasses on her nose and pressed down on the accelerator. They barreled down the street.

The BMW turned left and headed toward Route 70 at a fast clip. It was obvious she wasn't driving aimlessly around, just passing the time. No, she had a definite destination in mind, and Annie couldn't help wondering what it was.

Just when she thought Melinda would drive out of town altogether, the pastor's wife pulled into a strip mall. A small convenience store stood on the corner. She parked in front and hurried to a public telephone booth just outside.

Annie swung into the mall parking lot and parked a short distance away. She turned off the engine and settled back to watch.

The strip mall was about two miles from the center of town. The phone booth had a flared Plexiglas hood, and it occurred to her that anyone standing fairly close had a pretty good chance of overhearing Melinda's conversation.

The temptation was too much to resist. Annie got out and walked quickly down the sidewalk toward the phone booth. Dry, dead leaves, skittered by, blown by the wind. She drew closer to Melinda, who had her back to the glass storefronts. Her shoulders were hunched, and she pounded the metal shelf in anger.

"I told you, it's impossible," Melinda snapped. "I can't do that! What does it take to get through to you? God, we've been over this a dozen times. I can't do it!"

Annie halted about fifteen feet away and pretended interest in the window display: camping equipment, tents, stoves, lanterns, and the like. She had never been one for camping, anyway, and so had little trouble concentrating on Melinda's angry one-sided conversation behind her. Who cared about the advantages of fiberglass canoes over aluminum when she had a chance to discover what the pastor's wife was really up to.

"I can't! He'll find out. You're out of your mind . . . No, you don't know what you're asking. It's too dangerous. We don't have any choice." A pause while she listened, then, "Fine. It's over." She drew a long breath and went on in lower tones, "We both knew it couldn't last forever. That afternoon at Pasture Lake was wonderful . . . yes, I know. But he suspects, I'm sure he does."

Annie stopped breathing when she heard a definite click. Melinda had hung up the phone. She heard the woman's footsteps approach and felt completely exposed. At any moment she expected Melinda to tap her on the shoulder and demand to know what she was doing there. Had she followed her to the strip mall? Why? How dare she! Who did she think she was? A peeping Tom?

Annie leaned close to the store window glass, as if she could disappear into the camping display. She saw a reflection of her own face looming close, eyes covered by concealing sunglasses. She felt like a complete fool, spying on Melinda Pennyworth, and for what? She hadn't learned anything, not really; and if the woman noticed her, she'd look like a meddling fool.

Wonder of wonders, Melinda passed by without noticing her, and Annie was spared the humiliation of having to answer embarrassing questions. She started to breathe again. The woman got in her car and slammed the door in a fine display of temper. The BMW's engine roared to life, and she spun out of the mall parking lot, tires squealing.

A few feet away, the telephone began to ring. And ring.

Annie turned to stare at the phone booth, hesitating, wondering whether to answer it. The phone rang insistently.

It might be someone she knew. The veterinarian or someone else whose voice she'd recognize. If Melinda had been carrying on, maybe Reverend Morris had found out. That could have been a motive for murder.

The telephone rang. And rang. Eight, ten times. The convenience store wasn't busy, only one customer emerged and glanced curiously at the phone before walking off. Annie heard one ring more and decided to take a chance. She would pretend to be Melinda.

She snatched up the receiver and had little trouble achieving Melinda's husky whisper. "Yes?"

"You hung up on me," a man said in a voice threaded with anger. "What the hell's going on? I thought we—" He broke off, then growled suspiciously, "Hey, who is this?"

"It's me, of course." Annie put her hand over the mouthpiece, hoping the muffling effect would do the trick.

"Melinda?"

"Yes," she breathed, feeling like a character in a spy movie.

"You're not Melinda! Go to hell!" He slammed down the phone so hard Annie's ear hurt.

She hung up and backed away from the phone booth as if the receiver had turned into a cobra. *That voice. It was the same man who'd called her uncle's. The obscene phone call . . . he'd been trying to call Melinda.*

She got back into the Escort and drove back home. A series of images crackled in her mind: Murder, spilled blood, the metallic smell of it, the way it pooled . . . the neck torn open, a pair of frightened eyes glazed over. Was Melinda Pennyworth in danger, too? If she knew too much, she might be. Once a man killed, there was little to prevent him from doing it again, as often as he felt the need. Even in a state with the death penalty, they couldn't give you more than one lethal injection or strap you in and turn on Old Sparky more than once.

She was tired and had a splitting headache. Beside her, Claudius's tail was down and his ears were flattened. He was in a bad mood.

He snarled at a squirrel who ran along a telephone wire and leaped into a nearby tree. Annie groaned. The last thing she needed at this point was a display of temperament on his part. He didn't like squirrels, especially the ones here in Roswell; and from what she'd seen so far, he had a point. They weren't too bright—like the rest of the town's inhabitants—Melinda Pennyworth being a prime example.

"I can't hear myself think. Stop that racket."

He exhaled in disgust. Every bone in his large body expressed resentment. One thing they could agree on, she thought wearily: This was one hell of a way to spend a vacation—traveling across the country with someone you didn't like. And he'd made his feelings clear right from the start, that night back in New Hampshire when he arrived at her house. One look at her and he'd decided he didn't like her. Well, so what. The feeling was mutual.

But from his point of view, his dislike of her made perfect sense. Her attempts to make him feel at home had been clumsy. She'd offered him cheap generic dog food he'd sniffed suspiciously and ignored. He probably thought it was pig swill. In fact, his entire life this past month or more had been one long nightmare: dumped on her doorstep like a bag of dirty laundry, his adored Lydia missing, Tom drunk and angry.

All a dog asked in life was two squares a day, water, a walk, and a spot of affection now and then from his owner. Was that unreasonable? Annie didn't think so, but Lydia had gone away and hadn't taken her dog with her.

Claudius probably wondered if Lydia was angry with him. Had he done something to make her leave? He'd been careful about peeing and doing his business outdoors, so it couldn't have been that. Of course he had a few faults. He didn't know when to keep his big mouth shut. Barking at strange cars, and even those he recognized. Barking at people in the street, at any sudden sound. But he'd been protecting her, surely she knew that. It was what he was supposed to do. He loved her. He adored her. He'd lay down his life for her.

Yet she'd left him just the same, and here he was, stuck in the middle of nowhere with a loser he didn't respect and furthermore, refused to obey.

Things couldn't possibly get any worse.

His tail drooped as Annie let him into the house and shut the door.

Chapter Eight

"Well, here it is, Annie. The site where the alien spacecraft landed." Uncle Ira put his arm around her shoulder and looked around at the expanse of sand and scrub with a sigh of satisfaction. "Fifty years ago in our time, but for them . . . who knows? They've solved the problems of time and space, quantum physics. They achieved warp speed eons ago." He shrugged. "Probably they use worm holes. But never fear, Annie, we'll find out someday soon."

She tried to look enthused. Claudius, sitting disconsolately at her feet, yawned. As befitted rabid UFO believers, they were standing in the middle of nowhere. They'd spent the past half hour since they left the car back on the shoulder of Route 50, trudging over God only knew how many acres of sand and rocks.

For UFO fanatics, presumably the area was akin to Mecca. A rocky hillside with a few weeds and a stunted tree or two sloping beneath an empty sky. She looked up as a large black bird circled overhead. "What's that?"

He squinted upward. "Buzzard. Must be a recent kill around somewhere. Mountain lion or coyotes. Sometimes they don't eat it all at once."

She looked around nervously. "Mountain lions?"

"Don't worry, they don't usually hunt in the heat of the sun. He'll come back for the kill at dusk." He took out his handkerchief and mopped his brow. "Let me show you what we came here to see. People generally don't know this, but it's actually where the aliens landed first. The real McCoy. The debris field stretches literally over more than fifty square miles. They crash-landed on the ranch just over that arroyo. But the spacecraft hit that escarpment first, right up there where the rocks are scarred black. Then it skidded over the top of the hill and landed." He patted Annie's shoulder. "Too bad your aunt wasn't feeling up to coming along with us. We'll have to make sure we come out here again before you go back East."

"Great."

"You know, of course, that all the relevant government documents about the landing have unaccountably disappeared."

"Really?"

He uttered a grim laugh. "A stupid ploy that wouldn't fool a two-year-old. For heaven's sake, even the military has reported sightings."

"No kidding." She shaded her eyes with her hand and wondered how long he intended to stand out here in the blistering sun. Unfortunately, there seemed to be no limit to his UFO stories.

"The air force says electromagnetic waves from a far off galaxy would take too long to reach earth for UFO's to be real. Every time I see those guys on TV making lame excuses for why nothing ever landed here I roll on the floor laughing."

"Some of the stuff does sound weird, I guess."

"Darn tootin' it's weird. Swamp gas, my foot! We'd be idiots if we believed the government always told the truth. And they keep changing stories. First it never happened, then it was a weather balloon. Now we're supposed to think they put crash dummies in the balloon." He chuckled. "Folks have taken pictures they can't explain away, no matter how hard they try. The McMillan, Oregon, photos, for instance. A farmer's wife saw one just thirty feet overhead. Her husband snapped a picture, and guess what. The government interviews 'em, and all of a sudden—no more pictures. Some people think aliens are time travelers, but they don't know beans from bananas or shit from apple butter, if you get my drift. The spacecraft came from beyond the Pleiades, and that's a fact. Folks have seen 'em in Iran, Brazil, England, all over the world, and there are pictures to prove it. Okay," he conceded, "some are obvious fakes. Publicity nuts, I suppose. That Spanish fellow, Meyer, Mahoney, whatever. Anyway, his movies looked promising at first. A UFO flying over a pine tree, then one over a shopping center. Clear, no fuzziness, no blurring. He got pictures in broad daylight, which is extremely rare. Astonishing, really. Every time Mahoney set foot outside, there they were, flying around, practically hitting him in the head."

Annie heaved a sigh and thought about a cold drink. It had been hours since lunch, and even that had been less than filling. She'd fixed everything, following her aunt's special recipe: melted cheese sandwiches . . . low-fat American cheese on granola bread, canned peaches, and watery iced tea. If Aunt Hortense was dieting, everyone else was dieting. "Sounds too good to be true," she agreed, wondering if she dared stop at a Wendy's on the way home. A number one with lettuce, tomato, mayonnaise, or Thousand Island dressing with a slice of bacon. Her mouth started watering.

"Damn right it's too good to be true," Uncle Ira resumed. "He was clever enough to avoid the old double-exposure dodge, but he faked every damn shot. Pretty simple, really. He had a silver-painted cardboard model on a wire in front of the camera. One of his pals moved the wire from side to side, or maybe he had the thing on the end of a stick. If you look carefully, well, I'll show you the movies when we get home . . . you'll see it swings side to side like a pendulum. No real UFO would do that. No way, not in a million years."

"Of course not." She sneaked a look at her watch. "Goodness, it's after one. Aunt Hortense will wonder where we got to."

"Nonsense." He hitched up his pants and set off with a determined stride toward the hill in the distance. He yelled over his shoulder, "Shake a leg, Annie. We've barely started. I'll show you the radiation marks burned into the rocks. Would you believe it? They're still here after fifty years. It'll blow your mind."

She shook her head in the shimmering heat and trailed after him. The scarf that was keeping her hair out of her eyes kept slipping. She pushed it back with a distinct feeling of annoyance. What a great idea, not, she thought sourly. It trapped the heat like some damn solar reflector. She yanked it off and stuffed it in her jeans, then stomped after her uncle and decided she'd had enough of alien crash sites. Probably they were trespassing or some damn thing. He'd said something about the church owning the property, but she didn't care. There was something creepy about the place. The area was deserted, but surely there should be birds twittering, crickets or grasshoppers buzzing, going about their business. But nothing, only the noise of her feet crunching along the path. If it could be called that. It looked more like a drunkard's progress as it meandered along the dusty, rock-strewn incline.

Claudius grumbled loudly, heaved a tired sigh, and trotted along a few feet behind.

Yards ahead, Uncle Ira was striding onward like Hannibal crossing the Alps, waving his stick and pointing at relevant points of interest. "That's scrub oak over there and pinon pine. See that big rock? I found a bit of unknown metal near it last year, doubtless from the craft. Silver colored, tritanium alloy or some damn thing. Looks like aluminum, but it's much harder. You can't scratch it.

"That dried up yellow stuff over there is grama grass. Apaches used it for all sorts of things. It was kind of a one-stop drugstore. They brewed an herbal tea with it, made ointments, even used it as a yellow dye. And that spot over there by the foot of the hill where the rock's all streaked? If this were New Hampshire, you'd think possibly it was some kind of dark granite. But New Mexico's mostly sandstone. This area was below sea level a couple of million years ago." He grinned and tapped the ground. "We're walking on what used to be prime ocean-front property. About ten thousand years ago, it was a dangerous place. Mammoths and mastodons roamed this valley along with sabre-toothed cats and giant wolves. It wasn't always desert country, Annie. Aliens have probably been visiting this area for a couple of hundred thousand years. That's what happened to the dinosaurs, you know. It wasn't some comet wiped them out, it was aliens."

A hot breeze moaned through the rocky canyon like a mournful sigh. She drew a deep breath and stared toward a distant purple mountain peak. The spot felt almost haunted, with the mountain shimmering above the desert like a vision, and she wondered who else had stood here in the past, looking at that majestic view. Aliens, according to Uncle Ira.

God, she'd been listening to this stuff too long.

Sunlight bounced off the rocks and all around her bits of quartz sparkled in the dirt. She noticed an arrow-shaped sharp stone and picked one up. "What's this?"

"Hmm, could be a spear point some Apache warrior threw away. They hunted all over this valley a couple of hundred years ago."

Claudius dragged Annie over to a scattered pile of brown droppings. His ruff bristled and he growled as she tried to pull him away.

"He's got a head as hard as pig iron." Uncle Ira laughed. "Those are coyote droppings, by the way. Scavengers. They clean up whatever the mountain lions and buzzards leave."

His voice trailed off and she realized he was staring at something at the base of the hillside. From her vantage point she couldn't see what it was, but unconsciously, she began walking toward him. Weren't there snakes out here? Poisonous rattlers as thick as your arm with huge sharp fangs. This far from the highway, if he got bitten, how would she get him back to the car? People who'd suffered a snake bite shouldn't be moved. The venom traveled through the circulatory system. She read that somewhere in a *National Geographic* article. She couldn't remember the details, only that you were supposed to cut a cross in the wound and try to suck out the venom, then tie on a tourniquet. Or maybe it was the other way around.

Uncle Ira was poking at something near a big rock. It look like a black plastic bag, a garbage bag someone had thrown away.

Whoever had thrown away this trash bag had gone to a great deal of trouble to dump it here, a good quarter mile from the highway, she realized suddenly. He must have thought it would be months, even years before anyone found it. Maybe never.

Under the hot summer sun Annie felt goose bumps raise on her arms. Icy cold began trickling down her body, and she shivered uncontrollably.

Uncle Ira bent down to rip the garbage bag open, and Claudius lunged forward, all but knocking her off her feet. "Stop it!" she cried, yanking on the leash and forgetting every bit of excellent advice she'd digested from the dog books.

The dog kept fighting her, growling, jerking, and leaping this way and that as if he were demented. She looked over her shoulder. Uncle Ira had torn a hole in the side of the bag, and she saw an arm and the back of someone's head. A body.

He was staring at it, ashen-faced. "Oh, my God!"

Without conscious thought, she was flying over the path toward her uncle. Craggy rocks by the path caught at her feet and tore the leg of her jeans as she ran.

There was a gold bracelet on the woman's arm. She could see it glinting in the sun. She had to be dead, Annie thought. No one in her right mind would crawl into a garbage bag and lie down here in the middle of an alien crash site. Besides, how could she have tied the top with that orange twist tie? Impossible. It wasn't suicide.

Uncle Ira was still staring at the garbage bag. He shook his head and looked oddly blank, as if he couldn't quite take it all in. "My God, I don't believe it."

Annie ran up to him, panting heavily. Her ribs hurt. She had a stitch in her side. "It's a woman. Who is it? Anyone you know?" By this time, Claudius was sniffing the bag and its contents industriously. She hauled him off and said firmly, "Stay! And I mean it!"

He gave her a look that said who did she think she was kidding and followed her right back to her uncle and the plastic bag with its grisly contents.

"I said no!" She grabbed him by the collar and managed to drag him away again. "Here, eat this." Offering a biscuit as a bribe.

He grumbled but decided to eat it when nothing better was forthcoming.

By now Uncle Ira had managed to free enough of the plastic to see who the woman was. It was Jan Stalker. Her face was bruised and bloody. Her skin had an unhealthy gray tinge to it. She looked dead even though her eyes were open and staring.

Oh my God. This wasn't happening, Annie thought wildly. Another corpse. Worse, Jan Stalker lived next door to her uncle, and he'd admitted fighting with her over her choice of late-night TV programs. The police had a record of that. Jan had dialed 911 to complain about him. How would they explain this to the police? A coincidence? Somehow she didn't think Lt. Rhodes would believe it.

"My God," moaned Uncle Ira, "I opened the bag, my fingerprints are all over it. They'll think I did it."

"You had to open the bag, so your prints don't matter. Maybe her ex-husband killed her."

He eyed the dead woman doubtfully. "She looks like she's been strangled. There are bruises on her throat, and the side of her head's bashed in. Someone wanted to make very sure she was dead." He thought a moment. "You know, I think her ex had a gun. But wouldn't he have shot her?"

"Maybe not. The police must have revoked his gun license when he made those bomb threats. He probably doesn't have a gun now."

"That wouldn't stop him. Out here almost everyone has a gun, legal or not. I don't know, though. It's hard to picture Chuck Stalker doing this. He's a gutless coward."

He pulled the plastic back over Jan Stalker's corpse.

Annie forced her eyes away from the garbage bag and the disgusting flies already crawling all over it. She stared at the western sky, at the buzzard circling lower now, a black dot against the deep blue. But her mind's eye still held the picture of Jan Stalker's dead face. The pale, bulging skin beneath her staring eyes was laced by myriad tiny red dots. Broken blood vessels. And that terrible, sickening smell.

* * *

Aunt Hortense, for one, was not surprised at how Jan Stalker had met her end. "I told you. Didn't I tell you, Ira, that she'd get the wrong person mad at her someday?"

They were home now, sitting in the kitchen. While Annie called the police to report finding Jan Stalker's body, Aunt Hortense made a soothing pot of hot tea and reminded them of all the dire things she'd said that would befall their next-door neighbor due to her unorthodox lifestyle.

"I predicted," she went on with grim relish, "that woman would bring the wrong man home one of these nights. One of those dreadful lowlifes that hang around downtown by the art theater, preying on poor souls who don't know any better."

"We didn't find her by the art theater," Uncle Ira reminded her. "We went out to the desert, the UFO site."

"Oh, my God, no! You don't think it was aliens?"

Annie came in from the hall, overheard this last remark, and wondered if her aunt had ESP. For one fleeting, weak-minded moment it had occurred to her that aliens might have killed Jan Stalker. But common sense said it wasn't likely. Would they have gone to the trouble of stuffing Jan in the garbage bag? Did they have garbage bags? Or even garbage? She frowned. If they'd conquered the mysteries of space travel, surely they'd have solved a little thing like how to dispose of trash in an environmentally safe manner. And they wouldn't use plastic.

Uncle Ira patted Aunt Hortense's shoulder. "No, dear. The police will go out to the site and pick up the body. I don't think she died where we found her. The killer probably disposed of her there because it's so remote."

"But the police . . . won't they want you to take them where you found the body?" she asked, her brow wrinkled with worry.

Annie cleared her throat. "They're coming by to pick us up. I told them Uncle Ira wasn't in the best of health, but they said they needed a statement, so we have to go back out there."

There was an awkward pause. No one knew quite what to say. The truth was, Jan Stalker's death was undeniably inconvenient, coming so soon after Reverend Morris's death. Indeed, bodies were beginning to pile up.

"What's the use?" Uncle Ira slumped in his chair. "They can't wait to arrest me for Reverend Morris's murder. This will be all the proof they need."

Aunt Hortense got out homemade banana bread and low-fat cream cheese. "You could be working yourself up over nothing. Maybe Jan went out to the site and had a heart attack. You said it was quite hot."

"It was murder." The mention of the word made him wince. "She was strangled, hit on the head, stuffed into a garbage bag. That's not exactly suicide."

He sipped tea and looked glum. Aunt Hortense looked upset, and Annie ate a piece of banana bread without tasting it.

"Well, how about another cup of tea?" Aunt Hortense said after a while.

Annie got up to turn the stove on again, but Uncle Ira shook his head. "I don't think we have time."

They all knew it would be only a matter of minutes before the police arrived again. Lt. Rhodes would be asking questions and making nasty insinuations, and no stone would be left unturned in his search for Jan Stalker's killer.

It was almost three o'clock by the time the police took Annie and Uncle Ira back out to the desert. Shadows were lengthening and the cruel heat of the day was fading.

In the distance, the purple mountain peak still loomed majestically, and Annie saw the bulging black garbage bag lying in the dirt where they'd left it. A policeman was shouting and flapped his arms to keep the buzzards away, and she wondered when she'd stop feeling sick to her stomach. Other policemen were busy taking pictures, dusting for prints and traces of forensic evidence. But she was remembering Jan as she'd been at Reverend Morris's Remembrance dinner, a trifle tipsy, piling her plate high with overcooked ravioli. Laughing and eating with enjoyment, with no premonition of her own impending demise.

Annie frowned. Jan had said something about knowing secrets, and then she'd muttered something about hiding things in plain sight. She'd assumed it was just alcohol talking, but maybe Jan had possessed dangerous knowledge that led to her death.

"Looks like the actual murder was simple enough." Lt. Rhodes's eyes were hidden behind the usual dark glasses, but there was an edge to his voice. He didn't like murder and wouldn't stop until he discovered the killer. Unfortunately, just now Uncle Ira looked promising. "She was probably struck on the head first, then strangled. If she was drunk, she wouldn't have put up much of a fight. Of course, we'll know more after the autopsy."

Uncle Ira shifted his feet. He was sweating profusely and couldn't have looked guiltier if he'd worn a sign declaring : ARREST ME BEFORE I KILL AGAIN.

"Somebody should be notified about Jan's death," Annie suggested. "Has she got any family living around here?"

Lt. Rhodes shot her an irritated glance. "The department will take care of that. Notifying the family is official business. You two stay out of it."

"Of course," Uncle Ira agreed. "But we might be able to help with phone numbers of her relatives. She had a sister in Ohio somewhere. And there's her ex-husband, Chuck Stalker."

"The mad bomber? Jesus H. Christ. Just what we need." Lt. Rhodes eyed Annie with hostility. "We didn't have any trouble around here until you showed up. Roswell was a nice clean town. Quiet. People died in their beds of old age. They didn't get their throats torn out and their heads bashed in. And they didn't get strangled." She didn't have to answer that because he turned to the coroner and barked, "How long has she been dead?"

The coroner stripped off his gloves and lit a cigarette. "Can't say for sure. Maybe six, eight hours. Desert heat is a factor, of course. Rigor's well-advanced, but her eyeballs are still moist. I'll know better after we get her back to the morgue and open her up."

Lt. Rhodes nodded, then yelled to the men searching the area near the body, "Make sure you bag the hands. We might get some scrapings from the fingernails if she put up a fight."

Chapter Nine

In Annie's considered opinion, The Irish Rose Cafe was a terrible restaurant. As a place to stop for a bite it was convenient, but not much else. It was located on Route 50, a few miles out of town, on the highway heading west.

Annie and her two elderly relatives were celebrating the fact that Uncle Ira was still free as a bird. So far, the police hadn't arrested him. Besides, Aunt Hortense was facing bunion surgery in a few days and hadn't felt like cooking, so going out to dinner seemed like a good idea.

"Let's go someplace quiet and convenient," Aunt Hortense had suggested.

The Irish Rose Cafe was quiet, all right. But only because the food was dreadful, Annie decided as she stirred her bowl of French onion soup. It was lukewarm, thick and brown, with a lumpy glob of cheese floating on top.

The lighting in the cafe was dim, and the decor mostly brown. Dark brown booths with brown plastic menus. Acres of dark varnish sticky with smoke. Framed pictures of 1916 Irish patriots and photostats of newspapers of the day lined the paneled walls. They were mottled and yellowed with age. The men in the photographs wore baggy trousers, ill-fitting jackets, and caps that shadowed their eyes. They were all terribly young and looked uncertain, as if they hardly knew how to cope with the forces they'd unleashed.

"Damn Brits. Murdering sons of bitches." Uncle Ira was reading an Irish pamphlet he'd picked up by the door when they came in. The lead article was all about Bloody Sunday 1972. He looked disgusted.

"Don't let it upset you, dear. At least they're looking into it, finally. And they've signed that Good Friday peace agreement, too. Try some." Aunt Hortense held out a forkful of turkey. "It's quite tasty."

"The spaghetti's enough. I don't have much of an appetite tonight."

The waitress bustled up and put a dish of grated cheese on the table. She was dark-haired, overweight, and surly. "The chef says there's no more lettuce, so he can't make you a salad."

Momentarily at a loss, Aunt Hortense perused the menu. "Oh . . . well, I guess I'll have pickled beets instead."

That weighty issue decided, the waitress left with a swish of her large hips, and the discussion returned to the IRA and prospects for a permanent peace in Northern Ireland.

Uncle Ira muttered that he didn't hold out much hope for breaking the cycle of brutal violence. "Paisley's stirring the pot, like always. They're nothing but a bunch of fanatics. You wait and see. They'll be blowing each other up again before long."

"They've made some progress," murmured Aunt Hortense. "They signed that treaty."

"Oh, so you think that's progress? Well, you're wrong. Ireland had to change their constitution and legitimize Britain's occupation of the six northern counties. In effect, they gave 'em the whole ball of wax. That's progress? Not on your life!"

"At least they've stopped that awful bombing—"

"Bombing has nothing to do with it," he grumped. "It's a matter of principle."

Annie chewed a stale roll. It occurred to her that he was concentrating on Northern Ireland so he could ignore what was going on in Roswell. He was in denial, much the same as an ostrich sticking its head in the ground. And she could only think to herself that in the long run it wouldn't do any good.

She looked around, wondering idly if the cafe was an

IRA hangout. Possible, but not likely. It made sense that they'd prefer a seaport like Boston, Massachusetts, which had been a longtime hotbed of IRA sympathizers for the very good reason that a flood of Irish immigrants had settled there eighty-odd years ago.

Roswell wasn't Boston, but her aunt and uncle were Irish clear through to the backbone, and Annie figured that they'd probably found The Irish Rose by some kind of internal Sein Fein radar. She'd forgotten how very Irish they were.

The waitress came back and plunked down three glasses of water. She put her hands on her hips and inquired, "Is everything okay?"

Annie gnawed on another roll while Uncle Ira nodded. "Fine, we're all set."

"Lovely, everything's quite nice." Aunt Hortense's smile was serene, as if the gravy on her mashed potatoes didn't look like horse glue. The waitress marched away again, and Aunt Hortense went on, "It's nice here this time of the week. Quiet. Business picks up later in the week, though. Saturdays, they have a roast beef buffet. All you can eat for less than ten dollars. People line up. They pack them in."

"Like sardines," intoned Uncle Ira with a knowledgeable air.

"Really?" Annie tried to appear interested. "That's great."

"We don't buy or sell on Sabbath. It's against our principles." Aunt Hortense sawed away at the piece of turkey on her plate, making the table jiggle. "So, we don't come here on Saturdays, naturally; but it's a nice restaurant."

Annie noticed that her aunt frequently used the words "lovely" and "nice," as if they were a mantra. If she said it often enough, it would be true.

Pushing away her bowl of onion soup, Annie hoped it would stay down.

Her aunt noticed. "Don't you like it?"

"It's fine. Fine." Inwardly, she winced at her own use of the word. She hated herself for being a hypocrite. But what could she do?

Silence fell. She wasn't being much of a guest, but cheerful optimism seemed out of place somehow. Still, good manners dictated that she make an effort.

"After you recover from your bunion surgery, maybe we can drive up north and see some of the cliff dwellings."

Aunt Hortense smiled. "That would be real nice, dear."

"That's a great idea," Uncle Ira agreed. "It'd be terrible if you came all this way from New Hampshire and didn't get to see the sights."

Aunt Hortense forked up a bit of turkey and gave Annie a knowing look. "So, dear, is there a Mr. Right in your life these days?"

"No."

"What does your mother have to say about your being single?"

"She's not happy. She wants me to marry someone with a six-figure income and a Mercedes."

"Every mother wants that for her daughter. But they usually settle for some man with a motorcycle and end up living in a gingerbread house." She stared across the room. "Well, well, look at that. The pastor's wife. I wonder who she's meeting."

"It's none of our business," muttered Uncle Ira. He shook the container of Kraft grated Parmesan cheese on his spaghetti and dug in.

"Where?" Annie craned her neck but couldn't see anything but a sea of empty tables.

"The booth in the corner," hissed her aunt.

Uncle Ira heaved an annoyed sigh. "For God's sake, leave it alone. She's probably hungry. People get hungry, and they have a right to go out to eat."

Aunt Hortense leaned her formidable breasts on the edge of the table and glared at him. "Don't be a fool. A woman like that doesn't drive all the way out here to eat alone. Word gets around, and people start wondering if her marriage is up to snuff."

"Gossips, you mean."

"I am *not* a gossip."

"You could have fooled me," he grumbled.

Dying of curiosity herself, Annie sneaked a look across the room. Melinda Pennyworth was lighting a cigarette. She seemed nervous, and kept looking at the door, as if she were waiting for someone. Maybe the man she'd been talking to on the telephone at the strip mall.

"She's having an affair, of course," asserted Aunt Hortense. "The brazen Jezebel! It must be a terrible burden for the pastor, poor man."

Annie had a sneaking suspicion the pastor didn't have a clue where his wife was concerned. "Maybe he doesn't know."

Uncle Ira sighed in disgust and went back to the spaghetti on his plate.

"It can only end in tears . . . the silly woman." Aunt Hortense leaned forward to take another look at the Jezebel across the room.

The fat waitress was taking her order. After writing it down on her pad, she stumped off and soon came back with a tray with a cup and saucer and a pot of tea.

Aunt Hortense was incensed. "Look at that! Of all the nerve! She got better service than we did, and we've been here longer, too."

"Maybe she's been here before," Annie suggested. "Maybe she's a good tipper."

"Don't be ridiculous, of course she's been here before! This is probably where they have their illicit rendevous!"

Against his will, Uncle Ira glanced across at the booth in question. "One cup and saucer. If she's expecting someone, wouldn't she order for two?"

"Not necessarily. Maybe her lover said he'd be late."

"You've tried and convicted that poor woman of adultery without a shred of evidence."

In another minute they'd be going at it again, hammer and tongs. In desperation Annie snatched up the dessert menu. "How about some ice cream? I feel like a sundae."

"Ice cream is full of fats and triglycerides, a real killer," pronounced Aunt Hortense. "Try the rice pudding." Her smug expression intensified as she glanced across the room again. "Ha! Didn't I tell you?" It looked as if she was right, after all. The waitress was placing another cup and saucer on Melinda Pennyworth's table.

Abruptly, Uncle Ira put down his fork. "How can you bother with gossip when any minute now I could be arrested for murder?"

"Nonsense," said Annie bracingly. "The police know you didn't do it."

"Knowing you're innocent and being able to prove it are two different things," he retorted. "Thousands of innocent people are rotting in jail this very minute. And why? Because they were railroaded, that's why."

Aunt Hortense looked pensive. "What we need is a character witness. What if we have the church board speak to the police on your behalf? Wallace Hapgood, Roger Stubenville, and George Digby. As elders, they have a certain standing in the community. The police will have to listen."

"A fat lot of good that would do," retorted Uncle Ira. "No one with half a brain would pay attention to anything they say. Since last week when the proposal to sell artifacts was turned down, the latest bright idea is to go around the congregation, hitting everybody up for a pledge to pay off the steeple repairs. As if we're made of money."

"The Good Lord knows if we had it to give, we would," said Aunt Hortense. "But we're all in the same boat, putting off bills we can't pay."

"The pastor is a damn fool. He wants a laptop computer for his own use and thinks the church should pay for it. Did you hear about his latest hare-brained scheme to attract converts?"

Annie had to admit her ignorance.

"A motorcycle ministry. And what kind of churchgoers will hanging around bars attract? Hell's Angels, that's what. Last week he suggested a golf ministry, if you please. He must think we're a bunch of halfwits. He just wants the church to pay his greens' fees."

"He's out of his mind!" snapped Aunt Hortense. "The

church budget's already as loose as an old lady's girdle, no wonder he doesn't have a clue about his wife!"

"Don't talk like that!" After giving his wife a meaningful look, Uncle Ira reddened and said to Annie, "We don't usually fight like this. But what with Reverend Morris being murdered and then Jan Stalker, well . . . we're just not ourselves."

"It's understandable," Annie murmured.

"When you think about it," said Aunt Hortense, tight-lipped, "it's horrible. There's a killer running loose. A maniac. No one's safe."

Feeling a growing sense of unease, Annie leaned back and eyed her aunt across the table. What she'd said was true, of course. But the odd thing was that before now, she hadn't given a thought to the real possibility that they all might actually be murdered in their beds. After two vicious killings, were they becoming hardened, even accustomed to violent death? Or was it something else? Did they know subconsciously that they had nothing to fear because the killer had no reason to go after them?

It was an interesting idea. Annie thought hard. The mental picture of a crazed killer disappeared from her mind's eye. No, whoever he was, the killer had acted rationally, with a sure sense of self preservation.

The waitress, whose nametag read, "Ethel," reappeared by their table and took out her pad and pen. "Will that be all? Or do you want to see the dessert menu?"

"We'll see the dessert menu," Aunt Hortense said briskly.

Ethel marched off to the waitress station and came back with three small, plastic menus, which she distributed without further comment. From her disgruntled expression, it was clear that they were expected to hurry up about it.

Casting his eye down the choices, Uncle Ira muttered, "I'll have the pecan pie."

"You know what pecan pie does to your digestion," warned Aunt Hortense. "Have tapioca or the rice pudding."

Annie spoke up. "I'll have a strawberry sundae."

Ethel sniffed, but wrote it down on her pad, and after a moment, Uncle Ira, still looking mutinous, said he'd have rice pudding instead.

"Make that two rice puddings." Aunt Hortense beamed.

After Ethel cleared the table of dirty dishes, they sat back and relaxed. Uncle Ira grumbled that a man had a right to a vice or two, and that he wished he'd ordered a beer with dinner. At that, Aunt Hortense tossed her head and snapped that she wasn't stopping him, for God's sake.

A change of subject seemed in order. Annie cleared her throat. "I hope the dog is all right. I locked him in my bedroom." For a mercifully brief moment a mental vision of Claudius chewing up the bedspread and mattress floated through her brain. She lied. "I'm sure he's fine."

Aunt Hortense's jaw set in a firm line. "He'd better not get into anything if he knows what's good for him."

But, of course, Claudius had known nothing of the sort. Several books were without their covers when, an hour or so later, Annie opened her bedroom door. He stared defiantly from the middle of her bed. "Get off," she ordered.

He did so with a decided air of arrogance. Who wanted to lie on her bed, anyway?

She picked up the books, made a futile attempt to put the covers back on, and dumped the whole lot in the carton in the closet with the other books he'd eaten. It had to be the glue, she thought, not wanting to believe he'd behave in such a destructive manner out of sheer spite just because she hadn't taken him out to eat.

The simple truth was that he had his agenda, and her wishes about anything simply didn't register in his pea-sized canine brain.

Furious, she added up the probable cost of replaced objects. More than a hundred dollars so far. Good God. She'd be flat broke before she got back home. He lay on the rug and shot her a thoughtful look as she padded to the bathroom and brushed her teeth. Then she came back, undressed, and put on a nightgown. His eyes were shining with what she knew quite well was derisive laughter.

So she didn't look like Sharon Stone, with or without her clothes on. "Beggars can't be choosers. Laugh and you sleep in the hall."

He gave an elaborate yawn.

She was determined not to let him get to her. He was only a dog who, unfortunately, hadn't been taken out for his nightly walk. With a tired groan, she threw a coat over her nightgown, grabbed a flashlight, the sports section of yesterday's *Post* and his leash, and took him outside.

It was past eleven now, and the moon was up. The heat still rose from the pavement, but the worst was over, thank God. She hated heat. There was even a slight breeze. She took a deep breath and told herself to relax as she trailed after Claudius. Her flashlight beam played on the cement sidewalk. She sidestepped a discarded junkfood bag, which the dog sniffed, then lost interest in. He trotted on, his tail and head high.

They wandered on down the street, passing the hedge between her uncle's house and Jan Stalker's. She noticed that some lowlife had scrawled a picture in yellow chalk on the sidewalk. It was a man and woman. The woman was grinning idiotically, and her legs were wrapped around the man's waist. The man had an extraordinarily large penis. Crudely drawn, but very much to the point.

Underneath an admonition was written in foot high letters: God will not be mocked!

Presumably one of the congregation was responsible for this artistic statement. Elvira Stubenville? The woman was a Bible-thumping bigot with a bias against lace underwear, but was she nutty enough to sneak out at night to scrawl pornographic graffiti on the sidewalk?

On the other hand, it was pretty much on the level as the other stuff she spouted. Annie grinned and let the leash out a little as Claudius christened the drawing.

Suddenly, he lifted his head and stiffened. She held her breath and listened, turning to look down the street. In the distance, there was the noise of traffic, but in the shadowy darkness there was no one but her and the dog. Or was there?

She resumed walking, but slowly this time, still listening hard. Once she thought she heard a shoe scuff against the pavement across the street. She stopped. Maybe it was only the echo of her own footsteps. She walked on a little more quickly. Claudius's nails clicked and her running shoes brushed softly on the cement of the sidewalk, hardly making a sound.

As she turned the corner at the end of the block—the dog still hadn't done his business—she heard a noise from the other side of the street again, and, at the same moment, a car started up somewhere down the block behind her.

Claudius halted with a soft growl, and she took a quick look over her shoulder. If there was someone on the other side of the street, she couldn't see him. He had to be standing behind a tree. The street still appeared to be deserted.

Farther on down the block, ill lit by the infrequent street lights, she thought she saw a car moving slowly toward her. Its headlights were off.

She moved faster and thought. God knew muggers were everywhere these days, but here in her uncle and aunt's quiet neighborhood? At this hour of night? Just past eleven? The streets were more or less vacant, pickings were bound to be lean on this side of town. Wouldn't any self-respecting thief be downtown where the action was and potential victims were plentiful?

She started running, realizing she was too far from her uncle's house to make it to safety. But Elvira Stubenville's house was just ahead. The windows were dark. It looked as if they'd already gone to bed.

Annie didn't want to wake them, but if she had to, she'd scream and pound on the front door until they got out of bed.

Actually, at this point—what with that obscene drawing on the sidewalk—Elvira was the last person she wanted to see, but she had little choice. She sprinted up the front walk, ran up the steps, and dragged Claudius into the shadows of the porch, praying she hadn't been seen.

The car was still there, it had stopped fifty yards away with its motor idling. The driver was only a dark shape behind the wheel.

She heard another sound from the other side of the street.

As she crouched panting, by the front door, the headlights of the car came on, illuminating the figure of a man crossing in front of it. It all happened in a split second, but she thought she saw that he was wearing blue-striped trousers and a peaked cap. Was he a uniformed policeman?

The car drove away, slowly, its rear lights glowing red. It stopped, and the rear lights disappeared as it turned left at the corner. She leaned against the wall of the house and let her pulse beat return to normal. Thank the Lord he hadn't been a mugger. For just a moment she entertained the entirely irrational thought that she might be the killer's next target, that for some reason he was after her. She was losing it, she told herself. She was a stranger here. The only people she knew were her aunt and uncle.

The policeman came up the walk and flashed his light in her face. "Excuse me, Miss. You all right?" He moved the light slowly up and down the front of her coat, noting the lace hem of her nightgown.

She flushed and grabbed the leash tighter as Claudius started growling again. "Shut up. I mean the dog, not you, officer."

"It's Miss O'Hara, isn't it?"

"Yes."

"What are you doing here? This isn't your uncle's house."

"I know that." She went down the porch steps to join him on the front walk, noticing he was youngish, in his late twenties, with thick dark hair and blunt features. He looked like the same officer she'd seen earlier with Lt. Rhodes, when they'd searched Uncle Ira's potting shed. Lt. Rhodes had called him "George." "I was frightened," she explained. "I thought I heard someone following me, and I saw a car. The headlights were off."

"Maybe it's not such a good idea to walk around here this late at night, Miss." He smiled at her with utmost politeness, and somehow she found herself heading back down the sidewalk toward Uncle Ira's.

Inevitably, they had to stop for Claudius who squatted by a tree. Without comment, she scooped it up in the twist of newspaper and dumped it in a trash barrel.

The policeman waited while she accomplished this bit of business, then they resumed the night's stroll. As they approached Jan Stalker's house and the yellow drawing on the sidewalk out front, he played the beam of his flashlight across it and said, "Did you do this, Miss?"

"No, I did not."

"Do you have any idea who might have done it?"

She avoided a direct lie. "I've only been here a few days. I don't know the neighborhood."

"And you don't have a piece of yellow chalk in your possession?"

"No, and I didn't throw any chalk away, either."

"I didn't say you had, Miss."

She bristled at the note of disbelief in his voice. Doubtless, he'd been staked outside Uncle Ira's for hours, in case her uncle attempted to leave town. It was all Lt. Rhodes's idea, of course, she thought. A cloud of gloom enveloped her as she realized it was a stakeout. *He could hardly wait to throw Uncle Ira in jail.*

She thought, We'll just see about that. If I have to find the killer myself and drag him down to the police station, then that's what I'll do.

Suddenly she realized her hands gripping the leash were trembling, and the policeman was staring. She tried for a casual tone. "I gave up smoking a while ago."

"That's tough."

"Sure is." Her voice was almost normal now, and the rest of the stroll passed uneventfully.

A few minutes later, she let herself into the house just as the phone started ringing. She raced down the hall to the kitchen to get it before whoever it was woke up her aunt and uncle.

"Annie?" She had no trouble recognizing the deep, husky drawl. It was Bob Colfax.

"Hello, Bob." She kicked off her shoes and started to work on her coat buttons. "I was just going to bed. Is it important?"

"Sorry for calling so late."

He didn't sound particularly sorry, but she was too tired to argue. "It's okay, what is it?"

He was still in the middle of his explanation. "I tried to get you earlier, but you were out. I thought I'd just leave a message on your answering machine."

"Could you get to the point? I'm really tired. What do you want?"

"People around town are getting scared. Two murders, and the killer still on the loose. Rumor has it you and your uncle discovered the second body, as well—Jan Stalker. Is it true? Are you all right?"

"I'm fine." Ignoring his first question.

"Good. How about getting together for dinner. Tomorrow? We have a couple of decent restaurants in town."

"If you have The Irish Rose in mind, forget it."

"Well," he said, laughing, "I didn't think you'd been around town that long. Usually it takes a few weeks to hit the bottom of the barrel."

She waited until he stopped laughing and got straight to the point. "If you think buying me dinner will make me blab all I know, you're crazy. I don't know anything. I just happened to be in the wrong place at the wrong time, and I sure don't want to see my name in print."

"Did I say a word about trying to get a story out of you?"

"You didn't have to."

"Then I take it you don't want to have dinner tomorrow night?" He sounded disappointed.

"Not so fast. If you're buying, I might be willing."

"Okay." He hesitated, then went on as if he wasn't sure of her reaction, "Or I could make us dinner at my place. I'm a pretty good cook."

"Oh." She thought about that. She didn't want to give

him ideas, or did she? "Your place would be okay, I guess."

"Great. It's Highland Street, the Armstead Apartments. I'm on the ground floor in back. Come around seven. Good night, Annie."

"Good night." But he'd already hung up. "Shit," she muttered as she padded upstairs in her stockinged feet. Claudius followed silently. Her aunt and uncle's room was just down the hallway, but their door remained closed. They were asleep.

She went into her bedroom and shut the door, still thinking about Bob Colfax. He was good-looking. More to the point, he was bright and funny, which was important. She liked men who made her laugh. He was good at his job: talking fast and worming information out of people who didn't want to give it. She wondered if he was good in bed. He could be just what she needed at this point in her life. Charming, handsome, articulate. She knew he had a serious side. He seemed focused on his career and had made no bones about wanting to get to the top of the heap. She didn't think he'd ever been married. He didn't have that hangdog married look, and he didn't act like a divorced man, either. She'd had enough of divorced men. She'd dated one or two after her own divorce and was thoroughly sick of their constant moaning about ex-wives and alimony.

They'd seemed almost desperate about wanting to remarry. An attitude that annoyed her no end. Marching down the aisle again wasn't on her agenda, no way.

She looked in the mirror and sucked in her stomach until it looked flat as a board. Her figure wasn't great, but it wasn't bad, either. She wasn't tall, only five feet, six inches, and Bob was taller. Six-foot-three, anyway. They'd make a good-looking couple. He was about thirty-six, three years older than she was. Which was about right, she thought. And it would make her mother happy.

She raked a tired hand through her hair and frowned. All her life her hair had been straight as a string, but now she'd almost swear there was a slight curl to it. That couldn't be. She had to be seeing things. She turned away from the mirror and resumed brooding about Bob Colfax. Who was she kidding? She had no business thinking about beginning a relationship with anyone. She was far from home, as alien to Roswell, New Mexico, as if she'd dropped off the side of a UFO. Besides, look what had happened to her practically the moment she'd set foot in town: She'd found a body, a reverend who'd been murdered. And he was barely cold in his grave when she'd found another body—this time, poor Jan Stalker. So much for her plans for a peaceful vacation in the land of enchantment.

The next night around seven-fifteen, she parked the Escort in the Armstead Apartments parking lot on Highland Street. She'd covered all her bases and felt mildly optimistic about the next few hours. She was wearing a dress that made her look good. Not obviously on the make, but as if she'd cared enough about impressing him to climb out of jeans and into a dress. She had good legs, thank God, and by dint of talking fast and promising she wouldn't be out late, she'd managed to park Claudius with her relatives for the evening. Bless his doggy heart, he'd been only too delighted with the bribe: a big bowl of Aunt Hortense's leftover chicken pot pie.

She took a deep breath and walked around to the back of the brick apartment house, looking forward to dinner. She went up the steps and rang the bell. From inside, Bob's voice called out, "Let yourself in, Annie. It's not locked."

"Hello," she called and closed the door behind her.

"I'm in the kitchen," he yelled back, and she could hear the low strains of jazz mixing with the clatter of pots and pans. Something smelled good. She walked through the living and dining room to the kitchen at the back of the apartment.

"Mmmm, garlic." She smiled. There was a Smoky Robinson CD playing on the stereo.

"Garlic, my ass," he said, putting the lid back on a pot on the stove. He slipped his left hand around her waist. "Imported garlic, if you please." He dropped a kiss on her lips. "You get plain old domestic garlic with store-bought pasta. With what you're eating tonight, you get the best." He kissed her again, putting both arms around her. "I like your dress." He grinned. "Are you wearing a bra?"

"Not that it's any of your business, but no."

His grin widened. "Good."

"I thought you deserved a treat since you were going to the trouble of making dinner." She liked having his arms wrapped around her, but if she wasn't careful, he'd get ideas, and it smelled as if there was a very good dinner on the stove. "What have you got to drink?"

"Only the best for you, Annie. Get a couple of glasses down from that cupboard by the sink," he suggested, opening the refrigerator. He took out a bottle of champagne and began untwisting the foil at the neck. "Hey, I didn't know you had curly hair. It looks good."

She shrugged. "It was straight until the other day. All of a sudden I can hardly get a brush through it. I don't know what happened."

"You didn't lay out a couple of hundred for a fancy permanent?"

"No, it turned curly almost overnight, right after I went out to the desert with my uncle. He showed me where the alien spaceship landed, and we found Jan Stalker. When I got back to the house, my hair . . . was curly."

"What do you think happened? Some kind of weird, leftover radiation, or what?" He was smiling, but she didn't think it was funny.

"I don't know what to think."

"So how are things otherwise? Found any more corpses?"

She turned with two flutes from the cupboard in her hands. "Ha, ha. The cops are crawling all over Uncle Ira's neighborhood, which I suppose is only to be expected, considering everything."

"You can't make an omelette without breaking eggs."

"What the hell does that mean?"

"Nothing, but it's understandable that Big Brother is interested if you go around finding dead bodies."

"That's not funny."

"I didn't mean it to be." He smiled. "So, are you married? I don't see a ring."

"I'm divorced. What about you?"

"Never found the right girl." He eased the cork out of the bottle with a loud popping noise and filled the two flutes with the wine. "Cheers," he said, clinking her glass. "So why did you get divorced?"

She wrinkled her nose at the bubbles. "More to the point, why did I get married in the first place."

"Okay, why?"

"I was young and stupid. He was older and slick as a snake. He thought I had money, which I didn't. I thought he was honest, and he wasn't, not by a long shot. Our parting was mutual." She sipped from her glass. "Mmm, this is marvelous."

"It should be. It's vintage Krueger, sixty-eight, a present from the owner of the paper. He liked the story I wrote about Reverend Morris."

She raised her glass. "To the late Reverend Morris."

"Here's to the old boy, then. May he rest in peace." He drank some champagne and smiled. "Drink up and I'll pour you another."

"This will do me for a while." She smiled. He wasn't going to get her drunk if she could help it. There was no way of knowing what she'd say.

"Okay," he said, turning back to the stove. "Listen, go out on the terrace and let me finish up here. It'll be ready in a couple of minutes."

Against her better judgment, Annie poured more champagne in her glass and strolled through the French doors that led to a small, paved terrace. A table and chairs were set beneath a large tree. She sat in a chair facing the kitchen window so she could watch him making dinner. He moved around the kitchen as if he knew what he was doing. Chopping and slicing, adding seasonings and stirring something on the stove. No wasted effort. He was good at it and knew it. A bit of an unlikely thing for him to be good at, she thought as she sat and sipped his vintage champagne.

She relaxed and decided she was having a wonderful time.

He had laid the table in the dining room and pulled the curtains across the windows to make the most of the candlelight. The dinner was delicious: garlic and lemon chicken grilled to perfection, roasted potatoes and stuffed mushrooms, and an avocado and tomato salad with a spicy dressing that tasted like heaven. And the champagne was full and yeasty.

"This is wonderful," she said. "Where did you learn to cook like that?"

He smiled and refilled her glass. "I like to eat so I picked it up here and there. No big deal."

"You're wrong there." She sipped her champagne and looked around the dining room. Bob had good taste in pictures. Lovely old botanical drawings were hung on the sage-green walls. She wondered if they were souvenirs from one of his girlfriends or if he'd done his own decorating.

"You like botanicals?" he asked.

"Yes, these are charming."

"They're Swedish, eighteenth century. I have a thing for old books and prints."

"Oh." She couldn't help eyeing the silverware on the table and wondered if he had money.

He saw the direction of her gaze and shrugged. "I inherited a little, and I bought high-tech stocks when they were low. I do all right."

"Your accent though, it's Southern." She smiled. "Where are you originally from?"

"Virginia." He smiled persuasively. "Look, Annie, a friend of mine has a boat entered in the Great Schooner race off the Maine coast. I promised to crew for him. He has a beautiful boat, a one hundred forty-foot windjammer, nicely equipped. And he could use more help. How about coming along? We'd have a great time, and those boats are something to see. It's the highlight of the summer. Afterward, we could take a week or two and sail down the coast."

Annie thought for a minute. She'd done a little sailing, but never on anything as large as a one hundred forty-footer. And she'd never sailed in the Great Schooner race. She was pretty much a novice when it came to ocean sailing. Her cooking couldn't compare with his, so she'd be no good in the galley. Which left only one place where she'd conceivably be of some use, and she didn't know him well enough for that. "I don't think so," she said slowly. "Sounds like fun, but no thanks."

He raised his eyebrows, a bit surprised that she'd turned him down. "Too bad . . . Guess I'll have to find someone else."

She felt a sudden pang, which she told herself wasn't jealousy, and hoped the "someone else" he found wasn't female.

Sometime after eleven, she said good night and drove herself home. He'd suggested they make a night of it, and for a moment she'd been tempted. He was good-looking and made her laugh. It was impossible not to feel the pull of his sex appeal; but something made her decline. Her starchy New England upbringing, or the mental image of her mother rubbing her hands gleefully, anticipating a son-in-law in the offing. No, that wasn't it. The moment she'd said she didn't want to crew for him, the way he'd raised his eyebrows, as if he wasn't used to being turned down. That had done it.

As far as women were concerned, he was too sure of himself, and she didn't like that, not one bit.

She checked the rearview mirror once or twice, but no one seemed to be following. Hardly anyone else on the road, only a few cars and tractor trailers. She passed a few all-night gas stations, then drove past the Alien Museum. When the dancing chicken came into view, she turned down Elm Street to see the spire of The Neighborhood Church of the Celestial Spheres looming in the night sky. The dove weathervane atop the building pointed east, unmoving, and she noticed that there was no sign of the police detail she'd seen the night before. Either they quit at midnight, or they'd gotten better at concealment.

She parked in her uncle's driveway and let herself into the house, all the while wondering how many pairs of eyes were watching her from the dark.

Chapter Ten

"God in heaven, what a day I've had!" Mrs. Fielding wheezed as she dumped her purse and knitting bag on the floor and sat down in a chair in Aunt Hortense's hospital room. Her pear-shaped figure was draped in billowing, mid-calf length blue crepe, which failed to conceal stumplike ankles. As luck would have it, she'd just come from the Pounds Off Qwik weekly weigh-in at the church, and, having starved herself for the past eight hours, was more than ready for the feed bag. "Pass the chocolates."

Uncle Ira had gone off to park the car, and Annie made a corner for herself on the edge of her aunt's bed and watched the church ladies bicker over the candy she'd brought.

Mrs. Fielding's lips pursed in annoyance. In her opinion, Melinda Pennyworth was hogging the entire box of Russell Stover's. "Hurry up, Hortense can't eat before surgery, and we don't want them to go to waste."

"There's little danger of that. Everybody knows what goes on. The nurses take them." Melinda chose a cherry-filled chocolate from the gold-ribboned box and handed it over. "Anyway, are you allowed to eat chocolate on Pounds Off?"

"Of course. Not more than eight ounces during the week, but on weekends you can have all you want." Dragging out the afghan she was currently working on, Mrs. Fielding arranged it on her ample lap. She popped a marshmallow creme in her mouth and rummaged through the box with a look of displeasure. "Did you have to take the biggest one? There are only caramels left. I can't eat them."

"Never mind." Annie opened her bag, found a candy bar and gave it to Mrs. Fielding.

"Thanks." She unwrapped and ate it, savoring every mouthful.

They were in the outpatient wing of the hospital. No one expected Aunt Hortense to stay more than a few hours this afternoon, but Annie had brought along a couple of paperbacks just in case. You never knew. Her aunt was past sixty-five and had more than her fair share of health problems.

"Open the window," complained Melinda, fanning herself with her purse. "It's hot as hell in here."

"They don't open," said Aunt Hortense. "Everything's automatic. The price of progress, I suppose."

Annie went to the air-conditioning unit beneath the window and switched it on. A rush of cool air filled the room and everyone breathed a sigh of relief.

Aunt Hortense passed around snapshots of the ill-fated welcome home party for Reverend Morris, and they all commented on how handsome he was. What a loss to the congregation.

Just as Annie sat down on the edge of the bed again, in marched Elvira Stubenville, carrying a Bible. She cast a frowning look around, sat herself on a chair, and took off her hat. "I would have been here sooner, but I had a flat tire. The second one in a week. My Chevy Lumina needs new tires and a front-end allignment."

"You're a terrible driver," said Aunt Hortense, passing the snapshots her way. "Ira took these the night of the party. There's one of you that's quite nice, Elvira. Anyway, last week you drove over a curb. You told me yourself."

"That's not so. And even if I did, it was only a little bump. It couldn't have done any damage." Elvira flipped through the photographs, frowned, and flipped through them again. "Where's the one of me? I don't see it."

Aunt Hortense found it. "Your flowered dress came out really well. Ira's flash didn't work with the second roll of film, so these are all that came out."

Elvira said she hated that dress as it always made her look fat, then she glanced at the pastor's wife. "Actually, the first flat happened on Route 50 the other night coming back from the mall. Right near The Irish Rose, as it happens, so I was able to use the phone. Roger's too cheap to get me a cell phone."

Everyone nodded, conceding the known fact of Roger's penny-pinching ways.

With a sly expression on her face, and relishing what she was about to say, Elvira turned back to Melinda. "I noticed your car in the cafe parking lot. Having dinner?"

For a moment, Melinda looked blank, then gushed, "Why, yes. I thought I'd try the roast beef buffet, and it was really quite good. As things turned out, I had to eat alone. My husband was called to Mrs. Boroski's. She took a turn for the worse and thought she was dying."

"For heaven's sake," snorted Aunt Hortense. "Nobody ever died of shingles. She just wanted attention."

Annie was still pondering Melinda's slip of the tongue about the roast beef buffet. *The cafe only served the buffet on Saturdays.*

Meanwhile, Elvira flipped through her Bible. "Corinthians 9:7. 'God loveth a cheerful giver.' We should be grateful the pastor is so devoted to the congregation."

"The pain pills are wearing off," groaned Aunt Hortense. "My feet are killing me."

"They'll be coming for you soon," Elvira said knowledgeably. "Perhaps you'd like to pray now."

It was, Annie thought, giving the woman the benefit of the doubt, a suggestion kindly meant; but from Aunt Hortense's exasperated expression, it looked as if Elvira's welcome had worn thin. Her aunt was in no mood to cope with much more than getting through the next few hours in one piece.

Unfortunately, Elvira couldn't resist one more snide remark. "I don't care what people say, dear. You're having your feet done purely for medical reasons."

"What is that supposed to mean?" demanded Aunt Hortense.

"If you're bent on beautifying yourself, there's no escape from eventual hellfire. Believe me, God has no patience with that sort of thing. Neither have the aliens, for that matter."

They were going from one testy subject to another. Annie opened her mouth to pour a little oil on the waters, but before she could say anything, Aunt Hortense bristled. "How would you like to walk around on my feet, Elvira?"

Busy looking at the photographs again, Elvira didn't bother to answer. But when she noticed Melinda hurriedly gathering her things, preparing to depart, she said, "You're not going?"

"I have to pick up my son, Gerry, at the elementary school. He has a Cub Scout meeting." Melinda dropped a quick kiss on Aunt Hortense's cheek. "I hope the operation goes well. Bye, bye, dear."

With that, she departed, leaving behind the faint fragrance of Opium.

There was a pregnant silence. Then they all started talking at once. Elvira expressed fear that Melinda had strayed from the path of righteousness. With the Second Coming and the return of Our Friends from the other side of the Milky Way, Melinda was in big trouble.

Mrs. Fielding turned the afghan in her lap, starting the next row with puce green—she'd used up the last of the blood red wool, green would have to do. Offhandedly, she said, "Aren't they painting the elementary school this week? I read it in the paper—they've closed the school for a few days."

Annie thought back to breakfast this morning. Her uncle had read the paper and mentioned that the elementary school was being painted. Along with the comment that a good many mothers were bound to tear their hair out before long, what with the little darlings at home all week. An idle remark, since it didn't affect them—but it certainly affected Melinda Pennyworth.

"If she's picking her son up at school, she'll have a long wait," sniffed Elvira.

"I've always said she was a mite too free and easy with the truth." Mrs. Fielding wagged a fat admonitory finger. "That's the pastor's fault. He knew what he was getting when he married that woman."

"She lies like a rug when it suits her," Elvira agreed,

then added with a sly glance at Aunt Hortense, "If you ask me, Melinda's hair color isn't natural."

Aunt Hortense, whose russet locks were several shades redder than nature had ever intended, cleared her throat. "Really?"

"And she paints her face," Elvira went on, her tone making it perfectly clear that she didn't consider herself a gossip. Gossip was something lesser people indulged in. She smiled at Annie. "I've heard news about you that's somewhat troubling."

"Really?" Annie wondered what she was getting at.

"You've taken up with that newspaper reporter, a purveyor of filth!"

She managed not to laugh. "I'm not familiar with the newspapers out here, but I'm sure Bob Colfax isn't a purveyor of filth."

"They're little more than muckrakers, crucifying the innocent along with the guilty. They hate anyone with any religious beliefs. Mark my words, we'll be dragged into the gutter before this is done. I wouldn't trust that Colfax fellow as far as I could throw him."

Aunt Hortense eyed Annie worriedly. "Didn't you go out to dinner with him last night, dear?"

"Yes, I had a lovely time."

"I see." Elvira left an eloquent pause. "Which restaurant did he take you to?"

"I . . . we . . . he's a wonderful cook. We ate at his place." She regretted her words the minute they were out of her mouth.

"*Well!* Far be it from me to pry, but even the appearance of illicit behavior is bound to besmirch your poor aunt and uncle. Think of their reputation next time you feel the urge to indulge in wickedness and fornication."

"If I decided to have nonstop sex with Bob Colfax in the middle of Route 50, it still would be none of your business!"

Elvira eyed Annie's hair, which for some reason—ever since she'd been out at the crash site, as a matter of fact—had begun to curl wildly about her head. "I see you have a permanent. Very nice. Of course, God has taken note of it."

Momentarily nonplussed—she had her own ideas about why she'd begun to look like Little Orphan Annie, and she was damned if she was going to give Elvira any more ammunition—Annie decided to keep her big mouth shut.

"I'm not feeling up to an argument," said Aunt Hortense. "If Annie wants curly hair, it's none of our business. And where they had dinner isn't really important."

"How do you think *I* feel, having to bring all this up?" Elvira snapped in a voice rich with self-pity.

"I haven't got time to think about your nerves right now. I've got enough problems of my own," retorted Aunt Hortense, as a nurse came in with a tray and a hypodermic needle.

"I assure you, I take no pleasure in exposing licentious behavior of the sort that brought down the wrath of God on Sodom and Gomorrah, but it must be done. We are truly in the Last Days. The Good Book tells us we'll be tested with many false prophets. Of course, the hellfire they talk about will come from UFOs, the army of the Lord."

The nurse had no time for nonsense. She put the tray down on the bedside table, eyed the roomful of church ladies, and announced briskly, "Okay, ladies. Time to leave."

They bustled about picking up knitting, handbags, and assorted odds and ends—most of which belonged to Mrs. Fielding, who, besides working on the afghan, was crocheting several sets of place mats for Christmas. Annie kissed her aunt, who eyed the nurse distrustfully. "I can't think what's keeping Ira. Goodness gracious, how long does it take to park the car?"

"He must have run into one of his pals on the way upstairs. Don't worry. I'll find him and send him in."

Hypo in hand, the nurse marched over to the bed. "Say good-bye. You can finish your conversation after the surgery."

Aunt Hortense looked apprehensive, but managed a brave smile as they left.

It bothered Annie to leave her like this, but she had no choice. The nurse was brandishing the hypodermic with an expression of firm purpose on her face, so all she could do was wave. She took the elevator downstairs and found Uncle Ira in the front lobby, deep in conversation with the cleaning man. "Yes, bunion surgery," he was saying.

"Don't talk to me about bunions," the cleaning man said with a sigh. "I could tell you horror stories about my wife's feet that would curl your hair."

Uncle Ira nodded. They were two men who shared a common past of marriage to women with mysteriously complex female ailments.

She touched her uncle's arm. "You'd better go on up. They're getting ready to take Aunt Hortense to surgery."

The cleaning man went back to polishing the hospital gift shop window, and Uncle Ira hurried upstairs after saying he'd see her at home later on.

She stood there thinking for a moment. Claudius was waiting at home, she'd locked him in her bedroom. Presumably he was on his best behavior, if he was capable of such a thing. She had two choices: To go home right now and deal with whatever mess he'd made, or put off the inevitable for a few minutes and browse around the gift shop.

The gift shop won. "Hello," she said to the volunteer behind the counter. The woman nodded and went back to pricing stuffed animals. Annie strolled to the window beside the open door. The shop was fully stocked with cards, wrapping paper, ribbon, toys of all sorts, potted plants, even fake ones for those uninterested in caring for the real thing. She wondered if Aunt Hortense would like a plant.

From where she stood, she had an excellent view of the hospital's front entrance. There was a family approaching, and behind them, a man who looked disconcertingly like Lt. Rhodes. He had a uniformed policeman with him.

They walked up to the information desk, spoke to the volunteer on duty, then took one of the elevators.

Annie had a bad feeling about all this. Why would Lt.

Rhodes show up at the hospital? If he was visiting a sick relative, he wouldn't have another cop with him.

She headed toward the elevator. The arrow above it moved to two, then three. It stopped. Someone got off.

Aunt Hortense's room was on the third floor.

The stairs were quicker. Annie flew up them, and on third, banged the door open without regard for the sign admonishing visitors to be considerate as there were sick people here. Her eyes swept down the long hallway, past half a dozen semiprivate rooms. Her aunt's was at the end.

And there they were, Lt. Rhodes and his buddy, just going inside. Oh, God, she thought. That was all they needed.

By the time she reached her aunt's room, she heard her shriek of protest and Uncle Ira's voice saying that everything would be all right. She wasn't to worry. Then he came out, with Lt. Rhodes and buddy following close behind, in case he tried to flee.

"What's going on?" Annie demanded angrily. But she already knew.

"What does it look like?" Lt. Rhodes snapped, eyeing her balefully. "Stand aside. We're taking your uncle downtown for questioning."

"What for—he hasn't done anything!"

"That's what we're gonna find out."

Uncle Ira patted her shoulder. "It's okay. I don't mind. Take care of your aunt." His face was pale and his hands shook. Annie hugged him.

"I'll come downtown as soon as she's out of surgery. We'll have you home in no time. They won't get away with this."

"Let's go," said Lt. Rhodes. He grinned. "Not you, just your uncle."

Half an hour later, she was sitting in the visitors' lounge, cooling her heels, waiting for word of her aunt's condition. Lt. Rhodes had taken Uncle Ira off to the hoosegow and she'd comforted her aunt by lying and saying the police only wanted clarification on a few points. Aunt Hortense had already been sedated. She didn't ask what those points were, and Annie was careful not to tell her.

Half an hour crawled by. She read three dog-eared magazines without understanding a single word. Her mind was racing with unpleasant possibilities. An hour dragged by, then another. Finally a doctor came out, noticed her sitting there, and asked if she was Mrs. O'Hara's niece. Annie stood up and said she was.

"Your aunt's fine. But we'd like to keep her overnight, maybe a day or two longer. She's in recovery, but she'll be going back up to her room in another hour or so."

Annie didn't waste any time. She grabbed the first elevator, rushed down to the lobby, and outside. She was worried sick, nervous, and really didn't know what she was going to say when she got to the police station, other than they'd better let Uncle Ira go. Somehow though, she didn't think that would have the slightest effect on Lt. Rhodes.

Her acquaintanceship with Lt. Rhodes had been mercifully brief, but she'd had time to come to some conclusions. On the surface he looked unprepossessing and stolid. But behind those beady dark eyes lurked a policeman's dogged intelligence. Once he got his hands on a prime suspect, he'd never let him go.

The police station door shut behind her as she walked inside, her handbag clutched to her side. When the officer at the front desk glanced at her, she squared her shoulders, marched up to him, and said, "Where's Ira O'Hara?"

"You a relative?"

"Yes, his niece."

The policeman—his name tag read "Sgt. E. Dowell"—shrugged. "You'll have to speak to Lt. Rhodes, Miss. Why don't you take a seat." Indicating a hard wooden bench by the wall, he nodded and picked up the phone.

She sat there for twenty minutes before Lt. Rhodes decided to put her out of her misery and emerged from a door down the hall. "Well, well, look what the wind blew in."

She stood up. "Where's my uncle?"

"In good hands. We're not through with him yet."

"Is he under arrest?"

"Do you think he should be?" He shoved his hands in his pants pockets and eyed her with infuriating deliberation. Apparently in no hurry to get back to Uncle Ira.

"He's done nothing. While you're wasting time badgering innocent people, the real killer's walking around, scot-free."

"That's a matter of opinion. The good reverend's death was a little peculiar. Out here when it's murder, it's usually gunshot. Not . . . garden fork. Your uncle's the prime suspect, and we don't have much else to go on. Careless with his garden tools, is he?" He smiled.

"You know how that fork got over to the church. My aunt's already said she left it there after planting some flowers."

"That's what she says. Sounds a bit too convenient, if you ask me."

"It happens to be the truth. Someone else saw it lying there and used it to kill Reverend Morris. Not my uncle!"

Lt. Rhodes shrugged. "We could hold him as a material witness."

"What'll that accomplish? I'll get a lawyer and we'll have him out of here in an hour." She didn't know if this was possible, but figured the only way to get anywhere was to give as good as she got.

He laughed in her face.

She glared at him. "You think I won't? All I know is my uncle didn't do a damn thing and you're too stupid or too lazy to look for the murderer. You'd rather pin it on him than do your job. If you don't let him go right now, I'll call the newspaper and tell them exactly what's happened."

"Well—" There was a pause while he thought that one over. He shrugged again. "Guess it won't hurt to wait a bit longer. Sit down. I'll go get him, and you can take him home."

"It was absolutely horrible," said Uncle Ira in the Escort a half hour later, mopping his brow. "I thought they'd bring out the rubber hose any minute." Annie could see the experience had upset him terribly. She'd told him her aunt was staying at the hospital overnight, but was fine. The doctors were just being careful. Finally satisfied, he'd admitted that the police interrogation was something he didn't want to ever endure again.

"Well, you won't have to. They don't have a single bit of evidence against you."

"Other than my garden fork and the fact that I couldn't stand the sight of him."

"Probably lots of people hated him. Don't worry. Given time, they'll find out who really did it."

"God, I hope so," he said tiredly.

Once they got home, he went to check the mailbox while she let Claudius into the backyard for a quick run and went into the house. The telephone answering machine light was blinking. *Maybe it was Bob*. Her heart thudded with anticipation as she pressed the play button and listened to three messages, none of which was Bob, after all.

He could have called, she thought, annoyed and kicking herself mentally for even thinking about him. Granted, he was an attractive man and a good cook. Well, so what. He wasn't Wolfgang Puck, and it wasn't the end of the world if she never heard from him again.

She had more important things to worry about. Like how to keep Uncle Ira from being arrested for murder.

The back door opened, and he came in, still upset. He tossed the mail on the counter and glanced out at the garden. "What the hell is that?"

She joined him at the window. At first glance, everything looked normal, a serene oasis of green. Then clods of dirt appeared, flying over the tomato tepees like a barrage of tomahawk missiles. As they watched, one of the tepees received a direct hit and fell over.

Claudius.

They ran outside to find him industriously digging to China. He'd already wiped out two rows of lettuce and brussel sprouts, along with a row of pole beans.

"How could you? Bad dog!" Annie dragged him out of the trench by his collar. His muzzle and paws were covered with mud. "Bad dog!" He looked very pleased with himself. Not the slightest flicker of shame, not a twitch. He stared back at her as if he'd done nothing wrong, as if he hadn't just deliberately torn up fifteen feet of carefully tended vegetables.

Uncle Ira kicked a clod of uprooted brussel sprouts. "Gotta hand it to him, he did one hell of a job."

"I'm sorry." She gave her uncle a tense little smile. "It's all my fault. I never should have let him loose out here, but it's the last time I'll ever do that."

Uncle Ira grunted, eyeing the wreckage at his feet. "Damn fool dog."

Claudius scratched his ear with his hind leg, dislodging a clod of drying mud.

Embarrassed to the point of humiliation, she hauled him across the lawn and tied him to the tree, where he lay down in the shade and looked extremely pleased with himself as he watched them clean up the mess.

"Fool animal," muttered Uncle Ira. He was raking dirt back into the trench and stopped to wipe his brow. He stuffed the handkerchief back in his pocket. "That dog's nothing but a damned biscuit eater."

Annie didn't know what to say, so she stayed silent as she gathered up broken bean poles and tossed them in a pile. A few minutes later, her uncle seemed to have matters well in hand, and she lingered awkwardly, trying to make amends.

"I'm really sorry. Nothing like this will ever happen again."

"It had better not." He cast another baleful look at Claudius, stretched out in blissful comfort beneath the shade tree. "If he does, I'll kill him."

"I . . . I think he's really sorry he did this."

Uncle Ira uttered a snort of disbelief. "Like hell he is."

She was forced to leave it at that.

But she remembered the poster in Dr. Shepherd's office. Obedience classes for dogs, sponsored by the church. As soon as she went back in the house, she phoned the vet and signed up for the next session, which, as luck would have it, was being held that night, at eight o'clock.

"Just behave yourself," she told the dog as they drove

to the local high school. Ignoring that foolish remark, he stuck his nose out the window and sniffed the night air with gusto.

She decided to play it cool for the next hour or so. Anything she learned in class tonight would be a plus because, basically, she was starting from scratch. Whether Claudius would cooperate was entirely another matter.

Five minutes later, they were walking across the parking lot toward the gym. He'd peed on the Escort's rear tire and relieved himself by the curb, as if girding his loins for what lay ahead.

"Promise me you'll be good," she told him, noticing several other people and dogs congregating by the entrance to the gym. The dogs were sniffing one another, tails wagging in a convivial manner.

The idea that Claudius might do the same was laughable.

She made a wide berth around the group and led him inside. Three women were standing behind a table by the door, eyeing the assembled crowd of dogs and owners with mildly contemptuous curiosity. The nearest, with short, curly blonde hair and a no-nonsense manner handed Annie a registration form and a pen.

"Fill this out."

While she scribbled all the relevant information and handed over the sixty-five dollar fee, Claudius sat at her feet looking bored. The lessons consisted of ten classes, by the end of which Pam Hardaway—the woman with the blonde hair—and her two assistants, Molly Carson and Terry MacNeil, guaranteed that the dog would be trained to come when called, heel, and stay on command. No negative reinforcements were used. Only positive training. "A good dog is a well-trained dog."

Annie sincerely hoped so. She handed in the form.

"Well, well," muttered Pam, giving it the once over. "He's a mixed breed. German shepherd and huskie. I see." Exactly what she saw, she didn't say.

About to lie and say he was a wonderful dog and just needed a little training, Annie changed her mind. "Is there something wrong?"

There was a dead silence, which Claudius filled by yawning widely and then shutting his jaws with an audible click.

Annie pretended she hadn't heard that deliberate act of bad manners.

"No, not really," Pam said, exchanging glances with Molly.

"It's just that sometimes the mixed breeds . . . well, with purebreds you know their background and temperament," burbled Molly. "It's a lot easier."

"Some of the smartest dogs are mixed breeds," added Terry.

Annie noticed they avoided the term, "mongrel"—undoubtedly perceived as a mark of disrespect in some quarters. Well, she could live with that.

"At any rate, I'm sure he'll do just fine after a class or two." Pam made a dismissive gesture, as if brushing off the dictums of the A.K.C. as irrelevant, which perhaps they were. "We separate the group into beginner and advanced. The beginners are at the back of the gym."

She pointed, and Annie went, taking Claudius with her. So far, so good.

The gym began to fill up. The advanced class at the other end, seemed made up of about ten dogs. Retrievers, both black and golden, several cocker spaniels and poodles, big and small, a sheepdog or two. A mixed group, but one thing they all had in common was complete and utter attention to their owners. They walked docilely, tails up, ears perked, alert, eagerly waiting for the next command.

In contrast, the beginners' group consisted of ten or twelve barking dogs doing their damndest either to fight or escape. Claudius, having done his share of aggressive barking, zeroed in on a nearby sheepdog as a likely victim, so Annie hauled him back by the bleachers. "Bad dog! Shut up!"

He barked a few more times, but his heart wasn't really in it; the sheepdog was a good fifty feet away.

A lecture was in order. "Why can't you behave?" He yawned. "Look," she said. "We're guests at Uncle Ira's.

He's got enough on his plate, what with Aunt Hortense's surgery and the terrible murders. You're not stupid. You know exactly what you did this afternoon . . . wrecking his garden. We're both in big trouble."

She needed a sign that he was willing to meet her halfway—something—but he was now focused on a tan-colored Chihuahua. Making horrid little snuffling noises, growling, working himself up to launching an attack.

"No, you don't!" She gripped the leash and pulled him close by her left leg. Positive reinforcement seemed in order. She patted him and scratched his large ears in a show of affection. "Good dog, good dog." Trying to reinforce a so far nonexistent friendship.

Claudius eyed her for a moment, then swung his head back toward the Chihuahua now impudently yipping at him. If he got loose, the Chihuahua was a goner. Annie wound the leash around her wrist and prayed as Pam Hardaway marched to the front of the beginners' group and yelled, "Line up, folks. We've got a lot of ground to cover tonight."

With some apprehension and figuring the safest place to be was as far away from the rest of the class as she could get, Annie headed for a spot at the end of the back row. Much to her astonishment, Claudius got up and trotted along without a peep.

For the next twenty minutes, while Pam demonstrated the basics of heel, come, and stay, his eyes followed with intense interest. When it was time to put him through his paces, Annie was amazed to see that he did exactly as he was told.

At the break, Pam walked over. "He's a terrific dog." Bending to scratch his big, black ears, she asked, "What's his name?"

"Claudius. I'm amazed at how well he's doing. He's had training. He was a police dog for a while, but he was too stubborn and wouldn't obey orders. He's usually totally off the wall."

"Well, you've come to the right place. Control is what we strive for. With this dog, you have a greater responsibility than you'd have with, say, that cocker spaniel over there." Indicating a small taffy-colored cocker with a jeweled collar and a doe-eyed expression, Pam explained, "Claudius is a working dog, smart and easily bored. He wants to be worked. He wants to please you."

Up until that point, Annie would have agreed with her. But no way did Claudius want to please her. The only person he'd ever felt that way about was Lydia. He would remain loyal to her through thick and thin, no matter what. And there was nothing Annie could do about it.

"The trouble is he's not actually my dog. I only have him for a few weeks, a month at most. He's driving me crazy, tearing up books, chewing pillows. This afternoon he made a terrible mess and dug up my uncle's garden."

Pam gave her a long look. "Whether you have him for a week or a month doesn't matter. He's a fine, handsome animal. He has all the elements to behave perfectly, but he needs a strong hand on the leash. He wants discipline, he'll thrive on it. It's your job to provide it. Nothing negative, of course. Start by giving him treats when he does as he's told. After a while you'll find you won't need the treats."

After Pam walked back to the front of the class, Annie noticed with dismay that, anticipating the odd accident, the rest of the class had armed themselves with pooper-scoopers and bags. She took Claudius out to the car, letting him pee by a bush on the way. A quick search under the front seat turned up a crumpled McDonald's bag and an old newspaper. She told him to heel, which elicited an inscrutable stare but no movement on his part. She tried again, louder this time. "Heel!"

He looked away and ignored her, and she wondered what to do now. She mulled over what Pam had told her: supposedly, he wanted a strong hand on the leash and longed for discipline. Maybe. But she hadn't seen any sign of it. It was all too clear that he thought she was pathetic and inadequate. She'd never measure up—an attitude that annoyed her intensely.

It was a battle of wills, and she was damned if she'd let him win. One way or another, they'd go back to the gym, and he'd learn the rudiments of obedience training and good manners if it killed her.

She looked him straight in the eye. "Heel."

He gave her a considering look, then did exactly that.

When they reached the end of the row of cars, she heard loud barking and growling just ahead. They skirted two people trying desperately to untangle a dachshund and a Scottie. Claudius sneered, his body language conveying the message that he could eat them alive any time he felt like it, and they were just lucky he wasn't in the mood.

The break ended and class proceeded more or less in order. Claudius settled down, seemingly not at all bothered by being marched up and down the gym for no apparent reason other than Annie's whim. When an opportunity came to stand and rest, he was relaxed and genial, content to watch the other dogs. She had the impression he was noting and remembering each and every detail, storing it all away in his clever German shepherd–huskie brain for future reference.

Another hour passed. Pam noted the time and smiled at everyone. "Let's call it a night. We've made considerable progress. Perhaps one or two setbacks." She didn't embarrass the guilty parties by going into any of the grisly details. "I'm sure we'll do even better when we meet again, Tuesday night."

Slowly, the gym emptied of dogs and people, and Annie approached the table where Pam stood talking to her assistants. "It's obvious that the A.K.C. targets a few breeds every year," she was saying, "Everything's orchestrated. You can't convince me anything goes on that the board doesn't know about."

Molly looked worried. "I'll be in Texas next week. The Belgian sheepdog club is holding trials at Southfork Ranch all next week, with herding and pretrials Tuesday. I entered Frankie. With any luck I'll finish him by Friday."

"He's at peak form," Pam assured her. "He'll do just fine."

"He's worked hard for it." Molly beamed. "He deserves it. Well, about tonight's group. Let's get down to brass tacks. There are enough dogs for two advanced classes. You could split them up on Tuesday."

"Sounds good." Terry began to clear the table, stacking registration forms into a neat pile.

"That's a heart attack in the making." Pam said, nodding at a fat Scottie waddling out the door. "At least six pounds overweight. I told the owner he was killing the dog, overfeeding him like that There's no need for it. It's criminal, really."

"Excuse me," said Annie. "I was wondering if we'd get a certificate when the course is over."

"If your dog completes the course satisfactorily." Pam eyed Claudius who was smirking with self-importance. "He did pretty well tonight . . . on the whole."

"Yes, he did."

"You can't build Rome in a day," chipped in Molly. "A dog like that is smart. After a while he'll anticipate what you want him to do. Naturally, it'd be a different matter if you had one of the more stupid breeds."

"Why is he wearing that thing?" Pam frowned at the spike collar Claudius was wearing. Not entirely trusting him, Annie had exchanged it for the choke chain collar they'd used during the class.

"His fur is so thick he doesn't feel the other one. Besides, it was getting expensive. I bought three of them before I realized he was ditching them on purpose."

"What?"

Annie explained. "His fur is slippery. He runs, then stops on a dime, and tosses his head until the collar flies off."

"I told you he was smart." Pam smiled. "Stubborn, too. Drives you crazy, doesn't he? Right up the wall."

"That's right."

"Don't worry. You came to the right place. Actually, there are obedience booklets over at the church that you might like to study. We keep them downstairs in the library. The caretaker, John Barnard, could show you where they are." Her eyes sharpened and she darted another look at Claudius, then back at Annie. "My God, you found that dead woman and the minister."

They all stared at her.

"How awful," Molly whispered, practically pop-eyed.

Terry shook her head. "Do they know who did it? I mean, supposing there's only one killer. It's hard to imagine there are two murderers running around loose."

"It's downright terrifying." Molly shivered. "I'm glad I'm not involved."

"I'm not involved," Annie said loudly, fudging the truth a little. "I just happened to find the first body. My uncle found the second one . . . well, we were together."

"You don't have to explain anything." Pam didn't look happy. It was obvious she was wondering about the ramifications to her thriving obedience training business. Having a possible homicidal maniac in the class might prove downright embarrassing. What if it came out exactly who Annie was? Would Pam's pupils quit en masse, like rats leaving the sinking ship?

"What's done is done, I suppose," Pam said thoughtfully, then her manner changed. She was all business. "So, do you intend to remain in the class?"

If Annie had any doubts on that score, they were gone now. "I certainly do."

Pam shrugged, and Annie left the gym with her head held high and Claudius at her side.

Chapter Eleven

What else did she expect, Annie thought as she drove out of the high school parking lot and headed home. Her mouth twisted as she recalled Pam Hardaway's change of attitude once she realized who she was—a material witness in a murder investigation. It was upsetting and humiliating. A state of affairs she'd better get used to.

She drove down Elm Street, barely noticing the houses on the tree-lined street. It was a neighborhood that rolled up the sidewalks after nine. Here and there she caught the bluish flicker of a TV in an upstairs bedroom, but most of the houses were dark.

Jan Stalker's bungalow was just ahead. It showed no sign of life. The yellow-and-black police tape was gone. The investigation had moved on. She just hoped it hadn't settled on Uncle Ira.

Suddenly, Claudius, who'd been asleep in the back seat, got up and pressed his nose to the side window, and she turned to see what had caught his attention.

A faint light flickered in one of the first floor windows in Jan's house. Pale, almost ghostly, flickering behind the curtains. Someone was inside the house, using a flashlight. Whoever it was didn't want to be seen. Was it the killer?

Common sense said she should go straight to Uncle Ira's and call the police, but Lt. Rhodes wasn't exactly her number-one fan. Even if he wasn't on duty at this hour, he was in charge of the investigation into the murders. He'd be notified, and he'd land on her like a load of bricks. What was she doing spying on that house at this hour of night? Was she sure she really saw a light?

If they didn't find anybody, well then she'd made it all up. Her motive? Obviously to draw suspicion away from her uncle.

She pulled over by the curb and thought hard. What if that was Uncle Ira wandering around inside Jan Stalker's house? What if he'd decided to take matters into his own hands and do some sleuthing on his own? Aunt Hortense was in the hospital, and she was at the obedience class. He was home alone, worried sick, with time on his hands. Annie didn't need Elvira Stubenville to tell her what the devil did with idle hands.

Headlights approached and flashed by, a car going the other way. She sat and stared at the house across the street, weighing what to do. She had two possibilities. She could go home and forget all about it, or she could do some investigating.

She turned off the engine and groped around among the accumulated litter under the front seat for the small flashlight she'd had the forethought to bring along. Her fingers brushed several crumpled maps before she found it. She switched it on and noticed the light was fairly dim. Shaking it produced a brighter glow, but her heart sank. The batteries wouldn't last long.

She got out of the car, closing the door as quietly as possible. Claudius was coming with her. He'd be protection of sorts if she needed it. She opened the rear door and gripped his collar. "Don't make a sound."

His eyes gleamed at her, shining in the dark, then he swung his head to stare toward the house across the street. She felt his skin tighten beneath the thick fur, electricity coursing through him, the primal hunting instincts of his wolf ancestry.

Overhead, the rising moon cast a silvery glow through the trees. Annie hesitated, stomach churning, suddenly afraid. She wrestled with the urge to forget the whole thing, to get back in the car and go home.

The street held a graveyard stillness, a rectangle of almost perfect darkness where anyone could be hiding. Claudius stared at her, dark eyes glittering with challenge. He was daring her to cross the street with him. Was she a total wimp, a sniveling coward?

Stung, her fingers curled tightly around his collar. "Let's go."

They crossed to the other side. She was wearing dark clothes, a navy shirt, and jeans, all but invisible in the faint moonlight. But she felt terribly exposed, as if a thousand eyes were staring out of the dark, watching every move she made.

Ridiculous, she told herself. The people who lived on the street were all tucked up in their beds, asleep or watching the Sci-Fi channel. In this quiet neighborhood of manicured lawns and carefully tended vegetable gardens, people had better things to do than stare out their windows.

The front walk was just ahead. Avoiding that, she crossed the grass and slipped down the side path with the house wall to her left and the privet hedge to her right. Claudius padded silently beside her. She could feel his neck muscles tense beneath her fingers. He stiffened and breathed a low growl.

"Keep quiet! Not a sound!"

She felt him heave a sigh, but the growl wasn't repeated. They walked past a cluster of trash barrels. The shadowy bulk of the garage was some distance ahead down the driveway. It was odd that the police hadn't said anything about Jan's car at the time of the murder. There'd been no sign of it out in the desert when they'd found her body. So Jan hadn't driven herself there. She'd left it someplace else. Maybe it was in the garage.

Her mind raced. The killer could have picked her up, or she might have taken a taxi or a bus out to Route 50 and the desert. She frowned. According to newspaper accounts so far, no one had seen her in the hours before her death.

A veil of cloud crept across the face of the moon, and shadows deepened in the narrow alleyway as a faint breeze sprang up and whispered through the trees. She looked up, sensing something. She strained her eyes, but saw nothing but the upstairs windows staring back. The sensation of being watched intensified, and the hairs rose up on the back of her neck.

"Is someone there?" she whispered hesitantly.

Silence.

Then off in the distance, came the cry of some night creature, high-pitched, almost like a woman's scream of terror.

Claudius growled low in his throat. She jerked his collar. "Hush up!"

She stood on the back step, and glanced up at the second story again. Nothing but the creepy feeling of eyes staring back. She drew a deep breath, told herself not to be silly, and tried the door. It was locked, but a pale brown rectangle marked the lower right pane. At some point the pane had been broken, and Jan had replaced it with a piece of cardboard. It took only a second to rip it out. She reached inside to unlock the door.

It swung slowly open, creaking eerily in the night wind. She knew the house had more or less the same layout as Uncle Ira's. All the houses on the street did. There was a short hallway leading to the kitchen with back stairs on the left. The living room and dining room lay beyond. She slipped down the hall, shining the flashlight beam before her. The kitchen smelled of a mixture of Pinesol and old chili. A green dinette set sprang out of the dark. The stove and refrigerator were white, at least ten years old. A holiday brochure on the refrigerator door extolled the delights of Cancún, Mexico. It appeared that Jan had been contemplating an expensive vacation.

Annie filed away that interesting thought and tiptoed through the dining room to the living room at the front of the house. A dumpy couch and recliner. Two framed pictures of the desert. Except for the large TV, everything was brown. Like her aunt's living room. Maybe there was something in the water.

So far, Claudius had been content to look around quietly, but she had a sneaking feeling his silence wouldn't last much longer.

Just then, she heard a series of soft creaking noises overhead. *Someone was walking around the room over this one.*

She swallowed down a knot of cold fear and tightened her grip on the dog's collar, trying desperately to clamp a hand over his muzzle, but he lunged forward with a snarl, taking her by surprise and breaking free. He was gone. *Damn.*

He headed straight for the front stairs. She heard the click of his nails scrabbling on the wood floor. He started barking, and she yelled, "Claudius, here, boy! Heel!" Too late, he barked louder and raced upstairs. She ran after him, still calling his name, terrified that he'd get hurt. If the person upstairs had a weapon . . . God. She was only seconds behind him, sprinting up the carpeted stairs.

Out of the darkness above, a figure came rushing past, shoving her aside with brute force, knocking her off her feet. Almost involuntarily, she struck out with her fist, and felt it graze the man's face as she fell. It happened so fast, she had only an impression of a pale oval and black shadows where eyes should have been. Then her left shoulder hit the bannister, her cheekbone struck the edge of the step, pain exploded in her head, and she saw stars.

Every bone in her body seemed to hurt. Half-blind with it and swearing under her breath, she groped around until she found the flashlight on the step near her right knee, which hurt with a life of its own. She'd torn her jeans. Wonderful. She started to get mad. And Claudius, damn him, was still barking like mad upstairs somewhere.

From down the street came the roar of an engine starting, then the squeal of tires as the car sped off into the night.

She got to her feet somehow and made her way upstairs. Claudius's barking led her to a small room down the hall to the right. The door thudded as he threw his weight against it from the other side. He whined and barked. She opened the door, and he all but knocked her down as he rushed past her and raced downstairs, hellbent on futile pursuit.

She entered the room and moved the flashlight beam around. It looked like Jan had used this as an office. Stacks of magazines and newspapers covered every conceivable flat surface. A small bed had been pushed against the wall to the right, while an old cupboard stood in one corner, and a rolltop desk occupied the other. Straight ahead beneath the window was a long table with a computer on it.

The monitor screen glowed bright blue. The intruder must have turned it on, intent on reading Jan's files for some mysterious reason. Annie went over and scanned the lines moving up the screen. It looked like some kind of list.

The diskette was gone. She tried to type in a save command, which seemed to have no effect, and at the same time, frantically tried to memorize what she saw.

At that critical point, Claudius came racing back into the room, and before she could stop him, bumbled under the computer table, got entangled in the wires, and pulled the plug. There was a wheezing noise and the screen abruptly went black.

"Oh, no!" She groped around under the table and freed the dog, who was now whining, as if it was all her fault. "Damn, damn, damn." She looked around the office, thinking furiously. If Jan was like most computer users, she had kept copies of her diskettes. But when Annie found the two plastic boxes that appeared to contain them, none looked like the one now missing.

The list she'd seen on the screen had been old movie titles: *Singing in the Rain, Fatal Beauty, Spartacus, Gone with the Wind,* and so on. Maybe it was her video collection.

Fighting a sinking feeling, Annie looked around the cluttered office at the stacks of magazines and newspapers. It just didn't add up. If Jan Stalker had been organized to the point of putting her video collection on the computer, why hadn't she cleaned up her office?

Quite apart from that, why would someone creep into a dead woman's house to browse through a computer list of her videos? It didn't make any sense.

Suddenly, all hell broke loose as sirens sounded in the distance, growing louder and louder. Moments later, two police cars roared up in front of the house with flashing blue and red lights, and uniformed policemen poured out. They rushed up the steps. The front door banged open, and they raced inside. "Come out with your hands up!"

Annie, a veteran viewer of real-life cop shows, knew what was expected. She took Claudius by the collar and went out to the hall. "It's me, Annie O'Hara."

Lt. Rhodes was coming up the stairs. He looked extremely angry. "Christ, I should have guessed it'd be you. What the hell are you doing here?"

She tried to explain, but he wasn't having any. She was accused of criminal trespass, impeding an ongoing police investigation, and God only knew what else. If he decided to throw the book at her, and he didn't see why not, she'd end up in the slammer big time.

Red-faced, he paused for breath. "I told you," she said, going over it for the third or fourth time, "I saw a light upstairs and came in to check. That's all."

He glared at her, and she could hear the wheels turning in his head. He had no real proof of criminal intent. She was staying next door. She could have seen a mysterious light in the house.

He gave her a nasty grin. "You'll be surprised to hear that your uncle called 911 and notified us someone was prowling around the house."

"I was on the way home from an obedience class and saw the light. Maybe I should have gone home and called you, but I just thought—"

"No, you didn't think. If you had, you would have gone home and dialed 911. You just said so."

"Well, right. I realize it was stupid, but no harm was done except to me." She held up her torn right leg. "The intruder knocked me downstairs."

"So you say."

"Do you seriously think I threw myself down the stairs on purpose?"

"I guess not." He said nothing for a moment, and one of the uniformed cops came upstairs.

He cleared his throat. "The guy was parked down the street. One of the neighbors says he heard a car start up and take off like a bat outta hell about ten minutes ago. There are tire marks."

Lt. Rhodes chewed on that for a moment. "Okay, if

your story about the obedience class checks out, I guess you're in the clear."

"Good. Can I go now?"

"I'd like some answers first. Informally, of course."

She heaved a tired sigh. "What do you want to know?"

"This intruder you saw. What did he look like?"

"I don't know. He ran past me so fast, I didn't get a good look at him. He was just a big blur."

"Was it a man or a woman?"

"I . . . don't know. It could have been a woman." She tried to remember the shape of the shadowy figure, the height, anything, but it had all happened so fast. She shook her head. "Sorry."

"What about smell? Maybe perfume or shaving lotion?"

"I don't think so."

"You're not making this easy."

"I'm telling you the truth."

"You realize you're technically guilty of trespassing?" he said silkily. "I'd be within my rights if I took you downtown and booked you."

He was right. She was on shaky ground, but common sense was on her side. No one ever went to jail for checking on a neighbor. Even supposing that she knew the neighbor was already dead. She could be making sure thieves weren't cleaning out the house.

His face was set in a self-satisfied sneer. "God, I hate redheads. They're nothing but trouble. I should have known you'd screw up the investigation the first time I laid eyes on you. What the hell. Go on, take that damn dog and go on home. And don't come back or I'll throw the book at you."

"Thanks." Breathing hard and furious, she limped downstairs, Claudius padding by her side. She opened the door and stomped out, almost slamming it behind her. Her heart was pounding like a drum as she strode across the street to her car, got in, and pulled her car into her uncle's driveway and up the path to her uncle's back door.

That had been nasty, she thought as she let herself into the house.

Claudius rushed over to the water bowl and lapped hard for a good three minutes. Uncle Ira came in from the living room, looking worried. "Where were you?" Taking in her tumbled hair, bruised face, and torn jeans he said, "Good God, what happened?"

"I had a run-in with a mysterious intruder next door. Someone was going through Jan Stalker's house, and I got in his way."

"You could have been killed! These days thieves don't give a damn. They'd blow you away as soon as look at you!"

"I don't think it was a thief."

"Wonderful! Maybe you had a run-in with Jan Stalker's killer." Angrily, he sat her down and poured two brandies. "Bottoms up, and don't breathe a word of this to your aunt when she gets home or we'll never hear the end of it. The brandy's supposed to be for medicinal purposes."

"Okay." The alcohol burned its way down her throat to her midsection, leaving a warm glow in its wake. She put the glass down and leaned back, feeling safe for the first time in more than an hour. Her eyes drooped.

"It's late. Go on up to bed. Things will look better in the morning. Go on, now."

In the short time she'd been sitting there, she'd stiffened up. Every muscle in her body protested as she rose to her feet and made her way upstairs. She took a hot shower, hoping that would help. It did, but not enough. Her right knee was scraped and bleeding. She found a Band-Aid in the medicine chest and stuck it on.

When she closed the medicine chest door, she rubbed the mist from the mirror with a towel. Her tired face looked back at her. Wet red hair curled lankly to her shoulders, and her skin was bruised and purple around the right cheekbone. Basically, she looked like hell.

With great care, she managed to towel off and pull a Red Sox T-shirt over her head.

Claudius had already staked a claim on the end of the bed, and she was too tired to tell him to get lost. He watched without comment as she climbed under the covers and turned off the light. All in all, it had been an eventful evening. She'd managed to avoid getting herself killed, which was something, anyway. Things could be a lot worse.

Her mind raced. She remembered the list of movie titles on Jan's computer and wondered if she should have mentioned it to Lt. Rhodes. Unfortunately, the opportunity to do so hadn't presented itself. She'd been too busy trying to keep herself out of jail.

Her mind drifted, and she fell asleep sometime after two.

Annie woke in the dim morning light, shaking, ice-cold, her skin wet with sweat, her heart pounding. She'd thrashed and kicked the blanket off, imagining it was something horrible clawing at her feet. The nightmare faded as she let reality seep in. Oh, God. She winced. Her face hurt, her knee hurt, in fact there didn't seem to be any place on her body that didn't feel as if she'd been hit by a truck.

She got up and took a hot shower, and then, swathed in a thick towel, her hair still wet and tangled, tried to analyze her feelings about what had happened last night. What she felt was a mixture of anger, curiosity, and an awful tingle, as if from a distance, raw fear. It was oddly familiar.

She tried to match it with other frightening incidents in her past: that winter she'd lost control of her car and hurtled down the road, that terrible, slick feeling of the car's rear end whipping around one hundred eighty degrees, narrowly missing slamming into a tree. Her stomach had twisted with nausea, the car still in that sickening, crazy spin, her hands gripping the wheel. She'd fought for control, her only hope. But the snow-covered stone wall across the road had grown larger in the windshield, and the car shuddered as it slammed into the rocks. The front bumper had buckled in a metal-grinding crunch, showers of sparks flew upward, and she'd been flung forward, all but senseless. The seatbelt harness had tightened, and white-hot pain lanced across her neck and chest, squeezing the breath from her lungs.

There had been no time to scream. She'd been frozen with fear, and then it was over. The windshield wipers still clacking, clearing a greasy path through the falling snow, the radio still on, Mozart's *The Marriage of Figaro*, a waterfall of glorious music, and she'd never felt such a feeling of relief. She was still alive.

Skiing down Mt. Snow a few years ago: An expert trail, she knew damn well she had no business taking—sheer ice, with granite outcroppings and thick pine trees bordering the sheer drop. She was lucky she hadn't killed herself.

Even so, what she felt about last night was different.

She was mad, for one thing. Whoever came down those stairs and knocked her over—presumably Jan Stalker's murderer—somehow made it personal between them.

There was a knock at the door. It was her uncle. "Come on in."

He poked his head in. "You okay? How are you feeling?"

"Pretty good," she lied.

"That's a nasty bruise on your cheek. Maybe you should see a doctor. Does it hurt much?"

"No, I'm fine. Really."

For a moment he looked as if he was going to contradict her, then changed his mind. "I called the hospital. We can pick up your aunt after lunch. Speaking of food, how about some of my special blueberry pancakes? I guarantee you'll demand seconds."

"Sounds great. Give me a few minutes to get dressed and I'll help." True to her word, she pulled on jeans and a shirt and was downstairs before he'd finished mixing the pancake batter. He'd already started heating the frying pan, and the tea kettle was whistling as she got down plates and set the kitchen table.

He picked up one of the plates and inspected it. "Your aunt and I have had these more than thirty years. You'd think the flowers would have worn out by now."

But they hadn't. Indeed, they bore only a few chips

and nicks. "They were a good buy," Annie told him, smiling. "Most stuff you get today doesn't last ten minutes, let alone thirty years."

"That's true." His face bore a thoughtful expression. "When we bought those dishes, I was in the navy, stationed in Maine; and the Cold War was at its height. Nearly every damn weekend the base went on red alert. Sometimes I shipped out and didn't know when I'd see your aunt again. Maybe never. Back then we had to have a duffle packed and ready to go, right by the door." He paused in his reminiscing to pour pancake batter in the pan. It sizzled and hissed, and the fragrance of sweet blueberries filled Annie's nostrils.

"It must have been hard."

"You don't know the half of it. Once there was a Soviet sub seven miles off shore. The base went nuts, but the press and the public never got wind of it. The government covered the whole incident up. They did it all the time. We even had one of those experimental planes fly in, looked like a missile, weird as hell. Anyway, we were told to keep our mouths shut on pain of court martial. The official line was that the damn plane didn't exist." He flipped the pancakes. "Almost done. There." He slid them on a plate and turned off the stove. A moment later he sat down opposite Annie. "Dig in."

She forked up some of her pancake. It was delicious. "Strange to think the government was able to cover up something like a Soviet sub coming so close to the East Coast."

"Hell, that's nothing. Okay, maybe it'd be harder today, what with instant communication and all the computers. But back then they held all the cards. Look what they did here in Roswell when the UFO landed. Taking over, threatening everybody, scaring half the town to death. They have a lot to answer for." His face expressed deep gloom. "Actually, I take that back. The government still gets away with murder. That TWA 800 crash off Long Island a couple of years ago. Eyewitnesses along the coast saw a missile hitting the plane, and the bastards denied it. Said it was an electric spark in the fuel tank, even made them take dozens of planes out of service to check for a nonexistent defect. Lied through their teeth and got away with it again. The fact is, this nation is going to hell in a handbasket. Don't let anyone tell you different!"

After breakfast, she cleared the table and washed up, and he stomped outside to put in some therapy time in the garden. She watched him from the window over the kitchen sink as she scrubbed the frying pan. He seemed to be in his element among his leafy green brussel sprouts and tomatoes, hoeing away without a care in the world.

He came inside again, wiping his brow and smiling just as she put the tea cups away.

"We've got an infestation of slugs. Nasty, slimy things. Tough to get rid of. I'll have to pick up some beer."

"Beer?"

"They love the stuff. Works like a charm. Pour some in a pie pan and leave it wherever you see 'em. Once they get in, they're too drunk to get out. They drown."

They were interrupted by the front doorbell. Uncle Ira nodded. "That'll be Roger Stubenville. He said he'd be over some time today to check out my tiller. I don't think his store carries that type." He went to answer the door, and she followed him into the hall.

It turned out to be Mrs. Fielding with a covered casserole dish in her hands. She clumped inside, eyeing Annie's face. "My, that's a nasty bruise. How'd you do that, dearie?"

"I wasn't watching where I was going."

"Oh?" She raised an eyebrow in disbelief. "I thought I'd drop this off. Tuna and cheese. It's dreadful having to cook when you don't feel up to it. Er . . . how is Hortense?" She craned her neck, trying to peer into the living room.

"Fine, fine, we're picking her up right after lunch," said Uncle Ira.

"Tch, tch. Did they keep her overnight then? That's usually a bad sign. What did they find? Did they have to do a lot of expensive tests? An MRI? I had one of those last year when the disc in my back went. It was terrible, trying to fit into that nasty tube thing. I had no idea I was claustrophobic . . ."

Uncle Ira gave Annie a barely perceptible nudge. *Get rid of her.*

He led Mrs. Fielding, who was by this time listing her back pain symptoms and a half dozen various treatments and nostrums that hadn't worked, down the hallway to the kitchen. Annie was a little disconcerted by the woman's bold nosiness. Mrs. Fielding's beady little eyes didn't miss a trick as she checked out every inch of Aunt Hortense's domain.

"Isn't this a lovely, sunny room. And such a lovely view into the garden." Mrs. Fielding plunked the casserole on the table and sat herself in a chair with an air of settling in for a long, cozy chat. "You're the best gardener in town, Ira O'Hara. Bar none."

His face went pink as he grumbled a bit and hitched up his pants. "Well, I don't know about that."

"I do," she twinkled, her fat cupid's bow of a mouth screwed up in a flirtatious moue.

He shot her a look of sheer terror. He wasn't adept at small talk, and in a situation like this he was utterly lost.

Unfortunately, Mrs. Fielding was not. Oozing sweetness and light, she turned to Annie. "How do you like Roswell?"

"It seems to be a lovely town."

"Yes, the scenery is spectacular, what with the mountains and the desert. The only problem is the stupid tourists. Sometimes driving downtown is all but impossible. Summer isn't really the best time of year to visit."

"My vacation coincided with Aunt Hortense's surgery," explained Annie. "I thought I'd lend a hand with the chores and see some of New Mexico at the same time."

"I see." Mrs. Fielding's social manner slipped a little. Her fishing expedition wasn't turning out particularly well. "I'm sure your aunt is grateful."

They sipped iced tea, and Annie wondered when she could decently leave and call Bob Colfax. If he wasn't home, and at this time of day he probably wasn't, she'd leave a message on the machine. Friendly, but making it clear she wasn't chasing him.

Uncle Ira moved around the table, refilling their glasses.

Mrs. Fielding dabbed her mouth with a napkin and got down to business. "Elvira Stubenville called me this morning. She said she heard you'd been picked up by the police right there in Hortense's hospital room, and that they'd taken you away in a squad car. She also said there were dozens of police cars outside this house last night. Frankly, I was worried that you'd been, well . . . arrested."

Chapter Twelve

It took them another half hour to get rid of Mrs. Fielding, who seemed to think that if she didn't wring the last ounce of information out of them, she wasn't doing her sworn duty as the neighborhood gossip.

Finally, having run out of questions she could decently ask, she rose from her chair with a grunt and waddled off down the front walk. Annie went to the phone and dialed Bob Colfax's number. It rang three or four times, then his machine kicked in. His voice came on: "Hi, you know what to do after the beep."

It beeped. "Hi, it's Annie." A pause in case he knew dozens of Annie's. "O'Hara. Red hair, you had me to dinner the other night." That sounded suggestive, but it was too late, so she rushed on breezily, "Just wondered how you were. I . . . uh . . . had a really good time, and thanks." Frustrated—and knowing she was acting like a tongue-tied adolescent, she hung up.

The hell with him, she thought, wishing she believed it and hating herself for feeling like a fool.

She and Uncle Ira went downtown to the hospital and picked up Aunt Hortense at twelve-thirty on the dot. Time enough for her to eat the lunch provided if she felt like it. If not, Uncle Ira reasoned, they could rustle up something for her when they got home.

"I couldn't possibly eat," declared Aunt Hortense, as they bundled her into the car and asked if she was hungry. "How can I think about food? When that awful Lt. Rhodes took you away the other day, I thought I'd never see you again."

"Now dear," said Uncle Ira soothingly, "I told you, the trip to the police station was just a formality. Lt.

Rhodes hoped I'd remembered something about the late reverend's habits that might eventually lead to the killer. That's all." As a white lie, it was pretty weak, but Aunt Hortense wanted to believe it, so she calmed down and after another few minutes, said she was hungry after all, and wouldn't cream of asparagus soup be nice for lunch.

Unfortunately, when told that Melva Fielding had dropped by with a tuna casserole, her face reddened, and she announced loudly that she wouldn't eat anything that woman made if she were starving in Somalia.

"She was just being neighborly." Uncle Ira patted her shoulder.

Aunt Hortense limped past him into the house. "Nonsense, that woman's had her eye on you for years. Of all the nerve! First chance she gets, over she comes with a tuna casserole! I shudder to think what she would have tried if I'd stayed in the hospital a few more days."

"Well, at least we don't have to make dinner." A remark which Annie thought innocent enough.

Aunt Hortense reacted by dumping the contents of the casserole in Claudius's bowl. "I'll wash the dish and you can take it back to her. She lives on Oak Street, the house on the corner. You can't miss it."

"Fine." Annie decided to drop the dish off later. She'd thank her and say they'd eaten the tuna casserole, and that it was delicious. It was partly true. Claudius had devoured it without complaint.

Her day was quiet, but busy. Claudius had to go out after eating such a big meal, naturally; and afterward, Aunt Hortense demanded to be filled in about last night's excitement. Understandably, she was upset at the news that someone had been prowling around Jan Stalker's house, and even more upset when Annie confessed her part in the uproar. What was the neighborhood coming to? If they didn't watch out, they would all be murdered in their beds.

"Oh, no, dear," Uncle Ira reassured her. "The police will keep an eye on the place from now on. Annie will be more careful too."

Aunt Hortense mulled this over. She looked around and made sure her beloved cats were safe and sound.

Once she saw that they were both asleep on top of the refrigerator, she went back to the subject under discussion. To wit: Jan Stalker and anyone connected with her.

"What about Jan's husband, Chuck? Has he shown his face around town? I'd have thought he'd be Johnny on the spot, once he heard she was dead. I wouldn't put anything past him." She frowned. "I can't think why Jan married him. He made no secret of his drinking and womanizing. In fact, he had an illegitimate daughter a while back, which is why she divorced him. People thought it was because of his trouble with alcohol and that silly bomb threat, but that was just the tip of the iceberg. Actually, I can't think why the church let him in in the first place. We should set up a screening committee to make sure that sort of riffraff is kept out. Otherwise, there's no telling where it might lead."

Right, thought Annie.

The hours passed, and Bob Colfax didn't call. Annie fumed and decided she didn't care anyway; and Aunt Hortense, in some pain in spite of her medication and therefore somewhat out of sorts, sent Uncle Ira off to the store for chocolate ice cream. "None of that no-fat kind. I can't abide that stuff."

When he returned with the ice cream, they had an early supper of spaghetti and homemade tomato-mushroom sauce, which Annie made using fresh tomatoes from the garden. She did the dishes and then, making sure her aunt and uncle were busy watching TV in the living room—one of their favorites, a rerun of *This Old House*—tiptoed into their bedroom and slipped a key labeled CHURCH MASTER KEY off Uncle Ira's key chain, where it lay on the dresser. She told them she was taking Claudius for a walk, but didn't say where.

She'd spent a long time thinking about what she was going to do now that the police seemed to have zeroed in on Uncle Ira. Every instinct told her that if something didn't turn up soon, they'd invite him downtown for another grilling; and this time, he might not come home.

Clues to the real murderer wouldn't announce themselves. She had to dig them up. Which meant conducting her own investigation of the murders—and prowling around Jan Stalker's house in the dead of night hardly counted. She hadn't found anything, except that someone else—a mysterious intruder—had been interested in Jan's computer files.

The trick was to think like the victims, to try to see through their eyes. For instance, where would Reverend Morris have hidden incriminating evidence?

His office over at the church, of course. If he'd left anything in his car, the police would have found it already and probably arrested the killer. By deductive reasoning, then, there hadn't been anything in the reverend's car.

If something incriminating existed, it might be in his office, and that's exactly where she was going. There was always the chance the police might have missed something.

Claudius was her cover.

As Aunt Hortense liked to say, "might as well be hung for a sheep as a lamb"—and if there was time, Annie planned to search Pastor Pennyworth's office, too. If anyone questioned her presence, she'd say she was looking for her aunt's lasagna dish. No, on second thought, that might not work. A lasagna dish would probably be somewhere in the kitchen. She'd have to think of something else . . . ah, the obedience course brochures.

It didn't take long to walk over to the church. Claudius kept up a steady pace, almost as if he knew this wasn't the usual evening stroll before bedtime. When they rounded the corner of Idlewild and Elm, it was half past nine. In the street lights, the church looked ghostly white, looming behind the pastor's new, crooked sign. The grass of the small graveyard looked black among the tombstones.

She went around to the side door and tried Uncle Ira's key in the lock. It turned with a smooth click and the door opened. So far, so good. They stepped inside.

The door closed with a pneumatic whoosh. A rubber door stopper lay by the wall. Better safe then sorry, she thought, and propped the door open a fraction. Cautiously, she looked around. There hadn't been any cars in the parking lot, and no lights anywhere downstairs in the annex. Evidently, no church activities had been planned for tonight, though John Barnard might still be around. She thought she heard the faint whir of a floor polisher somewhere upstairs.

She shone the flashlight around the foyer as Claudius raised his head and stared down the hall toward the sanctuary. He stiffened, and she stood there listening, wondering what he sensed, but there was nothing.

The carpet on the slate floor was royal blue, and her feet didn't make a sound as she led Claudius down the hall toward the assistant pastor's office.

Suddenly, the outside door behind her opened, and a man's voice said, "Hey, Annie . . ."

It was Bob Colfax. Of all the bad timing.

Claudius growled. She jerked on his collar. "Shut the door and for heaven's sake, be quiet, both of you!"

"Why? What's up?"

"Nothing." She turned around and started back down the hall. "What do you want, anyway?" He hurried after her.

"I called the house a few minutes ago. Your aunt said you'd taken the dog for a walk. So I thought I'd drive around and find you."

"Well, you found me. So?"

"When you finish whatever you're doing, how about a drink?"

Any other time, she would have leaped at the offer. But not now, not tonight. She didn't feel like explaining what she was doing, either. She didn't think Bob would approve.

And she was right. He refused to be fobbed off with the lasagna excuse. For one thing, she wasn't going anywhere near the kitchen area, which he knew to be downstairs. So what was she up to? The Annie O'Hara he knew wouldn't set foot in this church without a very good reason.

He raised his eyebrows. "So give."

"When I tell you, you may not want to stick around."

"Why not?"

"Because I'm doing a little B and E."

"Whoa, you'd better think about that!"

"I have. The police dragged my uncle downtown and grilled him for three hours, then let him go. If something doesn't turn up soon, I'm afraid they'll arrest him."

He shrugged. "They must think they have something on him—"

"They've got nothing, damnit."

"Okay, they've got nothing. Maybe I'm a little dense, but what's that got to do with breaking into the church?"

"You'll see." She turned around and headed toward the back stairs, past a gray metal box on the wall, past several closed doors. The lettering on the next to last door had fancy gold script, three inches high: PASTOR PENNYWORTH. The door beside it had smaller lettering: ASSISTANT PASTOR.

"I'll bet it's locked," Bob said from over her shoulder.

From upstairs somewhere, she heard the floor polisher stop momentarily. She put a hand on the doorknob and hesitated, nervous. God, that was all she needed, for Barnard to show up and throw his weight around.

The polisher started up again.

She tried the knob. It was locked.

"I told you so," Bob said softly.

"I know what will open it."

"Oh?"

"If I'm right, that gray metal wall box holds a bunch of keys." Using Uncle Ira's master key, she opened the locked box. Inside were a dozen hooks loaded with various keys. Every one was neatly labeled. The one to the pastor's office was at the end of the first row. The one to the assistant pastor's office was right beside it. She took both.

"You're really not going to do this." Bob sounded astonished.

"Indeed, I am." Since it was closer, she changed her mind and decided to search the assistant pastor's office first. She turned the key in the lock and went inside. She told Claudius to lay down in the corner. Bob was still complaining. She could get in a hell of a lot of trouble. He knew what he was talking about. Cops had a nasty habit of arresting people who broke into offices. Did she want to spend the next couple of years in jail?

"God, Annie, we've got to get out of here before someone catches us. The janitor could show up any second—"

"He's busy upstairs. He doesn't even know we're here." She turned on the desk light. The office was mid-sized and held the usual complement of furniture. A battered desk, telephone, two chairs, a couple of filing cabinets, and a fan. On the wall, a painting of the church with what appeared to be a large, shining UFO hovering nearby. Golden rays emanated from the bottom of the UFO, evidently blessings from above. A small closet in the far wall contained several boxes of hymn books and a bottle of hair gel. Reverend Morris's church vestments were arranged neatly on hangers.

Annie searched the office thoroughly, looking for clues, for anything. Jotted notes, bills, love letters tied with pink ribbon . . . even doodles. She found a stack of sermons in the bottom drawer. The focal point of most of them was that the congregation should pray for another visitation from Our Friends beyond the Pleiades.

With weary exasperation, she got down on her hands and knees to look under the desk and found only a few dust bunnies. John Barnard hadn't cleaned this office. Maybe the police had ordered him not to.

Satisfied at last, she ignored Bob's plea that they should get out before they were discovered and all hell broke loose. She picked up Claudius's leash and went to search the pastor's office next door. Bob trailed after her, still upset.

This was the larger of the two offices, the furniture clearly new. A large desk, a lamp, a clock, two comfortable chairs, a closet with vestments, a mirror on the back of the closet door. She went through the desk and didn't find anything incriminating, but there was a pile of snapshots. She shuffled through them, realizing with a start that they must have been taken the night Reverend Morris had been killed. His welcome home party. Here he was smiling, arms around two stout, middle-aged ladies. Another shot caught him talking seriously to Uncle Ira, who had his head down and looked grim. More ladies, lots of blue and purple rinsed hair. Pastel, acrylic flowered dresses, toothy smiles. Wallace Hapgood in the background with a plate of food—so all his talk of not attending church dinners was a lie. He was chatting with Roger Stubenville. Mrs. Fielding with a bigger plate. Elvira Stubenville at one of the tables, sipping tea. One of George Digby and the late Reverend Morris. John Barnard helping to clear the tables. Five or six more shots of the same party.

Bob sat down in the swivel chair and stared at Annie until she was forced to look at him.

"We have to get out of here. You have to stop this," he said worriedly.

"Someone has to help my uncle. If I don't, no one will."

"Okay, look, we'll go someplace and get a drink. You'll calm down and feel better in no time. Come back in the morning if you have to. Get permission to look around. Searching the church like this is crazy."

"You think I'm crazy?" She shut the last drawer with a slight bang.

"No, that's not what I meant. You're as sane as the next person. It's just that . . . well, you're not thinking clearly. You're under a lot of strain, and it shows. You need to calm down. You look tired."

She looked in the mirror. He was right. She did look tired. Lines of strain showed on her pale face.

"Annie, I haven't known you very long, but . . . I care about you."

"Oh?"

He smiled and stood up. Gazing at him across the room, she felt an unbearable yearning. All those wonderful things she'd hoped would come true when she married Lenny. Suddenly, they seemed real again . . . attainable.

Bob walked over to her and put his arms around her. His fingers cupped her chin, holding it still as he kissed her deeply. The sense of wonderment grew inside her. Warm, glowing. Like a fire, sizzling along her nerve endings. She was melting, relaxing against him. Happiness filled her. She'd waited a lifetime to find him . . .

Then Claudius, tired of all this standing around, got up and bumped the back of her legs. When that didn't get the desired effect, he bumped her again. She grabbed the edge of the desk and pulled back, out of Bob's embrace.

Claudius stared at her, beady-eyed. He wanted to go out.

Bob moved closer, nuzzling her neck now, one hand stroking her hair, the other caressing the small of her back.

Claudius growled.

It wasn't going to work. She pushed Bob away and grabbed the dog's collar. "Okay, you win."

Bob was breathing heavily. He stared at her. "What's wrong?"

"I don't know . . . the timing's all wrong. Certainly the place." She sighed. "And Claudius has to go out."

"Wouldn't you know. Well, I shouldn't have kissed you like that. I didn't mean to," he confessed. "It just happened."

"Why?"

He ran an exasperated hand through his hair. "How the hell should I know? You affect me like that. Seeing you looking so worried. My God, what am I going to do with you?"

"Nothing. I can take care of myself."

"I know that. Look, why don't we finish this discussion someplace else?"

"I don't have time. I have to finish looking around in here."

"You're hell-bent on getting into trouble, aren't you?" She nodded, and he sighed. "Then what about your aunt and uncle? Think of the shame they'll feel if you get caught. It'll be all over town. People talk. They'll never live it down. In fact, the cops will probably think your uncle put you up to it."

"No, they won't."

They stared at each other a moment, then he looked away. "Well, I guess that's that."

As he stepped toward the door, she burst out, "Don't you understand? There's no one else to help my uncle."

"Annie," he said impatiently, "the cops will finish the investigation and arrest someone. Hopefully, it won't be your Uncle Ira. But you'd do a lot more good spending your time looking for a lawyer."

"What a nasty thing to say! For God's sake, Bob . . ."

"I'm being honest."

She had nothing to say to that.

He hesitated. "I'm going. Are you sure you won't come with me?"

"No," she said emphatically.

Frowning, he left the office. She moved to the window to watch as he walked down the church steps and got into his car. He didn't look back as he drove away.

Claudius was pacing back and forth, he still had to go out. Absently, she stuffed the snapshots in her pocket and picked up his leash. "Okay, we're going."

Not fast enough to suit him, of course. He grumbled as she glanced at the clock. It felt like a lifetime, but only an hour had passed since she'd left the house. She turned off the lamp and waited, listening for the sound of the floor polisher. But all was quiet. Well, the office door was closed. John Barnard could still be polishing floors upstairs. From where she was standing, she could still see out the window overlooking the parking lot and the graveyard beyond the hedge. She froze and looked again.

Someone was standing in the shadows of the parking lot, watching. It could be someone taking an innocent evening stroll, but she didn't think so. A week ago, before all this happened, she wouldn't have thought twice about someone standing on a shadowy street. But not now.

Thankful that she had Claudius along, she relocked the office and left the church. If she had any plans to walk quietly home, they disappeared in an instant. Claudius barked loudly and tore down the street after the person in the shadows, who turned and ran. In the dim light from the street lamp, Annie, panting as they hurtled along the sidewalk, saw that the person was shorter than she was, smaller. Somehow, though, she didn't care. She was angry. Frustrated. She wanted to see who it was and wring the truth out of him.

The person they were chasing darted through a gap in the hedge and ran through the graveyard. Claudius leaped forward, Annie followed, hanging onto the leash like grim death. They were gaining.

Over the thick grass, past rows of gravestones. One with an urn, another with a weeping angel. Up ahead was the bulk of a marble mausoleum. The person they were pursuing ducked behind one of the columns and disappeared into the darkness.

She stopped, hauling in Claudius, who leaped and jumped, eager to get going. She strained to hear past her own thudding heartbeats. Hadn't there been a metallic grating noise—like a mausoleum wrought-iron door opening?

She could let Claudius off the leash, and in moments it would be over. He'd bring down whoever that person was. And probably tear him to bits. Unfortunately, Annie didn't know the command to make him stop. What if the person had simply been out for a walk, and for some reason got frightened of the dog and ran. If Claudius bit him, he might sue. That she didn't need. No, it was smarter to keep the dog under control, at least for now.

That decided, she started forward again, Claudius straining on the leash with all his might. Despite the cool evening air, she was sweating. It was dark in this part of the graveyard. The only light came from the streetlamp on the corner and her flashlight, which was growing dimmer by the minute. She reached the mausoleum and put a hand on the door. It swung open. That same rusty, grating sound. The person she was chasing had hidden inside.

She peered into the inky blackness. Surely, there was something darker in the far corner. The shadow of her prey moving slowly sideways, trying not to make a sound.

Her eyes adjusted to the faint light from the small stained-glass window high on the opposite wall. She could make out the shapes of two tall, iron candlabra beside the center aisle. There were three graves on either side, with brass name plates and handles on each drawer. Cautiously, she took a step inside. Claudius growled, then snarled, lunging at the person in the corner. Annie grabbed at an arm and felt thin material under her fingers. A woman's arm.

She pulled, and the woman stumbled and half fell against her, crying out in alarm. "Get that dog off me!"

For a moment, Annie's heart seemed to stop beating, then started up again from sheer relief. She knew that voice.

It was Elvira Stubenville.

"Let me go! I'll have the police on you!"

Annie let go of her and, careful to keep a tight hold on Claudius, took a step backward, out of the mausoleum. "Why were you spying on me?"

"I was simply taking a walk." Elvira's voice gained confidence as she came down the steps to the grass. "What were *you* doing in the pastor's office?"

"I wasn't in his office."

"Yes you were. You could get into a lot of trouble."

"I was just looking for my aunt's lasagna dish."

"I don't believe a word of it," Elvira sneered triumphantly.

"I don't care what you believe." That said, they seemed to be at a stand off. Elvira muttered something to the effect that Annie had better watch her step from now on and hurried away through the graveyard.

Annie had no choice but to leave, too, taking Claudius with her.

She walked home down Idlewild Circle.

Why had Elvira been standing out there in the dark, watching her? It didn't make sense. But then, nothing that woman did made any sense.

Annie remembered a movie she'd seen years ago: *Don't Look Now.* Julie Christie and Donald Sutherland in Venice. Their child had drowned. He was restoring church frescoes and she consulted a blind psychic who warned of danger . . . death. A dwarf preying on visitors and tourists, dressed as a child. Hideously murdering.

The movie had ended with Julie Christie in black, following Donald Sutherland's funeral gondola.

Why had she remembered that now? Because she was essentially a visitor, too?

She reached her uncle's house and quietly opened the back door. Claudius padded inside and immediately lapped from his water bowl. Annie shut the door and locked it, letting the feeling of being safe and sound at home steal over her.

On her way downstairs to breakfast the next morning, she smelled coffee perking and eggs frying. Aunt Hortense had resumed cooking with a vengeance.

A stack of pancakes was waiting on the table, along with burned toast, orange juice, sausages cooked to a rocklike consistency, and soggy hash browns. Annie sighed. "You're supposed to be resting. I was going to make breakfast. I can't possibly eat all that."

Aunt Hortense would have none of this. "Nonsense. I can get around pretty well, and I like cooking." She slid two leathery eggs and a couple of charred sausages on a plate and plunked it on the table. "You need some fattening. Men like women with a little meat on their bones."

There was no use arguing, her aunt wouldn't be happy until she put on a good fifty pounds. She dug in as her aunt poured a cup of tea and sat down. She'd already decided not to mention last night's run-in with Elvira Stubenville unless she absolutely had to. For one thing, she'd have to admit she'd sneaked into the church. And why.

"Your uncle's already out in the garden. Putting in more peas." Aunt Hortense slathered a piece of toast with a thick layer of butter and grape jam and took a bite. "How are the obedience classes going? I don't see much change in that dog of yours. He's still as stubborn as a mule."

"He's smart enough," Annie admitted. "Maybe too smart. The trick is to get him to do what I want."

"You can lead a horse to water, but you can't make him drink."

"Exactly."

The back door opened and Uncle Ira came in. He was in great good humor, rubbing his hands. "Ah, food for a hard-working, honest man. In case you're wondering, beer did the trick. I caught more than twenty of those goldarn slugs."

"Wonderful, dear." Aunt Hortense got up and slid more bread in the toaster. "Sit down and have a cup of tea."

Annie glanced at the wall phone, wondering whether to call Bob or not. She suspected she'd burned her bridges pretty thoroughly.

Aunt Hortense asked curiously, "Are you expecting a call?"

"No. Although, I'm a little surprised Lt. Rhodes hasn't called. I thought he'd want to grill me more about the other night."

"Nonsense. Anyone with half a brain can see you're telling the truth about what happened. There was an intruder at Jan Stalker's house, probably a sneak thief. You simply went to check on things. Nothing wrong with that."

"That's right," put in Uncle Ira.

"The thing is, I didn't tell them everything." And she still didn't intend to. Last night's burglary at the church was a deep dark secret, and she meant to keep it that way.

Uncle Ira gave her a worried look. "Why not?"

"He didn't give me a chance. I was too busy trying to stay out of jail."

"Still," said Aunt Hortense pensively, "it's dangerous to keep things from the police. You could be accused of hindering their investigation. What didn't you tell them?"

"The man on the stairs . . . I think it was a man." Annie thought back, trying to remember the shape of the figure who had knocked her down. "He got into Jan's computer in her upstairs office. There was a list of files on the screen, and I tried to save it; but Claudius got tangled in the computer wires and pulled the plug."

"Oh, my," her aunt murmured.

"Hell, it ain't your fault," snorted Uncle Ira. "Just call Rhodes up and tell him. They've got plenty of computer experts down there. I'll bet they scare up that file and find what it's all about before you know it."

Annie gave him a hopeful smile. "You really think so?"

"Sure."

Aunt Hortense nodded encouragement. "Why not call them right now, dear?"

Breakfast was congealing on her plate, which was just as well since Annie had just lost her appetite. She got up and went to the phone.

It took less than a minute for the police to locate Lt. Rhodes and get him on the line. "Yeah, what is it now, Ms. O'Hara? Broken into any more houses lately? Or did you find another corpse?"

"I forgot something I should have mentioned the other night."

"Oh, yeah? Well, what is it?"

"Jan Stalker's computer was on when I went upstairs. The intruder must have been going through her files, looking for something."

"Like what?"

"How should I know?"

He gave a snort of disbelief. "I thought you had all the answers. You and that uncle of yours. Every time I turn around, there's another dead body, and guess what? You're the one who's found it. We could be pardoned for thinking both of you might be more than innocent bystanders."

Anger washed over her in a hot wave. She gripped the receiver hard. "Look, I called this morning because I wanted to cooperate, not to listen to sarcasm."

"Keep your shirt on. I was just letting off steam. You've no idea the number of crackpots calling. Maybe it's the full moon."

In the heavy silence that followed, she sensed he was deciding what was judicious to reveal, considering that she was a material witness to not one, but two homicides.

"Okay," he said grudgingly. "I guess it won't hurt to

tell you we already brought the computer downtown. Our experts are going through the contents of the hard drive."

"So I needn't have bothered calling."

"That's right. The best advice I can give you, Ms. O'Hara, is to keep your nose clean and stop finding dead bodies. I don't know about the cops back East, but we frown on that sort of thing here in New Mexico."

She stood there, doing a slow burn.

"And, Ms. O'Hara, one thing more. Keep that dog of yours on a leash."

Chapter Thirteen

They buried Jan Stalker on a rainy afternoon. The church congregation didn't turn out in force as they had for Reverend Morris's funeral. Still, considering Jan's somewhat checkered past, Annie thought as she walked into the church with her aunt and uncle, it wasn't a bad showing. There were at least fifty people scattered among the pews. She followed her aunt and uncle into one about halfway down the aisle.

Bruce Wolf was at the organ, playing suitably mournful music. Annie looked around the church. There were stained-glass windows of rose and amethyst—the more familiar Biblical scenes and one or two that looked suspiciously like alien pilgrims being converted somewhere beyond the Pleiades. A bluish glow seemed to fall over the faces of the assembled mourners.

"We just made it," whispered Aunt Hortense. "I hate to be late to funerals."

She nodded and looked toward the altar. The good ladies of the church had done Jan Stalker proud. Tall candles and twin vases of calla lilies stood at each end. Pastor Pennyworth, attired in black robes and looking solemn, approached the lectern. He smiled. "Dear parishioners and friends of the deceased, we are gathered today to say good-bye to one of our own, Juliet Stalker. A woman some would say had a troubled past, but in whom I saw the heavenly spark of goodness. Despite her ups and downs, the Good Lord did not give up on our Juliet, and neither did I. Indeed, many's the afternoon we sat in my office wrestling with the devil."

A great deal more of the same followed. Pastor Pennyworth fancied himself an orator and looked forward to occasions where he could display his mellifluous voice to advantage.

"The pastor trained in Africa and Russia," confided Aunt Hortense. "This is his first ministry, actually."

"He's an idiot," Uncle Ira muttered. "The national conference always sends the failures off abroad for seasoning. They do mission work. Nobody wants them. No wonder this is his first church."

Annie was somewhat disconcerted with the news that there was actually a national conference of Celestial Spheres' believers. She'd thought the church was sort of a one-shot Mom-and-Pop operation.

She looked up as the pastor introduced a second speaker—a tall black man with an ingratiating grin and the unlikely name of Elijah Wacker. He was from The Islands.

His voice was impressively deep, and he spoke with great feeling. Rolling cadences issued from his mouth. His eyes flashed. There were murmurs of agreement and appreciation. He waved his hands and rolled his great brown eyes, and the congregation reacted even more warmly. Some broke into tears, mopping their eyes and nodding. Others cried out, "Amen, brother!"

He stepped down to wild applause and stamping feet.

Annie hadn't understood a word he'd said.

Aunt Hortense assured her that was of no account. The main thing was that Elijah Wacker had a good heart and meant well. Uncle Ira was more cynical. "Let me put it another way. Pastor Pennyworth put Wacker in an administrative position. The poor sap does all the work and gets minimum wage. If he's lucky."

Annie frowned. "That's awful."

The congregation sang a few hymns, and then Bruce Wolf launched into a rousing version of the dead woman's favorite tune, "Chattanooga Choo Choo." Their voices rang out in joyous rhythm, and just as they got to the line where the conductor yelled all aboard, she noticed a man sitting up front near the flower-draped coffin. He wore an ill-fitting, new-looking navy blue suit and dabbed his eyes every once in a while.

"Chuck Stalker," sniffed Aunt Hortense, noticing the

direction of her glance. "I don't know why he bothered to come."

"He's probably hoping Jan didn't take his name off her insurance," Uncle Ira snickered.

It was exactly what Annie thought, but since several ladies in the row in front turned around to glare at her, she didn't say a word.

Thunder rumbled as they drove to the cemetery. The heavens seemed to open up. Rain poured down in sheets. Annie opened her umbrella and held it over her aunt and uncle as they walked across the grass toward the grave. To the left was a pile of newly turned earth half-covered by a green plastic cover. It was reddish and raw-looking, and rain ran down in muddy streams. A hundred feet off to the left under a clump of trees, two grave diggers in overalls and yellow slickers leaned on their shovels and smoked. A couple of police cars were parked down the hill, and nearby, a man with a camera crouched beside a tombstone and snapped pictures. Somehow, Annie didn't think he was a reporter from the local paper.

They hurried into the tent and had to stand in back as the first arrivals had taken all the available seating. The canvas rustled eerily in the wind. Annie shivered and turned up the collar of her raincoat. Pastor Pennyworth was hunched over the open grave, intoning the prayer for the dead. In his black coat and hat, he looked like some great bird of prey.

It suddenly struck her that there was something surreal about all this. The assemblage of teary-eyed mourners by the open grave, a fair number of them hypocrites who'd never extended a helping hand to the deceased when it might have done some good. The long arm of the law lurking nearby, waiting to pounce when and if the killer made a false move. She peered over the decent black hats and balding heads at the metal lid of the coffin. Her mouth went dry and cold panic formed a knot in her stomach as reality set in again with a vengeance. The poor woman was truly dead. She and Uncle Ira had found her out in the desert, discarded as if she'd been so much garbage.

Just a few days ago, she'd been alive, laughing, talking. Presumably looking forward to the future. At the pot-luck supper for Reverend Morris, she'd even made a feeble joke about being a dumb blonde who was smarter than she looked. And then something about secrets and hiding things. Annie frowned. Whatever she'd meant, it had gone with Jan to her grave.

Chuck Stalker stood by the pastor. Rain dripped down his face. He wore glasses with thick, black frames, the lenses enlarging his pale eyes. His navy suit was a little short in the sleeves, and his black loafers with tassels looked new. He shifted his weight as the pastor droned on, and Annie wondered if his feet hurt.

He had a pencil-thin moustache and his hair, what there was of it, was greasy and black. He'd brought a Styrofoam cup of coffee to the cemetery. He put it under his folding chair, along with a smoldering cigarette.

When the pastor was done, Chuck smiled and stepped forward to shake his hand. The short service was over, and the pastor hurried away across the wet grass. Chuck stood and looked at the coffin, newly lowered into the earth. A little smile crossed his hard face as he bent and picked up a handful of earth. He tossed it in with an air of grim satisfaction.

Aunt Hortense whispered to Annie, "I think we should talk to him. It's the decent thing to do."

Uncle Ira nodded. "After all, we found the body."

Annie frowned, but followed along after them as they stumped over to the grieving widower. She slowed her steps, wondering if this was such a good idea; but by the time she caught up to them, Uncle Ira had already introduced himself and Aunt Hortense. "The important thing is," he was saying, "that Jan's at peace."

Chuck smirked. "Amen to that."

"Well, it's not the sort of thing we really should be discussing at her funeral," said Aunt Hortense, "but the sad truth is that your ex-wife was a troubled woman."

"You can say that again," Chuck agreed without much compassion. He reached into his breast pocket and brought out a crumpled snapshot. "Our wedding photo-graph. We were happy, but it didn't last. The truth is

Jan wore the pants in our marriage. She had a mind of her own, and it didn't take me long to figure out where I stood. I kept my mouth shut and did what she told me." He tapped his dead wife's beaming face. "You can see it in her eyes right here. She cracked a mean whip."

"I never saw that side of her," Aunt Hortense murmured, somewhat taken aback. "Although at the potluck remembrance supper for Reverend Morris, she seemed a bit . . . well . . . under the weather."

"Drunk as a skunk?" suggested Chuck, who believed in calling a spade a spade.

"She'd had one or two, that's true. But I saw her at the church annex a few days earlier and she looked more herself." Aunt Hortense delicately avoided all mention of the fact that Jan had been going at it hot and heavy by the pizza oven with the caretaker, John Barnard.

Chuck snickered. "I saw her at the Oaken Bucket a few months ago. She was so bad off she was doing blow jobs in the alley for drinks."

"None of us is perfect."

Certainly not Jan Stalker, thought Annie.

"She made mistakes along the way," Aunt Hortense went on. "But quite naturally, she wanted to find her way to God's salvation. I respected her for that. Lately, it seemed things were looking up for her."

"That's so." Uncle Ira nodded. "Although she was still hitting on men."

Aunt Hortense frowned and nudged him to shut up.

"Hmm." Chuck's good mood seemed to have evaporated. He fingered his pencil-thin moustache and looked thoughtful.

"Er . . . had you seen much of her lately?" hazarded Aunt Hortense.

"No, well, I've been . . . away. I was sent up for a few months a while back—check kiting, no big deal. But Jan—Juliet—that was her real name. Jan was just a nickname. She was never one for visiting jail, and I wasn't much of a Romeo." He retrieved his cup of coffee and cigarette from underneath the folding chair. "We'd split, anyway."

Annie gazed at the wedding photograph, which Chuck

had tossed on the chair. Evidently, they'd been married by a justice of the peace. Jan bulging fore and aft in a tight red cocktail dress with a low neckline, an expression on her face of extreme satisfaction. Chuck, by her side, looking trapped and vaguely embarrassed.

He breathed out a stream of smoke, his eyes narrowed. "Like I said, she was hell on wheels. She knew what she wanted and didn't care who she had to stomp on to get it."

"She wasn't a bad person, not really," Aunt Hortense protested feebly. "She had her good points."

"Few and far between, I can tell you." He flicked his cigarette away and glanced up at the dripping sky. "Lovely day, ain't it. She could have been more considerate and picked a day when the sun was out. But what the hell, I always say there's something about a funeral that makes you feel alive."

Aunt Hortense straightened her back. "Your ex-wife didn't choose the time and day of her death, Mr. Stalker. She was murdered."

"So it seems." He sniggered. "Guess she pushed somebody too far. From what I heard down at the Oaken Bucket."

They left the grave and walked toward the cars parked down the hill. Chuck walked confidently, whistling merrily between his teeth. His chest stuck out, and his new shoes squished through the wet grass. He looked very much as if he saw a rosy future opening up before him. "I got some ideas of my own who she was bugging, but I'm gonna play my cards close to my chest."

Uncle Ira frowned. "If you know anything, I suggest you go to the police at once."

"You think they're gonna come across with some green?"

"Green?" asked Aunt Hortense.

"Cash," Chuck explained obligingly.

She stared at him in disbelief. "You can't be serious."

His face suddenly took on a secretive look. "You're right. Ha ha, I was just kidding."

"Well, you'd better be careful," huffed Uncle Ira. "Jokes like that could be dangerous."

Annie watched as Chuck Stalker hurried away under the dripping canopy of trees. He was driving an old clunker of a car, rusted and spewing a considerable amount of bluish smoke from the exhaust. He rattled away down the bend, and she turned to help her aunt and uncle into their car. They drove off wearing twin expressions of disapproval, commenting that water sought its own level and that it was only a matter of time before Chuck Stalker ended up in the gutter, doubtless a fate he richly deserved.

Annie walked to the Escort. Claudius was sitting in front with his nose to the glass, leaving smears from one end to the other and barking ferociously at a squirrel in a nearby tree. She opened the door and shouted at him through the cacophony, "Get the hell in back!"

For a moment he looked as if he wanted to argue, then changed his mind, shut up, and jumped in back. She got in, conscious of an expectant silence—except for the panting, of course—and eyes boring between her shoulder blades. "Okay, you win." She turned the key with a familiar sinking feeling. She'd sunk to bribery again.

Hating herself for being so weak, she went out of her way to drive down Highland Street and past the Armstead Apartments on the way home. There was no sign of Bob's car in the lot, and the curtain at his kitchen window hung still and lifeless. So he wasn't home. Well, she hadn't planned to call him again, anyway.

She detoured to McDonald's, bought a couple of burgers and fries, which she split with Claudius, and went on home, feeling frustrated. Jan's funeral aside, so far it had been a wasted day. If the police had anyone else in their sights as the prime suspect in the murders, they weren't telling anyone. They'd been at the cemetery taking pictures. Uncle Ira, still under suspicion, undoubtedly would figure prominently in all of them.

She let herself into the house and heard her aunt and uncle in a low-voice conversation somewhere upstairs. The kitchen smelled good. Aunt Hortense had put a roast in the oven before they'd left for the church. It looked like life was slowly but surely returning to normal, but she took off her wet raincoat with a terrible feeling that it wouldn't last.

That night Annie came awake with a start at 2 A.M. Aunt Hortense was shaking her shoulder. Pale light from the street light filtered through the softly blowing curtains at the window. Slanted shadows played against the walls. She sat up groggily, noting the lines of worry on her aunt's face. "What's the matter?"

"Someone's out there in the backyard. I heard noises. It sounded like the potting shed door. I don't want to wake your uncle. He'd go out there and get killed."

Annie looked around. Claudius was nowhere in sight, which was unusual. "Maybe the dog got out." She climbed sleepily out of bed and pulled on a sweater and a pair of jeans.

"No, he'd be barking."

"It's still raining." Annie said, looking out the window. She pulled on her sneakers. "Maybe the wind blew the shed door open."

Her aunt followed her downstairs, holding her bathrobe together over her bosom. "Yes, maybe that's it. Would you go out and check, dear? I hate to ask you, but I don't know what else to do."

Annie nodded and walked through the darkened kitchen to the back door. It was open. She turned back to her aunt. "Did you open the door?"

"I may have, honestly, I don't know. It doesn't catch sometimes. I didn't check it before we went up to bed. Oh, dear, the dog could have gotten out, I suppose."

Indeed, he could, Annie thought sourly. But if he had, why wasn't he barking? She took a flashlight from the drawer and went down the back steps. Cold rain fell on her shoulders.

Aunt Hortense had switched on the back porch light. Silvery drops fell in driving sheets.

Annie called for Claudius, whistling. A loud "woof" and a sudden thrashing in the bushes by the potting shed was her reward.

She walked across the wet grass. The pool of light from the house was behind her now as she moved into the shadows near the shed. Trumpet vines by the back porch fluttered in the rain and screened out any remaining light from the house. She took a few steps forward and banged her shins against a wheelbarrow. "Shit!"

"Do you see anything?" Aunt Hortense's whisper floated across the misty backyard.

"No." Annie pushed aside the vine and promptly bumbled into a daylily bed, the long leaves soaking the legs of her jeans. She backed out into a puddle. A stubborn branch got in her way, and she batted it out of the way, wondering if Claudius had chased the poor cats out here.

The weathered wood of the potting shed was dark with rain, and the lilac bush beside it swayed in the wind, rustling, whispering at her from the shadows. Belatedly, Uncle Ira had bolted a two-by-four across the door, but she saw at once that it was missing, and the door hung open a crack.

She stepped closer, thinking this was really weird. She shone the flashlight into the ink-black hole of falling rain and pushed the door open. Something was definitely wrong. She moved the light around the interior of the potting shed, suddenly uneasy. Maybe Aunt Hortense really had heard someone out here.

She moved the beam to the left, and saw the orderly shelves of pots and trays, the pegboard with its row of tools. Her sneakered feet made no sound on the brick flooring. She held the light over compost and fertilizer barrels, half expecting to surprise someone crouched here at the far side of the shed, but no one was hiding behind either of them.

The bricks looked a little dirtier than usual, though. Clumps of dried red clay. Uncle Ira must have dug a new vegetable bed. Pretty deep, too, to get all the way down to clay. She wondered what he was planting.

Maybe asparagus.

A soft, creaking noise as something moved behind her. Startled, her heart a knot in her throat, she whirled and shone the light in the corner. A small stool was lying on the floor, and . . . *God . . . someone was hanging from the roof beam in the corner!* The body of a man sagged from a hangman's noose.

She screamed.

For one horrible moment, she thought it was Uncle Ira. He was wearing the old jacket that he kept on the hook behind the door. The body swung slowly, turning toward her. She was frozen with fright, then the shadowy face revealed itself. The ragged hair was straw stuffed in an old pillow case, the lopsided eyes, nose, and mouth drawn on with black magic marker. *It was Uncle Ira's scarecrow.* Someone had carefully rigged the scarecrow from the beam.

It was a warning.

Aunt Hortense woke Uncle Ira, who exploded with fury when he heard what was hanging in his potting shed. He blamed himself for not keeping a better eye on the backyard. The idea that some bastard had the gall to do this. They weren't safe in their own home. Annie gave up any thought of going back to bed and put on the kettle. Someone would have to call the police.

Uncle Ira objected. "They don't have to know about this. It probably has nothing to do with the murders, anyway."

Her aunt nodded. "It could be a wicked prank. Maybe some neighborhood boy with a cruel streak."

"Maybe," said Annie, not believing this for one minute.

Uncle Ira sighed, his white hair wild about his head and his glasses askew on his nose. "What the hell is the world coming to?"

Claudius, resting in the aftermath of his nocturnal adventure in the backyard bushes, lifted his head and let out a funereal howl. Annie gave him a sharp nudge with her foot. "Shut up."

"Well," said Uncle Ira, looking at Annie again. "What should we do?"

There was a small silence in the kitchen, and she decided it was time to restate the obvious. "We have to call the police. This might not just be some cruel prank. I was in Jan Stalker's house. Maybe the man I saw is her killer. He thinks I know something, and this is a threat. Shut up or else."

Uncle Ira had already come to the same conclusion. He just hadn't wanted to deal with it. Reluctantly, he went to the phone. When he came back, he'd smoothed his hair down and looked, Annie was glad to see, more like himself.

They drank tea and nibbled on bagels and cream cheese, and in due course, the police arrived.

Lt. Rhodes stomped inside after surveying the shed's contents. He usually looked businesslike if rumpled, but at this hour, his hair was slightly disarranged and the knot in his tie was shifted to one side. His jowls were dark with stubble. "Christ, why the hell did I get called out for this?"

"We thought it might have something to do with the murders." Uncle Ira's voice was harsh with nervousness. "It could be a warning of some sort."

"The murderer hung the scarecrow in the shed because you know something?" Lt. Rhodes looked from Uncle Ira to Aunt Hortense. "Well, what is it?"

"N . . . nothing," Uncle Ira protested. "Truly, there's nothing we could possibly know. It's terrible."

"That's right," said Aunt Hortense. "Terrible."

Lt. Rhodes opened a notebook with another muttered curse and took out a pen. "Okay, tell me what happened from the beginning. And make it snappy."

So Annie recounted the night's events, starting with Aunt Hortense's waking her around 2 A.M. because she'd heard a noise outside.

Her aunt nodded agreement, adding that she hadn't woken up her husband for fear that he'd do something stupid.

Uncle Ira frowned at that disclosure.

"Well, you would have gotten down your old service revolver, Ira. You know you would." She trembled with indignation. "You probably would have fallen out there in the backyard and shot yourself, and then where would we be?"

Where indeed, thought Annie.

At the mention of the revolver, Lt. Rhodes's eyes narrowed. "Go get it. Do you have a permit?"

"Y . . . yes. I, that is, I don't know if I renewed it this year." Uncle Ira got up and left the kitchen. They heard his slippered feet reluctantly heading upstairs. A few minutes later, he came back with the revolver and a slip of paper.

"Is it loaded?"

"No."

"Good." Lt. Rhodes checked anyway, then handed the gun to the uniformed cop by the back door. "You're lucky. The permit expires next month." He crooked a finger at Annie. "You, come outside and show me exactly what you did."

It was all very dreary. Annie went over her movements until her throat was sore, and Lt. Rhodes, standing in the shadowy shed, with his eyes flicking like a lizard's to the corner where the scarecrow still hung from the beam, finally ran out of questions.

"Jesus H. Christ." He hunched his shoulders in thought. "The press gets hold of this, they'll have a goddamn field day."

It seemed to Annie that they were drifting off the subject at hand. "My aunt and uncle are very upset about this. They're frightened."

"They should be. There's a killer running around loose. We'll take pictures and cut it down. It might just be evidence in the investigation."

They went back to the house after that. Lt. Rhodes's face wore an expression of grim seriousness. It was sinking in that maybe Ira O'Hara hadn't killed anybody, after all.

After the police left, it was too late to go back to bed, and Annie and her aunt and uncle sat around the kitchen table, playing gin rummy.

The clock with the Felix face on the shelf over the stove chimed the small hours, and Uncle Ira threw his cards down and rearranged the stacks of pennies in front of him. "I think they need a good shuffle." His losses couldn't have added up to much more than the price of a bottle of brandy that between them they'd almost managed to consume—Aunt Hortense having decided that in the circumstances, a drop or two wouldn't hurt.

The cats woke up, jumped down from the refrigerator, and demanded to be fed. Loudly. Aunt Hortense ladled out identical portions of special low-calorie food from the health food store and patted Violet, who purred and wove herself around her legs.

Aunt Hortense smiled. "Violet's a wonderful mouser. She has a very particular call she uses when she catches something and drags it into the house."

"I'll bet." Annie yawned.

Uncle Ira, who'd been pondering aloud the likelihood that whoever hung the scarecrow in the shed was the same person who'd done away with Reverend Morris and Jan Stalker, drained his glass. "So where was I?" he mumbled, realizing blearily that he was incapable of talking and shuffling cards at the same time.

"You were telling us that it might not be a threat to keep our mouths shut," prompted Annie. "You said the cats or Claudius might have interrupted the killer. If they saw him return the hand fork, he might think they could identify him. Then he'd have to kill them, too."

"Violet isn't a threat to anyone," said Aunt Hortense worriedly. "She's very intelligent, but she can't really talk."

As if trying to give comfort, Claudius had parked himself at her feet. He might have a sympathetic streak, but Annie doubted it. Her aunt tended to drop crumbs on the floor.

"By golly, that's true." Uncle Ira nodded. "That damn cat is smart as a whip. A hell of a mouser, too."

"Not like Daisy. Now she's never been much of a mouser." Aunt Hortense took another sip of brandy. "She doesn't go outside much."

"That's right." Uncle Ira nudged Annie to be sure she was listening. He'd caught her yawning and didn't want her nodding off.

She blinked and sat up straighter. "Daisy probably prefers her food in a can or a box. I don't blame her."

Having confirmed that she was paying attention, Uncle Ira eyed his empty glass and said with an air of surprise,

"You know, it's a damn good thing that neither Morris or Jan Stalker was shot, or I'd be in big trouble. There are a hell of a lot of thirty-eight's around. It'd be just my luck if that was the caliber of the gun used. Rhodes would accuse me of cleaning it afterward and hiding it in the linen closet."

Aunt Hortense looked upset and Annie hurriedly chimed in, "No use borrowing trouble. Just be thankful they were strangled and stabbed." That hadn't come out quite right, but she was too tired to think straight. "I just wondered, are you planting an asparagus bed?"

He frowned. "No, why?"

"I saw some red clay in the shed. Usually a layer of clay is down pretty deep, a couple of feet anyway. I thought you must be digging a new bed."

"Nope, I've got plenty to do with the beds I'm tending already." He riffled the cards and gave a mirthless smile. "Annie, you never should have gone outside alone. What if you'd surprised him while he was hanging up the scarecrow?"

"Don't scold her," muttered Aunt Hortense. "She was very brave."

Annie shook her head, remembering how dark it had been, and the way the shadows had moved in the corner of the shed. "I wasn't brave. I was just blind stupid."

Chapter Fourteen

Annie didn't see Bob Colfax again until two days later, when she was taking Claudius for the usual four o'clock stroll. Bob drove by. When he saw her, he pulled over. "Hi, stranger."

"Hi, yourself."

He raised his eyebrows. "I take it you got lucky and didn't get arrested the other night."

"That's right. I didn't." She smiled and heard herself telling him about Elvira's spying on the church. How she'd chased the woman into the mausoleum and caught her.

"You're kidding."

"No, I'm not. God only knows what she was up to. The woman is nuts."

His manner changed. He became serious. "Forget about her. We should talk. My source at the police department says you ran into an intruder at Jan Stalker's."

She nodded. "Whoever it was practically knocked me down the stairs." Claudius sniffed the base of the tree and decided it would do. He lifted his leg.

"So what happened?" Bob demanded. "Did you see his face? Could you tell who it was?"

"No. There's not much more to tell. He got away. I have no idea who it was."

"But the cops think it was the killer?"

"Probably. I don't know. Maybe it was Jan's ex."

"Chuck Stalker doesn't need to sneak into that house. All he has to do is wait until the dust settles, then take possession of everything."

She shook her head. "He can't do that. They're divorced."

"Jan didn't bother to show up for the final hearing, and it was canceled. I checked the court records. The divorce never became final, so Stalker inherits everything."

Annie stared at him, wide-eyed. Did Chuck Stalker know his divorce hadn't been final? At her funeral, he'd talked about her as his ex-wife.

"Come on, Annie. We need to put our heads together and come up with a plan to solve these murders." He slid his arm around her. "My source also says your uncle's scarecrow was found hanging in the potting shed with a noose around its neck. What the hell's going on?"

"I don't know. I didn't find anything at the church, and I don't know where to look next. What am I going to do? The police suspect my uncle. He and Aunt Hortense are scared to death. They can't take much more."

"I've been thinking." He squeezed her shoulder. "If we go through what we know, we might come up with a few leads."

"This isn't just a pitch for a juicy interview?"

"No. And I'm sorry about running out on you the other night at the church, but I draw the line at felonies. God knows what would have happened if we'd been caught. I still feel bad about it, though. Let me make it up to you. How about it?"

Reluctantly, she let herself be talked into having coffee with him, and they drove to a cafe on King Street, for a brainstorming session. Claudius stretched out on the seat beside her, snoozing. Annie was content to just sit and listen while Bob talked.

He was full of ideas. "The victims' characters are crucial to the murders. These weren't random acts of violence."

"You're saying they asked for it?"

"In a sense."

"I don't get it."

"There has to be a reason someone was searching Jan's house. Think. What else did you see that night?"

"Her computer was on. He must have been looking through her files."

"Like what?"

"I didn't have a chance to find out. Claudius got tangled in the wires and unplugged it." She shrugged. "The diskette was gone, too."

"What was on the screen?"

"A list of movie titles. *Gone With the Wind, Fatal Attraction*." She tried to remember the rest. "There were more, but that's all I can think of off the top of my head."

Bob nodded. "Jan liked old movies, but I thought she was more into books. Horror. Dean Koontz, Stephen King. Edgar Allan Poe was one of her favorites. I got to know her last year. She worked part time down at *The Post*. Typing. She liked to play games, too. Had a histrionic streak a mile wide. Nothing was fun unless it was complicated." He got out his wallet as the waitress came by and dropped the bill on the table. "What else?"

"That's all. Here, let me get it." She reached into her jacket pocket for her wallet, and felt something else bulky in her pocket.

The pictures she'd taken from the pastor's desk.

Bob pushed their coffee cups aside and spread them out. "Looks like a church function. A party or potluck. Everyone's having a good time."

"Here's Jan." She picked up a snapshot. The dead woman, glass in hand, was laughing at something Reverend Morris was saying. John Barnard could be seen in the background, talking to Uncle Ira. "I'll bet these pictures were taken the night the assistant pastor died. There's a banner over the door in this one."

The banner read: WELCOME HOME, REVEREND! Underneath was a man bending to put a tray of food on a table. The next picture, snapped seconds later, showed him—John Barnard—walking away.

"They really rolled out the welcome mat." Bob sorted through the rest of the pictures. "Everybody who's anybody in the church is here. Elvira and Roger Stubenville. Wallace Hapgood and his wife. Your aunt and Mrs. Fielding. The pastor and his wife. Sad when you think about it. Here's Morris, having the time of his life, and a couple of hours later, he's dead."

"The church doesn't hold with drinking alcohol."

Annie examined the picture of Jan with the glass again. "In this one, Jan looks like she's already had a few. She must have been drunk that night. I wonder . . ." Annie told him about Jan's drunken babbling the afternoon of Reverend Morris's remembrance supper. "She said she knew secrets someone would pay plenty for. Then she laughed and said she was a lot smarter than people thought."

"The cops took her computer," Bob pointed out. "So we'll have to forget that for the time being. But Jan's house is still there. If we could get inside, we could look around. Maybe find something. There's a good chance the man you saw the other night didn't get what he came for."

"Too bad we don't have a legitimate reason for going inside." She narrowed her eyes. "But that shouldn't stop us. Somebody has to go through her things so they can put the house up for sale. You know, throw out junk, save the good stuff."

"It doesn't matter," he said glumly. "Members of her family will do that."

"Not necessarily. Jan doesn't have any family left, other than Chuck." Annie thought a moment. "He won't bother to clean the house, but the good ladies of The Neighborhood Church of the Celestial Spheres could do it. The funeral committee probably offers help every time somebody in the church dies. My aunt might even be on the committee."

"That's a hell of an idea."

"Aunt Hortense just had a foot operation, so she can't be expected to clean the house. It's hard work, dirty, too. But I could do it. I'd have a legitimate reason for cleaning the house, and there's nothing the police could do about it." On the other hand, it sounded too easy. Really, this was no way to solve a mystery. She and Bob were playing detective. Looking for clues that probably weren't there. "I don't know," she said. "Maybe it's not such a good idea."

"Come on," he urged, "it would only take an hour or two. You wouldn't really clean the place, of course;

though it might look good if you took a pail and mop with you. You never know."

She frowned. "The other night you were upset when you caught me in the church, now you can't wait to get me to snoop around Jan's house. I don't get it."

"This isn't a felony. The other night was. Look, you have the perfect cover and your aunt will back you up if necessary." He meant, if things got sticky and she were discovered. "Not that I expect you to run into trouble. People die all the time. You're right. Friends and family clean out the house. All you have to do is let things die down for a day or two, then go in and search the place."

It sounded so simple, so achievable, and besides, it was a good idea. Not to mention Bob's deep voice with that treacherous warmth luring her on. She was putty in his hands. The idea of snooping in Jan Stalker's house in broad daylight, searching for whatever the intruder had been looking for, at first glance, seemed preposterous. Silly, even. But when he looked at her with those clear dark eyes, he had a way of undermining her common sense. After all, she wanted what he wanted. An end to these horrible killings. Her aunt and uncle's lives would go back to normal. They wouldn't have to worry about being arrested. The goal was praiseworthy, no one could argue with that.

He smiled again, and her resolve to stand firm against his blandishments began to crumble. "I know what you're thinking, Annie. All I'm after is a big story. Well, sure, I'm just doing my job as a good reporter. What's wrong with that?"

What, indeed? she thought sadly.

"I like being a journalist. It's an immensely rewarding job. Hard work and long hours, but with any luck, I'll get to the top."

He was telling the simple truth. He was ambitious, and one way or another, he'd hit the big time. He'd work for CNN or one of the other TV networks. He'd write a best-seller, a tell-all book about celebrities he'd interviewed—inside stuff—and the public would eat it up. Naturally, he'd never look back.

But you couldn't make an omelette without breaking

eggs, and for some reason right at this moment she felt remarkably fragile.

He reached across the table and took her hand again. "I have a good many talents, Annie. I can read palms." He turned her hand over, running a gentle fingertip down her skin. "Your love line . . . very well developed, but somehow I already knew that. Let's see, here's your life line." His fingertip slid across her palm.

Her skin tingled, and a vision of them embracing in bed floated through her head. She shook it off and tried to pull her hand free.

He wouldn't let go. He smiled. "What are you scared of? Your life line runs right across your palm, without a break. You'll live a long, long time. Nothing to fear there. Your heart line is deep and passionate. You're one hell of a woman."

He was stringing her along, but he was so persuasive. His forefinger caressed her palm while his thumb stroked the inside of her wrist with a sensual circular motion.

Her mouth went dry. Her heart was thumping like a drum. She opened her mouth and licked her lips. Bob's eyes watched her, and she could tell what he was thinking. God, she knew exactly what he had in mind.

For a moment she closed her eyes and imagined what it would be like to lie down on his bed and welcome him to her arms as her lover. They would make love without inhibition, without any guilt, for whom would they be hurting? No one. They were free to indulge in a brief love affair.

She was lonely and vulnerable. Far from home, and whom could she talk to, really? Her aunt and uncle were terrified out of their wits by the deadly events of the past few weeks. They didn't deserve more worry and fear. Bob was right. She had a positive duty to try and find out who the murderer was, and if there were any clues hidden at Jan Stalker's house, it would be the logical place to look.

Bending his head, he kissed her wrist. "You're lovely. And shy. I like that."

Her heart all but popped out of her breast as his lips caressed her skin again. The message couldn't have been clearer. *Quid pro quo.* They'd have great sex, and she'd do what he wanted. Still, she hesitated. "I don't know. Searching the church was one thing. At least that was after dark. This would be in broad daylight. Something's bound to go wrong."

"Nothing will go wrong."

She pulled her hands free, frustrated and almost angry. "It'll never work." Why didn't he just go away and leave her alone? What an idiot she was, hanging on his every word. He teased her with charm, and led her on with lies. She knew it . . . and yet her body was responding whether she liked it or not.

"Let's go back to my place. I'll make us a couple of drinks, and we can talk it over. Come on, you know you want to." He took out his wallet and reached for the check. "Let's go, sugar."

That did it.

She wasn't going back to his place and have sex. Already her mind was telling her how wonderful it would be, her healthy body was singing the siren song of the flesh, and warmth was flooding her solar plexus, but she wouldn't go. She knew quite well that what she really wanted was to strip herself bare-ass naked and go into his arms. To feel his hands on her skin, caressing her body. She was certain she'd have a wonderful time. Feeling his skin against hers, the hot furnace of his breath against her cheek, kissing her until she didn't care about anything else.

But she wouldn't go, not now. He'd called her "sugar."

"I don't think so, thank you."

He looked a little surprised, then shrugged. "All right, that's okay by me. You want to play coy a little longer. No big deal. But about searching the house, Annie . . . it's just the opportunity we've been looking for."

She thought about it. "It's dangerous—"

He cut her off. "I take it back."

"What?"

"I was just thinking how special you are, bright, willing to take chances. Guess I was wrong, though. You don't have what it takes."

That stung, as of course, he'd meant it to. She gazed at him speechless for a second, then gathered up the snapshots and shoved them in her pocket. "I've never been called a coward before."

"There's a first time for everything."

"Not for that." She stood up and tossed a ten-dollar bill on the table. Enough to cover the check and the tip.

He eyed her quizzically. "You look mad, sweetie. What's wrong?"

"You're smooth as silk. You always get what you want, and I don't like it."

"Come on, it's the way the world works. What's not to like?"

"Nothing, I guess. Okay, Bob. Don't try so hard. I'll see what I can do about getting into Jan Stalker's."

Why not? He was right. It was a chance to kill two birds with one stone. If she got lucky, she might find something that would lead straight to the killer. Two murders would be solved, and her uncle's good name cleared. What wasn't to like.

Repressing a smile of great satisfaction, he drained the rest of his espresso. "That's great. Call me when you decide to go. I want to help, of course."

"Sure." She looked at her watch. "Right now I've got to go. It's late."

"Hey, you're not mad, are you?"

"No." She smiled. "You can't change a leopard's spots, I guess."

"What's that supposed to mean?"

"Think about it, sugar."

Chapter Fifteen

"You want to do *what*?" Aunt Hortense demanded, her eyes round with astonishment.

"I want to go next door and search the house."

The dinner dishes were sitting in the sink. Annie started washing up, while her aunt wiped down the kitchen table. With her uncle out of the house—he'd gone downtown to the garden center to purchase more seeds—she'd decided to seize the opportunity to talk to her aunt alone. Uncle Ira would take a dim view of her plan to break into Jan Stalker's. Her aunt was a practical soul. Once she understood everything, she'd see things differently, Annie was sure of it.

"Someone probably should clean up Jan's house," she concluded a few minutes later. "Why not me? I could look around while I dust and vacuum. It's perfect."

"I don't know. The police told you not to go near the house again."

"They won't know anything about it. Think how wonderful you'll feel if I find a clue that leads to the killer. The police will leave Uncle Ira alone for good." Tempting bait, and her aunt weakened.

"We . . . ell, I am on the funeral committee. We try and help out when a church member dies. We prepare a funeral meal, or if they have a wake, we make refreshments."

"Okay, I'll go next door, and if anyone says anything, you say you sent me to clean up. You were going to do it, but you're recovering from surgery."

Aunt Hortense frowned and put the last plate away in the cupboard. As she passed the window, she twitched back the curtain and stiffened. "Look at that! The nerve of that man, she's not cold in her grave and he's already picking over her bones!"

"Who?" But Annie already had a sneaking suspicion who it was.

"Chuck Stalker! He's backing a van up to the front door. He'll take everything worth pawning and leave the rest." She paused thoughtfully. "If you're serious about searching that house, dear, you'll have to go over there right now."

She handed Annie a mop and a bucket. "Jan may not have been the tidiest housekeeper, but there are bound to be cleansers in the broom closet. If Chuck gets difficult, tell him Jan had an insurance policy through the church, and you need his signature. Oh, you'll think of something clever."

It was time for Claudius's nightly walk. Annie clipped his leash on him, collected the mop and bucket, and went next door. Chuck's van had been backed up practically to the front porch. It looked like he planned to take out something heavy. Like Jan's TV.

She assumed a suitably churchlike expression and rang the bell.

The door snapped open and light flooded the porch. "Whaddaya want?" he snarled.

"My aunt would have come. About the insurance and helping out with the house," Annie began, indicating the mop and bucket, "but she just had an operation. We need to clean, you know, wash the floors and dust, vacuum, that sort of thing. The house should be neat as a pin when you put it on the market."

Warring emotions chased across his weaselly face. The urge to call her an interfering bitch and slam the door, greed, astonishment at the likelihood of somebody showing up and actually offering to do something for free. Greed won out. He opened the door a trifle wider. "What's this about insurance? So far, all I've found is chicken feed, and I'm still her husband." He smirked. "How do ya like that. The divorce never went through, so I'm her legal heir. Any money's mine."

"Naturally, the church has a copy of the policy she signed. Fifty thousand." Annie went on, mentioning an amount off the top of her head. "Enough to pay her last expenses and any outstanding bills and charge cards, that sort of thing. Unfortunately, it's been misplaced over at the church. I'm sure Jan kept a copy with her other papers."

Chuck had already pawed through her desk and found nothing of interest—just a pile of bills he sure as hell didn't plan to pay. He narrowed his eyes. "So what you're sayin' is you wanna come in and clean, plus look around for this insurance policy?"

"That's right, Mr. Stalker."

"Well, I guess that'd be okay." He opened the door wide. "There's some cleanin' stuff you can use in the kitchen."

"Do you mind if I bring my dog? I can't really leave him outside." Chuck indicated he couldn't care less, and she stepped inside.

The front foyer was a cramped little hall, made smaller by a stack of boxes piled in one corner. Annie was amazed. Chuck was a model of efficiency. He hadn't been in the house a half hour. It just went to show what a person could do when properly motivated.

The grieving widower hitched up his pants, suddenly expansive. "I got here a little while ago and there's a lot I need to do. If you wanna go upstairs, Jan's office is at the top of the landing. Kinda messy, but I guess that won't bother you, ha, ha. That's what you're here for."

Dispensing with the idle chitchat, which in any case wasn't going to buy baby any new shoes, Chuck went back to the onerous task of unplugging and carrying the 30-inch TV out to the van. Annie dumped the mop and bucket in the kitchen and hurried upstairs.

Claudius's nails clicked on the wood floor beside her. He grunted and flopped on the rag rug just inside the bedroom door. "Stay there and be quiet," she ordered. He heaved a resigned sigh, his nose on his paws, apparently content to watch.

She yanked open the closet door and peered inside. Jan's clothes, and there weren't all that many, were hung neatly from hangers. Nothing interesting here, if you didn't count the fact that Jan had thought sleaze was trendy. She shut the door. Nearby, on the floor, was a pair of sling-back shoes, one on its side looking as if Jan had just kicked them off. By the bed were a stack of paperbacks. Tom Harris and a big Tom Clancy. And a notebook with figures in it. Thirty thousand, crossed out, beneath it, fifty thousand, also crossed out. Under that, one hundred thousand. Underlined.

It was proof that Jan had been thinking about money before her death, but that didn't prove anything. Annie decided to check out the contents of the rolltop desk.

The gods were on her side. Just as she noticed the desk had a key and was probably locked, she saw that Chuck had anticipated her. Unable to find the key himself, he'd broken the lock. She pulled the top up. A packet of photographs fell on the floor, then a mass of papers slid forward, almost engulfing her. She picked up the photographs first.

Jan had taken them the night of Reverend Morris's party. There was the same banner in the background. The same faces, same silly grins. Uncle Ira, looking aggrieved as Aunt Hortense took a piece of chocolate cake away from him. Wallace Hapgood talking to John Barnard. Then Melinda Pennyworth, looking blonde and beautiful. The pastor with his arm around Reverend Morris. Elvira, Mrs. Fielding . . .

She'd seen all this before.

She turned her attention to the papers in the desk. Some were bills, others seemed to be newspaper clippings, pages from the personals. Jan had circled some of the ads in red. Annie ran her eyes down the pages: "WM, five-six, slim, Warren Beatty lookalike, likes outdoors sports and a good time. Seeks someone who like fun and games. Write Harry, box 5451." And another: "WM, 45, looks physically younger than age. Enjoys working out, boating, swimming, movies, travel, etc. Hard-working, financially secure, occasional drinker, drug-free. I'm easy-going. Looking to meet F, 30–45, pear shape preferred for relationship leading to committment. Likes leather and SM, into big, blonde women. Dominatrix okay. Write Clark, box 2347."

There were other symbols, the meaning of which escaped Annie. However, she suspected they were pornographic in nature. She didn't have time to feel embarrassed for Jan, whose motto as far as sex and sensual gratification was concerned seemed to have been any port in the storm. Besides, the question was purely academic now, since Jan was dead. She put them aside, thinking she'd ask Bob what the hell those symbols meant. She straightened and looked around, rubbed her aching back. Jan's dressing table was loaded with enough bottles of perfumed creams and ointments, and over-the-counter treatments for various skin conditions—evidently, she'd had both dry and oily skin and a foot-odor problem that would have made a polecat proud.

But this wasn't finding any clue to her murderer. Annie went back to the desk. In one of the cubbyholes, she came across a sheaf of letters from various men. They looked like replies either to ads Jan had placed herself or part of an ongoing correspondence. She read a couple. They were pathetic, really. Letters from lonely men looking for love or at least sex in all the wrong places. They were signed with first names. Mike, Marlon, and so on. Intent on looking through the rest of the cubbyholes, she put the letters down on a nearby pile of magazines.

Just then, from downstairs came a series of thuds and bangs as Chuck dragged a nice overstuffed chair out of the house and humped it to the van. Annie straightened with a frown, thinking absently that he'd turn every stick of furniture into firewood before he was done. It happened in slow motion. Her elbow struck the precariously balanced magazines, and they slid to the floor.

An envelope was sticking out of one of the magazines. She picked it up and took out the letter. It was crumpled a little. She frowned, skimming down the page. It was a reply Jan had received from one of the personal ads:

"Dear Juliet"—evidently Jan had used her real name—"it was real nice to get your letter. We could get it on, but I need more than empty promises, if you know what I mean. We have a lot in common, I can tell. I like it slow and smooth, to take time and explore all the angles. You want a lot, but if I have to, fifty thousand isn't out of the question. But I need time. Meet me at The Irish Rose out on Route 50, on Wednesday at 2, and we can talk things over. Love, Michael."

Annie frowned and read it again, then looked at the envelope. Box 3221 was scrawled in the upper lefthand corner, and the postmark was local, marked ten days ago. Someone named Michael, undoubtedly the killer, had lured her out to the cafe by the desert. Suddenly shaking, Annie read the letter a third time, barely able to take in the meaning of the scrawled words. A chill slid down her spine. The Irish Rose . . . she and her aunt and uncle had eaten there a few nights ago. It was located just a few miles from where she and Uncle Ira had discovered her body.

On that fateful Wednesday, Jan had kept a date with death.

The sharp crackle of the envelope in her pocket made her skin crawl. Whoever had written it had deliberately planned and carried out her murder with no more emotion than if he'd swatted a fly.

Chapter Sixteen

Annie knew she'd eventually have to turn Jan's letter from "Michael" over to the police, but not just yet. She had a better idea. There was a phone on the dressing table, and before she had a chance to change her mind, she dialed Bob's number at his apartment. He picked up after three rings. "Hi, it's Annie. Jan was using the personals in the paper to meet men, and one of the letters looks like it's from the killer. He signed it, 'Michael'. There's a box number on the envelope—3221. See if you can find out who's using it."

"Great!" There was a pause while he thought a second. "Look, I'll get on it right away. Where are you? Still in Jan's house?"

"Yes." She glanced toward the hallway as a sudden muttered imprecation floated up the stairwell. "Stalker's downstairs. I'm supposed to be looking for an insurance policy."

"Don't take any chances. Do what you have to and get out of there."

"Okay, but there might be other letters from Michael. It's worth looking around some more."

"Yeah, the more evidence we come up with, the better for us. We wrap it up and hand the killer over to the cops. Hot damn, Annie! It's so close, I can smell it!"

Claudius gave a sudden low rumble and stood up. She gave him the hand signal, which he proceeded to ignore. "Down!"

Bob muttered in her ear, "What?"

"Nothing. When do you think you can check the personals?"

"I'll try and do it in the morning, but it'll be tough.

The paper doesn't open until eight-thirty, and I have to be in Alamagordo by nine—a criminal trial. The world's oldest and dumbest crook. He's eighty-five. Tried to break into an ATM machine by ramming it with his car. The case is pretty much cut-and-dried. A cop was standing on the corner and saw the whole thing. But knowing the antiquated court system, the trial will take up most of the morning, so I'll be stuck there. If I run late, chances are I won't be able to check Box 3221 until two or three."

She didn't want to wait. "It's too important to put off until tomorrow afternoon. I'll go down first thing in the morning, right after they open."

"Well . . . okay," he said, a shade reluctantly. "*The Post* is on the corner of South Virginia and Route 70. A big old stucco building, you can't miss it. The ad office is in the annex on the second floor."

"I'll find it without any trouble. Will they give me the letters in the box without identification?"

"Probably not. It's set up to protect privacy, and they check a master list. But the boxes are in the wall opposite the front desk, so you should be able to see them without any trouble. In the meantime, have you got any ideas about Michael's identity? What about the letter? Anything in it ring a bell?"

"You mean motive?"

"Yeah, or opportunity. The what, when, why of how he killed her."

"He talks about money and a meeting out on Route 50, near where we found the body."

He laughed. "It's hardly conceivable that she'd get a letter like that from an innocent man. She went out there expecting a big payoff."

Claudius looked toward the door and growled again, and Annie grabbed his collar

"The letter was his hook," Bob went on. "Odds are he killed Morris, and she saw him do it or else she just had a pretty good idea who he was. This is turning into one hell of a lead! No way I'd hand this to the cops on a silver platter. There's nothing here yet that would help them anyway."

From the doorway, Chuck Stalker shouted, "Hey! I didn't say you could use the phone!"

Annie swung around, fright pumping ice through her veins. He was glaring at her. His eyes glittered with suspicion.

There was a tense silence. Bob's voice said tinnily from the receiver, "Annie, what the hell's going on?"

She hung up the phone. Her hand shook. "I . . . I called the church to see if the insurance policy had turned up."

"Oh, yeah?" Chuck eyed her with disbelief. "So where's Jan's copy?"

"I looked in the desk, but didn't find it."

"You wanna know what I think? I think you're nothin' but a goddamn liar. There ain't no insurance policy. Get outta here right now or I'm callin' the cops."

"I'm not lying. I told you, my aunt had a foot operation—"

"I don't give a hoot in hell about any damn foot operation." He hitched up his pants. "And now I think about it, you don't look like one of them Holy Rollers."

"Mr. Stalker, I really need to find the copy of that policy. Or you won't be paid."

That last remark gave Chuck pause, but only for a moment. "Yeah, well I think I'll look for the policy, myself." He stared at her red hair for a moment, mulling things over. He made up his mind. "I never seen a church-going' bitch with hair like that. Who the hell are you, some kinda weirdo who gets off on goin' through dead people's stuff? Get the hell outta here!"

She drew herself to her full height. "You don't want me to look for the policy?"

"You got that right," he sneered.

"Fine. It may not even exist anymore. Your wife may have had second thoughts about paying the premiums. Maybe she canceled it and ripped it up."

"Like hell! That money's mine!" He balled his fists. "I ain't gonna be cheated outta what's legally comin' to me!"

"I hope not." She was dismayed to hear a faint note

of fear in her voice when she was trying so hard to sound indifferent.

A nerve in his cheek twitched. "Either way, bitch, I'll tell you one thing. It ain't none of your goddamn business. I told you to get out, and I ain't sayin' it twice!"

He stepped forward, so close she could smell his sour breath.

She said a hasty good-bye and, taking Claudius by the collar, went downstairs. The heavy stumping sound descending behind her indicated that Stalker didn't trust her to exit the house on her own. She raced out the front door and heard it slam with a thunderous crash.

Hurrying past the van, she noticed it was parked at an angle on the grass by the front porch. Its back doors yawned wide and bits of furniture, a rolled up rug, several nice lamps, and the TV were stuffed inside.

But like a stuck video playing over and over in her mind, Chuck Stalker's outraged face followed her through the hedge and up the back steps into Uncle Ira's.

She went indoors, and her aunt fell on her with outstretched arms. "Thank goodness, you're safe. What did he say? Not that you can believe a word out of his mouth. He's nothing but a lowlife. He beat up some street person last year, robbed him. Put the poor man in the hospital. Oh, Annie, I'm so glad you're all right. I watched the house the whole time you were gone. If he'd laid a hand on you, I'd have called the police right away."

She sorted through her aunt's babbling. "Stalker threw me out."

"Never mind. You're all right, that's the main thing." But Aunt Hortense was still upset. "My, I almost forgot. Elvira Stubenville called a little while ago. She wants you to call her back."

Annie sighed. What could that woman possibly want—advice about replying to alien transmissions through her dental work?

She hoped she sounded reasonably calm a few minutes later as Elvira picked up the phone. "It's Annie O'Hara. I'm returning your call."

"Yes, I . . . I'd like to get together with you this evening for a little chat. It might be extremely advantageous for both of us. I . . . don't like to talk about people—and no matter what you think, I wasn't spying on you the other night."

"You could have fooled me. Why did you run away?"

There was a pause, then Elvira said, "That's not important. We need to talk in private. Not over the phone. Meet me at the Gondola restaurant on the corner of Main and South Streets. Tonight, nine-thirty."

That was all Elvira had to say. Annie thought a moment, then agreed to meet her. She hung up. It was definitely peculiar, Elvira asking to talk to her. Could it be that the woman had remembered something about the murders? Maybe this was a break in the case. Well, it wouldn't hurt to meet her at the Gondola and see what she had to say.

Annie got to the restaurant early. The main entrance led through the bar, so she ordered a beer and sat at a table where she could see the door. Fifteen minutes passed. She ate some peanuts and drank her beer slowly, making it last. People came and went, but no sign of Elvira. She glanced at her watch. Elvira was late. It was almost eleven. An hour and a half late. She ordered another beer and decided to give her another ten minutes, then she'd go home.

She waited another twenty-five minutes and gave up. She was tired and a little down. Tonight had been nothing but a big waste of time.

She saw the flares and the blue and red flashing lights through the trees that bordered the road on the way back to Idlewild Circle. She saw them long before she had to slow down for the long line of cars waiting at the police barrier.

She let out a groan. It was past midnight. This was all she needed. A mile or so behind, the road widened at the junction with the highway. Just ahead, there was a sharp curve and the shoulder of the road sloped steeply downward past a long line of shrubs and trees.

A motorcycle policeman in an orange vest was placing more accident flares in the road. Three police cars blocked the oncoming lane, their blue and red roof lights flashing eerily against the night sky.

A tow truck was backing down the slope toward a car lying in the ditch.

Something, she didn't know what, made Annie get out of the Escort and cautiously make her way along the shoulder of the road. Traffic sounds receded. Down the steep slope she went, her feet slipping on the damp grass.

There was a battered Chevy Lumina at the bottom of the ditch. The front end of the car had slammed into a large pine tree. It looked as if the car had rolled over more than once—the windshield was smashed, glass sparkled in a thousand fragments in the thick grass.

A fire truck and an ambulance waited up on the road. Half a dozen police and firemen were working to right the Chevy, rocking and heaving the car from side to side.

Elvira drove a Chevy Lumina. The other day in the hospital, just before Aunt Hortense's operation, they'd mentioned it. They'd said what a bad driver Elvira was.

"Hey, you!" shouted one of the uniformed policemen. "Get out of here—get back to your car!"

"I was on my way home. I saw the accident. The car may belong to someone I know."

The policeman sighed. "Christ. This is all we need." Wiping a muddy hand across his face, "Look, lady. Get back in your car. You don't want to see this."

"If she's my friend, someone should let the family know."

He shrugged. "Go ahead, then. See for yourself. The car took the bend too fast, slammed into two trees, and flipped over, ending up down here."

"Do you know the driver's name?"

He nodded. "License says Elvira Stubenville. Lives here in town. Eighty One Idlewild Circle."

"Oh, my God—was she alone?"

"Yeah, luckily"

"Is . . . she badly hurt?"

"Geez, what do you think—an accident like this. She's dead, lady." He gazed back down the slope and shrugged. "We're lucky she didn't kill someone else. She was plastered, tanked to the eyeballs."

"Drunk?" That didn't sound like Elvira. One of the church doctrines was no alcohol. Besides, Elvira had been on her way to the Gondola, not on her way home from some bar.

"There was the better part of a bottle of scotch all over the driver's seat." As he spoke, two EMTs loaded Elvira's body on a stretcher and carried it up to the waiting ambulance. They slammed the doors and drove off. No sirens, no flashing lights. They were in no hurry now.

Stunned, Annie looked down at the car. The police had finally righted it, and a mechanic in overalls was wriggling under the Chevy to attach a chain to the front axle.

"Watch it, they're gonna move the vehicle back up on the road."

When she got home, the first thing she did was call Bob and tell him Elvira was dead. She explained that she'd expected to see her at the Gondola, but Elvira had never showed. He let out a slow whistle, then said he'd check with his police contact and get back to her later.

When Annie hung up, she turned around to find Aunt Hortense standing there in her bathrobe. Obviously, she'd heard every word. She demanded to know what was going on.

So Annie told her.

"Elvira dead? *Drunk?*" Aunt Hortense sat down. "Impossible. I'm shocked. Utterly shocked. I can't believe it."

"The police said there was liquor all over the front seat."

Aunt Hortense looked dazed. Her eyes filled with tears. She got up. "I'll tell Ira. Then I'll get dressed and we'll see if there's anything we can do for Roger. Has he been told?"

"I don't know."

"A police car drove up a little while ago. For a minute I thought they were coming for your uncle, but they went over to the Stubenville's. The poor man. They must have brought the news."

A short time later, Annie watched from the window as her aunt and uncle went over to the Stubenville home. They returned about a half hour later, saying that Roger was terribly upset, so stunned that he couldn't believe Elvira was gone.

In the midst of sorrow, Aunt Hortense was already busy making lists of things to be done. Of course, the funeral would have to be held at the church, along with a remembrance potluck. Roger would probably want her buried in the church graveyard. As to flowers, perhaps a donation to the Church Millennium Fund would be better. Poor, dear Elvira having been chairwoman of that committee.

"Well, that's enough to get things started," she said as the phone rang.

Annie got it. "Hello?"

It was Bob calling back and he had news. "There's something odd about the accident. Elvira suffered internal injuries as well a broken leg and three broken ribs. Slamming into the steering wheel crushed her chest. The car didn't have an air bag. The thing is, she was short, an inch or two over five feet. The driver's seat was pushed well back when they got her out of the car. Her feet couldn't have reached the pedals."

"So she wasn't driving?"

"The cops don't think so. Rumor is that she may have already been unconscious from a series of blows to the head. Whoever hit her, drove to the side of the road, arranged her behind the wheel, poured whiskey on the front seat, and put a brick on the accelerator before jumping out. Maybe he counted on the car catching fire, but that didn't happen."

"My God . . ."

"For the time being, the cops don't want this to come out. So I'm writing it up as a straight accident story. If the killer thinks he got away with it, he may get careless. In the meantime, don't forget to check the personals tomorrow."

"Don't worry. I'll be at the paper, first thing in the morning."

So far, the police hadn't questioned where Elvira was headed in the Chevy before she died. If they found out Annie waited for her at the Gondola? Well, she'd worry about that later.

The next morning, after showering and getting dressed, and leaving Claudius at home—he was busy eating the breakfast leftovers anyway—she drove off toward the center of town.

The heat of the day hadn't built up yet, and traffic on Route 70 wasn't too bad, so she made good time and soon turned down South Virginia Ave. *The Post* was located in the building just ahead. The architecture looked like a throwback to eighteenth-century Spanish; fortresslike beige stucco and a red tile roof. The front door was massive and heavily carved. She hit the brake and swung into a parking spot across the street.

For at least ten minutes she sat there, eyeing the newspaper building's imposing front door. A steady stream of people went in and out—it was a busy place. She chewed her lip. How to get the information she wanted? What to say . . . as little as possible. She'd take out an ad.

Hurrying across the street, she went up the front steps and paused to get her bearings. The foyer wasn't really a room. It was an elegant chamber, high-domed, with an ornate gallery that ran all around the ceiling perimeter. Lush green plants cascaded from overhead baskets. The air-conditioning kicked on and cool air brushed her face as she made her way upstairs and pushed opened two heavy oak doors marked ADVERTISING ANNEX.

A glance around the room showed that it was almost deserted. An elderly man was reading the morning paper, hunched over a table in the corner, and a teenage girl was sweeping the floor. Behind a long counter, a stout woman with brassy blonde hair was chewing gum and sorting through a stack of pink memo slips. She snapped her gum and gave Annie the once-over. "You want something?"

"I'd like to take out a personal ad."

The woman handed her the form for the ad and pointed to a pen attached to a chain. "Ten dollars for fifty words or less. For a double ad, fifty-one to one hundred words, it's thirty dollars. Fill this out. There's voice mailbox, but that's extra. If you don't want to use that, you put it in the ad. Just write 'no voice mail' as the last three words."

"You don't publish names and addresses?"

"No, but we need a name and address for our records. Strictly confidential. Nobody's gonna see it but me."

"Good." Annie began to fill out the form, at the same time covertly eyeing the rack of cubbyholes on the wall opposite. They were labeled and numbered. Box 3221 was in the top row, at the far end. It was empty.

Her spirits sank. No damning letter. She hadn't really thought it would be that easy, but she couldn't help feeling disappointed.

Never mind. She'd concoct a letter to "Michael." Keeping it simple, yet with enough information to draw him out. She'd set up a date to meet him. Then they could notify the police, and the trap would close. Because of the limitations of a personal ad, the letter had to be written in the same code Jan had used.

She had to find the original ad.

She cleared her throat, and the gum-snapper scowled. "You want something else?"

"I need to see last week's paper."

"The personals?"

"Yes."

The woman reached under the counter and found a copy. She plunked it down. "That's a dollar-fifty. I'll put it on the final bill."

Annie took the paper and retreated to the table where the old man was sitting. She sat down and began a search of the personals' column, skipping the male entries, concentrating on females. "Introverted bohemian. SWF seeks SWM, kind and muscular, 25–35. Interests include movies, gothic and horror. Likes to experiment in various sexual practices. Voice mailbox #307539."

Although it mentioned horror movies, Annie was sure

the author wasn't Jan. By no stretch of the imagination had she been introverted, and there was nothing in the ad hinting about murder.

She scanned down the page "Dana, Hello, I live in Roswell. I'm a scorpio, 40 years old. I love sports in any kind of water, love fun and making people laugh. I want to be serious, but then again, I don't. Voice mailbox #303653." Repressing the thought that the author might do better if she made up her mind, Annie decided it wasn't Jan.

"Let's get hot together. 2nd year law student, 5'7" with long, strawberry blonde hair. Call me and state your case. Voice mailbox #302447." Clever, but again, not Jan.

Neither was the Georgia peach with the sense of humor who wanted sex outdoors, or Kristal who liked hot group sex, or the Hispanic female with green eyes. The "model living in Roswell" looked promising. She was "strong-willed and needed spanking," but again, no mention of anything remotely connected to murder.

She read through page after page of Naughty Marissa's, Amanda's, and Chelsea's with the hots for men with muscles, longing to be kinky in hot tubs or sculpted in the nude. Who knew how to have fun . . . and big men were a plus.

Whatever else they were, they weren't Jan.

She turned to the last page, and there it was, sandwiched between "Lorrie, the avid skier and one-man woman, who was sexually submissive, divorced three times, and still looking for the man of her dreams," and "Samantha, the college-educated, hot French stripper who was into pastries and profanity."

"I know who you are. I saw *Fatal Attraction* twice, and I need aid and comfort. Please write, Juliet." The box listed was the same one Michael had replied to.

Annie found a pen and pad in her purse and jotted down notes. Juliet was Jan's real name. Chuck had laughed about it at her funeral. Jan had died because somehow, she knew who'd torn the reverend's throat out.

The mental pictures this conjured up remained vivid

and horrible: Jan in that plastic bag in the desert. The heat. That sickening smell. Buzzards. And the reverend's body behind the dumpster . . . Claudius sniffing, his paws and muzzle smeared red, and Morris's corpse, eyes glazed in death, the gaping wound in his throat, blood everywhere.

Jesus, enough of that. She rested her head in her hands for a moment, and when she looked up, the old man across the table was staring at her across the top of the sports' pages, obviously wondering if she was going to get sick or worse.

"I'm fine, just a little tired," she muttered.

He gave her a look that said if she threw up in his direction she'd regret it, and went back to the box scores. She picked up the pen again and began writing a letter to Michael from Juliet's friend. She missed her dead pal, and she knew that Michael probably missed her, too. They had a mutual interest in movies. Especially *Fatal Attraction*. Why not get together in the church parking lot to talk things over . . . Thursday night, about eight.

It took a good half hour, but she worked at it until she had it exactly right. A woman's handwriting would be a plus. Michael would think she was as foolish as Jan—and as easy to silence.

She addressed it to Box 3221 and walked back to the counter. "This is for Box 3221."

The woman snapped her gum twice with an air of weariness. "I thought you were gonna post an ad."

"I decided not to, after all."

"So, you still owe a dollar fifty for the paper."

Annie paid up and was in the act of closing her purse when she had an idea. "Do you know what the man who rented Box 3221 looks like?" She smiled. A little charm might work wonders.

The woman was not impressed. "I told you, it's confidential."

"But . . . how about whether he's dark haired or blond. Couldn't you tell me at least that much?"

The woman jutted her chin. "No, I couldn't."

It'd been a long shot, but worth a try.

Annie left the newspaper and drove back to the north side of town. The streets were laid out in a grid, with the sprawling downtown section strung out from Route 285 in the north to Hondo Park in the east, and the Broadmoor shopping center, not far from her aunt and uncle's neighborhood.

As she drove by the shopping mall and the orderly rows of cars, she couldn't help thinking how ironic it was. Air-conditioned bliss and high-priced goods—a place to spend an idle hour or two. As it was, she hadn't set foot in the mall and probably wouldn't. Nothing about this so-called vacation had been normal. People getting murdered right and left, with the police at a standstill.

The letter to Michael was risky, but at this point it looked like the only way to flush him out. If it worked, Uncle Ira could go back to weeding his garden in peace. If it didn't work, they'd have to think of something else to keep the police from arresting him.

When she got back to Uncle Ira's she noticed Bob's car parked out front. She ran up the steps and let herself in, eager to tell him about the letter to Michael.

Chapter Seventeen

"You left a letter in Box 3221 already?" Bob said, surprised. He was sitting at the kitchen table with her aunt and uncle, who'd just returned from helping Roger Stubenville make funeral arrangements for poor Elvira.

Aunt Hortense looked worried. "I wish you hadn't done that, Annie. It's too dangerous. We should turn this matter over to the police. Half the time they don't know beans from apple butter, but they're all we've got in a situation like this. Besides, it's what we pay our taxes for."

A slight quaver in her voice made Bob and Annie exchange glances. If they didn't talk fast, the whole thing could slip away. He got up and paced restlessly. "We'll turn it over to the cops in a day or two, I promise you that." His voice rang with sincerity, and Aunt Hortense's face cleared. Here was a man whose byline appeared twice a week in Roswell, a man, after all, she could trust.

"I don't know," muttered Uncle Ira, not convinced. "I don't want any more trouble. Given half a chance, they'll pin the murders on me."

Annie put her arm around him. "That's why we need to find out all we can before telling Lt. Rhodes."

"What exactly did you say in the letter?" Bob asked.

"I said I was a friend of Juliet's—that was her real name, the one she used in the ad. I said we had a common interest. I mentioned *Fatal Attraction* and suggested we meet Thursday night at the church."

"Sounds good. How's he supposed to reply?"

"I used Jan's box number."

"Okay, I'll check it daily."

She thought of something else. "What if he doesn't reply? What do we do then?"

"Let's not go down that road until we have to. We can try to contact him again, or just turn it all over to the police."

As a backup plan, it sounded feasible, but from Bob's expression, she realized that, despite all his protestations to the contrary, it was the last thing he'd agree to.

She decided to change the subject. Why had Elvira been killed? Whatever she'd wanted to talk to Annie about that night at the Gondola, presumably had led to her death.

But what could it have been?

She sighed. "The only things Elvira ever talked about were her prayer lists, the Second Coming, alien broadcasts through her dental work, and how I was going straight to hell."

"But she said she knew something that might be advantageous for both of you," Bob reminded her.

"I can't imagine what it was. Now she's dead, and I'll never know."

Somewhere upstairs were the sounds of two Siamese cats snarling and glass breaking. Aunt Hortense went upstairs to make sure her sweeties were all right.

Uncle Ira got down the brandy and they all had a drink. The Felix clock over the refrigerator chimed softly, and Annie looked at Bob. Time was running out.

They waited for Michael to reply.

The post box remained empty. No letters from Michael.

By Wednesday, the tension was unbearable.

Michael held all the cards. He could afford to let the Thursday deadline slide. In fact, it was to his advantage. Then he could strike without warning. And suddenly, with dawning horror, Annie realized she was a sitting duck.

He'd killed three times, and now she was the bait.

That night after dinner the phone rang. Aunt Hortense handed her the phone. "Some man asking for you."

Stomach churning, "Yes?"

Soft laughter. Then a muffled voice. "You wrote me a letter."

Michael.

She felt frozen. She could hardly get the words out. "Who is this?"

"We don't want to get ahead of ourselves here."

"I don't like anonymous phone calls."

"Too bad. I make the rules."

"Tell me what you want, or I'll hang up."

More laughter. "Oh, I don't think so. You need to talk to me."

He was right. She swallowed and whispered, "Is this Michael?"

"Too fast. What are you afraid of, Annie? I like it slow and smooth." His disgusting, wet snigger made it perfectly clear what he meant.

"If you're Michael, I knew a friend of yours with expensive tastes."

A tense silence. She could almost hear him thinking on the other end of the line. Then he muttered, "Let's say I am this Michael. So what?"

"Like Juliet, I have expensive tastes, too."

He laughed again. "That ain't nothing to me. So you wanna be a rich bitch. I'd like to be freaking Superman, but it ain't gonna happen, and who the hell cares, anyway."

"You're going to help me get what I want. I think you'd better start caring," she retorted. "I'll be over at the church tomorrow night at eight. If you're smart, you'll meet me there. We have a lot to talk about."

"Like what I did to Morris and Juliet? It took them a long time to die. Morris had more blood in him than I thought."

Fear rose in her throat. Her instincts told her to be quiet and listen. The more he talked, the more he gave away. She held her breath.

He whispered, "Did you like the present I left for you the other night?"

"No." She closed her eyes against the vision of the

scarecrow hanging from the noose in the shadows of the shed.

She wondered if he'd say anything about killing Elvira, but he didn't. Well, as far as he knew, he'd gotten away with it and everyone believed her death to be just another drunk-driving statistic. Cooperating with the police, the paper had listed it in the obituaries as "Tragic highway accident."

He grunted, "Instead of the church, let's make it The Irish Rose Cafe. If I decide to show up, I'll make it worth your while." There was a slight click. The phone went dead.

Annie turned to her aunt as she replaced the receiver. "That was Michael." Her voice was barely a whisper. "He took the bait."

"Oh, my God," her aunt cried. "We ought to call the police right now."

But Annie was already calling Bob.

They decided to let it play out. Thursday was the deadline.

Chapter Eighteen

Thursday night, Annie walked into The Irish Rose at seven forty-five. Claudius was by her side, heeling for once. The waitress eyed him sourly. "What's that supposed to be, lady? Some kinda guide dog? You don't look blind to me."

"He's a guide dog for the Helping Hands Organization," Annie informed her, skirting the issue of whether she was sighted or not. "I'm meeting one of the other members here. Has he arrived?"

She gave her name, but after checking the list by the phone, the waitress shrugged. "No sign of anyone looking for you. Take a seat. If someone shows up, I'll show him over to your booth."

Annie slid into one by the front window. While she ordered a coffee and sat back to wait, Claudius settled himself under the table and put his nose on his paws. When the coffee came, she found she couldn't drink it.

Why was she so frightened? Common sense said they'd covered all the angles. Bob was outside in his car, waiting for Michael to show up. Their plan was foolproof. When she gave the signal, he'd call the police on his cell phone. The Roswell police weren't stupid. They ran down every tip. They'd be here within minutes, and it'd be all over. Nothing was going to go wrong.

Still, her hands were icy with sweat. She rubbed them on her jeans. Minutes crawled by. The cafe began to fill up with the evening crowd. A few couples, several people on their own. Through the window, she could see shapes of cars outside in the lot. Bob was parked off to the side, some distance away from her Escort. The idea being that if Michael were watching, he'd think she'd come alone.

Waiting. She tried the coffee, but it was cold now and strong enough to peel paint off the wall. She pushed it away and looked at her watch. Well after eight. He wasn't coming. He'd teased her with that possibility on the phone, probably getting off on it. If she shut her eyes, she could still hear his muffled laughter. *Damn him.*

The waitress came back with a carafe of coffee. "Want a refill?"

"No."

The waitress frowned. She didn't appreciate customers occupying space without ordering. "How about a muffin?"

"Okay, bring two muffins and water." Outside, it was so dark, she couldn't make out Bob's car. But she knew he was there, somewhere in the shadows. It was the only thing she had to hang onto. Her lifeline.

The muffins had been grilled flat, with browned scorch marks and sodden with dripping butter. She gave the whole lot to Claudius who didn't care that the muffins didn't have any nooks and crannies. She drank a glass of water and thought about Jan Stalker. Had she sat in the same booth a week or so ago, waiting for Michael, thinking her fortune was made? One hundred thousand, that was the figure scribbled on the pad by her bed. *And her face with those horrible lifeless eyes in that garbage bag.*

After a while the sick knot in Annie's stomach eased, and she looked at her watch. Almost nine-thirty. He wasn't coming. She knew it.

Just then Wallace Hapgood came in. He sat down in a booth across the way. He looked nervous and kept drumming the table with his fingers. Looking around. The waitress approached and he ordered. He leaned back and glanced over at Annie. For a second she thought he wasn't going to move, then he got up and came over.

"Mind if I sit down?"

"Be my guest."

He smiled. "So, what are you doing all the way out here by the edge of the desert?"

"I thought I'd take a drive." Her voice was steady, but under the table her hands were locked together, nails driving into her palms.

"Have you heard anything new about the murders?" He leaned back, seemingly relaxed and calm. But she felt a distinct sense of tension coming from him.

She shook her head. She couldn't have said a word if her life had depended on it.

"Everyone at the bank talks about nothing else. It's a nine days' wonder downtown." He put his hands on the table. The nails were square and shiny. He had big hands.

Annie shivered, wondering if he'd wrapped them around Jan Stalker's neck and squeezed the life out of her. She prayed soundlessly.

Wallace looked around, annoyed. "Where the hell's the waitress. I ordered the ribs. They're not bad here, barbequed. They give you a big portion. Not like some places. The Mill Restaurant on the other side of town. You been there yet?"

"No."

"Don't bother then. People go there for the pecan rolls. They make them from scratch, and they're very good. My wife got the recipe from the chef, but they don't taste the same. She doesn't have a light touch with pastry."

She couldn't figure him out. He sat there as if the only thing on his mind was his dinner. Gathering her courage, she said, "Do you read the personals in the paper?"

"Lovelorn columns?" He laughed. "No. That's just a racket."

He was making her work for it, enjoying every minute. A wave of anger flooded her veins. "I put an ad in the personals. I'm supposed to meet somebody here tonight."

"You'll regret it." He eyed her with pity. "They're all the same, people you meet through ads. In it for one thing and one thing only. This man you're waiting for will take you for every penny you've got and then some.

When he's done, you'll be lucky if he leaves the fillings in your back teeth."

"Maybe you're right." Suddenly, she was certain he wasn't Michael. The voice on the phone hadn't been louder than a husky whisper. Wallace Hapgood's voice was higher in pitch. Of course, he could be faking it now, but she didn't think so. He acted as if he really didn't know what she was talking about. In fact, he was looking at her as if he thought she had a screw loose.

Providentially, at that point the waitress appeared with his order, and Wallace got up and went back to his table. Annie was left more or less to her own devices, which meant that she checked her watch every few minutes, wondering if she should give up and leave. Michael wasn't coming. The killer had stood her up, and her sensible half was so relieved, she could hardly think. Now she could go outside and tell Bob she'd done her best, but it was no good. They'd have to let the police handle things from now on.

With a distinct sense of relief, she paid her bill and took Claudius outside. Where was Bob's car? She peered around the half-filled parking lot. What did she really know about him, her mind whispered suddenly. An icy drop of perspiration slid down her spine.

He wanted fame, attention, success. *Maybe he was a charming psychopath. Maybe he was Michael.*

She went numb. *He couldn't be the killer. She'd know.*

But killers didn't wear the mark of Cain. The face of evil looked like any other face. Reassuringly normal, like someone you saw everyday, like the man next door.

She glanced back through the doors of the cafe at the patrons inside. Any one of them could be Michael, watching her and waiting. Even now he could be deciding to strike when she least expected it—perhaps when she walked to the car. God, she wished she'd told Bob to park closer to the entrance.

A couple came out of the cafe and walked past, eyeing her curiously. Claudius lunged forward and stuck his nose in the man's crotch. "Sorry." She hauled the dog away and ordered him to behave. His response was to yawn and snap his teeth in that annoying habit of his.

It was stupid to stand around here all night, she thought, finally giving up and dragging him across the lot toward the car. Maybe she should have called the police herself from the cafe. An idea that held more appeal with each passing minute. She could tell Lt. Rhodes everything and dump the whole mess in his lap. Even now it wasn't too late, she thought. Bob would be furious, naturally, but he wasn't putting his life on the line. She was.

The red Escort looked almost black in the dim light of the parking lot. She opened the back door, and Claudius jumped in. She rolled the window down halfway, closed the door, and put her hand on the front door handle.

A sharp pain pierced her back suddenly. She twisted away, letting out a scream, but it was too late. A man's hand covered her mouth as he pulled her back against him. "I've been waiting for you," Michael whispered. "I don't like to be kept waiting."

She twisted desperately, but her struggles only angered him. He shoved his arm up under her chin, and she couldn't breathe. Her lungs were burning and bright spots danced before her eyes. *God help her, she was going to die.*

"How does it feel, bitch? Knowing I can kill you with one shove of my knife," he muttered, twisting her so he could see her terrified face.

It was the church caretaker, John Barnard.

He grinned at her, and somehow the knife point was now under her left eye, sliding upward, pricking her skin and drawing blood. She screamed, but there was no sound, just a roaring in her head. The terrible strength of him, shaking her like a ragdoll. Choking her. Grinning, enjoying every minute of her agony.

The knife dug in deeper. Instinctively, she shrank back, terrified witless, a thin line of blood trickling down her face. "I'm not gonna kill you here. You're gonna die in the desert like Jan Stalker." He shoved her in the car behind the wheel and got in the passenger seat. "Drive, you goddamn bitch."

She was crying now, soundless sobs that shook her body while she fumbled to find the keys and get the right one in the ignition. John Barnard shoved the knife up against her right breast, and she shuddered. The engine caught, but she was so frightened she couldn't keep her foot steady on the accelerator. The Escort bucked backward like a mad thing and stalled.

Barnard slapped her face hard. "Think someone will see you and call the cops? Think again. People mind their own business out here. Nobody cares whether you live or die."

Where was Bob? Frantically scanning the parking lot as she started the engine and drove slowly toward the highway—hoping against hope that he'd see her. *God, he had to see her.*

"Turn right on the highway and head out to the desert. If you try anything, I'll stick this knife right in your heart and twist it good." He laughed. "I'll cut off both your tits first. That I'll enjoy."

Her mind filled with wave after wave of terrible images. She couldn't block them out. He was going to kill her. But first he planned to torture and mutilate her.

The Escort raced through the night.

She risked a look in the rearview mirror. No following headlights. Bob hadn't seen her leave the parking lot. She was truly alone.

Barnard moved the knife until it was just under her chin, shoving it in, cutting her. She could feel warm blood dripping. Nothing, she could do nothing. She was helpless, driving to her own death. Hanging onto the wheel for dear life. How much longer? Not long. She sobbed, her body shaking with blind terror.

"Crying? Don't worry, it ain't far. Turn off at the next side road on the left." She almost missed it in her fright, and he slapped her so hard her ears rang. "Try that again, and I'll kill you right now."

They'd left the highway and careened down a secondary road, the Escort jouncing over the ruts. Frantically, she tried to think. As long as life remained, there was hope. She couldn't afford to panic. She had to remain in control.

The road abruptly narrowed before the twin beams of the Escort's headlights, dwindling away to a ragged cart track. She had no idea where they were. The desert lay vast and silent under the bowl of the starry night sky.

"Stop right here. We've gone far enough off the road. Nobody's likely to see us." The knife pricked the skin of her neck, and he grinned.

Her teeth were chattering. She stepped on the brake. Ice cold now. She couldn't feel anything. The Escort stopped and she felt oddly disconnected, as if someone else were at the wheel. She swallowed past the digging knife point and croaked, "Why are you doing this?"

"It's a long story." He leaned over and took the key from the ignition. It was so quiet, she could hear the tick of the engine cooling beneath the hood. Coyotes howled in the distance. "Let's take a walk."

Desperately trying to think of some way to stall, she pleaded, "Let me go. I won't tell the police. You can get away."

He grabbed her arm. The knife in his left hand, up under her right breast, cutting her. *God, it hurt like hell.*

"Let me go . . . I won't tell anyone."

He laughed. "Cut the crap. You're gonna die, and you can thank your goddamn uncle."

"Why?" She prayed silently. Claudius in the back seat. He must be asleep. If he woke up and saw what was happening, would he help her? *Oh please, please . . .*

"The church owns land out here. They found some metal from the UFO. It's harder than steel. You can't scratch it. I know, I tried. It's flexible, some kind of miracle metal." His face twisted in white-hot anger. "I told 'em we could make millions with it. Sell it to some steel company. We could negotiate a deal, get royalties. The church would be rich. They turned me down cold. Goddamn fools."

Keep him talking. As long as he talked, she'd stay alive.

"But why kill Reverend Morris?"

He shoved her forward over the rough ground. "The night of the party, I asked him to intercede for me with the elders. Make 'em see things my way. We'd all be rich. He laughed in my face. Who did I think I was? He called me a stinking bum, a nobody . . . I saw red and grabbed the first thing at hand, your uncle's hand fork.

Morris looked damned surprised when I tore his throat out. Fell down like he'd been pole-axed. He was dead before he hit the ground. Your uncle was the perfect patsy. It was his fault I killed Morris anyway, he's the one persuaded the rest of the elders not to sell the metal, so I waited a day or so, then put the hand fork back in the shed. I figured the cops would find it, and he'd be arrested."

"What about Jan Stalker?" She whispered. He stopped walking, and fear set her heart hammering until her ribs ached.

"I asked her to help me out, give me an alibi for Morris's death. I told her I'd been drinkin' all night. At first she went along with it, then started to get suspicious. Said she'd taken pictures at the party. They proved I'd killed Morris. I had to change my shirt . . . there was so much blood. So I went home, changed into another shirt and came back to the church to help put the chairs and tables away. Jan said her pictures proved I'd done it. I told her I'd spilled food on the first shirt, that's why I'd changed. But she didn't buy it. First she hinted around about money, and I pretended like I didn't know what she was getting at. She didn't stop. She put that ad in the personals. Blackmail. So I lured her out into the desert, and the stupid bitch came sweet as you please." Barnard laughed. "When she knew what was happenin', it was too late. She started screamin'. I bashed her in the head, then strangled her. I dumped her body where your uncle was sure to find it. I knew he'd take you out there to show you where the UFO landed."

"W . . . was that you in Jan Stalker's house that night? What were you looking for?"

"She tried to make me let her go, said she'd left a letter naming me as Morris's killer. The cops were sure to find it." Barnard shrugged. "I checked the computer first, figuring if she really had that letter, she'd have saved a copy in her files. She was big on movies, said that's how she listed the men she was dating. First names the same as the lead actors in each movie. So I answered her ad, using the name, Michael; she said it was *Fatal Attraction* . . . like Michael Douglas. She was right about that." He looked around. "This is far enough. Might as well kill you here as anywhere else. It don't make no difference to you. Stop walkin'."

"Wh . . . what about Elvira? Why did you kill her?"

"She was spyin' on me. Said the same thing. She had proof I'd killed Morris. Pictures of the party. She was going to the police with them. I bashed her head in with a brick, dumped a fifth of whiskey on her, then crashed the car." He laughed. "Killin' her was a freebie. The cops don't have a clue."

From thirty feet away, a wolflike spectral shape stalked from the shadows. It was slowly gaining ground, its eyes watching without mercy. With her peripheral vision, Annie caught a glimpse of movement. *An animal . . . Claudius.*

"Claudius! Help!"

She saw the razor-tip glinting as Barnard raised his arm, then the dog leaped at him. A blur. It all happened at once. Annie, still screaming, desperately twisting away from the slashing knife, and Barnard aware that this huge and snarling creature was almost on top of him, wheeling and stumbling backward.

Claudius hit him square in the chest, knocking him off his feet. The knife flew away into the dark. The dog roared and lunged for his leg, tearing and ripping his pants.

"Christ! He's gonna kill me! Get him off of me!" He fought to get free of those slashing teeth. "God damn it! He's tearin' my leg off!"

Annie swept the sandy earth with frantically searching hands. *The knife . . . where was the knife . . . Oh, God . . .*

She couldn't find it.

Barnard was trying to crawl away, kicking furiously with the leg Claudius didn't have a death grip on. He screamed a series of curses that had little or no discernible effect. Claudius continued to rip away at the gory mass between his jaws.

"Jesus, damn it! He's tearin' my leg off!"

Fighting back panicky sobs, Annie groped around, hoping to find the knife or a rock, something she could use as a weapon. *What if Barnard found the knife first and stabbed the dog, then came after her?*

There was nothing she could use.

She turned as Barnard staggered to his feet. He started after her, limping, his face a mask of rage—Claudius growling, gathered himself for another attack. "Bitch! I'll kill you with my bare hands!" Barnard was almost on top of her. He grabbed her arm.

Terrified, Annie twisted out of his grasp and ran for her life. Her feet thudded on the uneven ground, mesquite tore at her jeans, ripping her legs. Racing away into the night, half bent over, her breath coming in gasps, she tried not to make a sound. If she didn't make any noise, maybe he wouldn't find her. *Oh, God, please don't let him hear me breathe.*

Barnard wasn't far away. She heard his running footsteps as he crashed through the underbrush. In the distance, Claudius barked. The barking was coming closer. She crouched behind a rock, rigid with terror as Barnard stopped and looked around. Long moments passed while he stared at the rock.

She squeezed her eyes shut and prayed with all her might, and a minute later, he limped a short distance away to the left.

"I'll find you, bitch! The desert's full of snakes. Rattlers. They'll get you if I don't! Don't think you can get away!"

She pressed against the rock, hoping he was wrong about the rattlers. *Thank God he didn't have a flashlight. Thank God, maybe he wouldn't find her.*

Suddenly, bright lights streaked across the night sky. A meteor shower—celestial fireworks. One seemed to shoot almost overhead, Annie heard the whoosh of its passing, parting the air, its light extinguished mere feet from the ground. Instinctively, she ducked.

Claudius raced around, barking. He'd lost interest in attacking Barnard and was free to run his heart out. He raced around in circles, snapping at the lights in the sky, then darting off here and there, sniffing at bushes and rocks, stopping to lift his nose to the desert wind.

Annie glared at him, outraged. Just when she was

starting to have a little respect for him, he forgot all about Barnard, leaving her at the mercy of a cold-blooded killer. He was useless!

Barnard yelled again, but his voice grew faint. She lay there, crouched in a ball, shivering with shock. "If I get out of here alive, I'll kill that dog!" Then from a distance, came the sound of the car starting. Cautiously, she lifted her head up and peered over the rock. The Escort's headlights pointed east toward town, bobbing up and down, growing smaller. Barnard was driving away, leaving her there.

For twenty minutes, she didn't dare move in case it was a trick and he came back, then she dragged herself upright and called the dog. It took her a half hour to persuade him to come to her. Eventually, he dashed close by, and she caught him by the collar. "Heel, you traitor!"

He wasn't happy about it, but he came along without too much grumbling. She was so tired, all she could do was stagger down the dirt road, back to the highway. There was no traffic to speak of, and when a few cars appeared, terrified it was Barnard searching for her, she ran to the side of the road and crouched down, trying to hide. Cars whizzed past heading to town, tractor trailer trucks going the other way in a haze of exhaust. Then silence, with only the keening of the desert wind.

She was too exhausted to think straight. One foot in front of the other. Stumbling, falling. Picking herself up again and going on. Claudius padded along beside her as she stumbled back toward town. Then the car appeared around a bend in the highway. She'd missed the glow of the headlights until she was caught in the glare. Too late to run. Too late to hide. The car slowed and came to a stop.

"Annie! Thank God, you're safe!"

It was Bob. Waves of sweet relief flowed over her, and she was crying like a baby.

He bundled her into his car, made sure Claudius was in back, and turned the car around. "I'm really sorry about what happened. It was a dreadful mix-up, but what matters is that you're all right."

She wiped her eyes with the edge of her sleeve. "Michael was John Barnard, the church caretaker."

"I . . . know. When I realized you'd left the parking lot, I tried to follow you; but it was too late. I called the cops on the cell phone. By the time they arrived, Barnard was heading back to town, alone. They picked him up. At first he denied everything, but he couldn't very well explain what he was doing driving your car. Finally, he admitted he'd left you out in the desert somewhere, and I drove around looking for you."

She leaned back and watched him drive, stupid with exhaustion. "What happened when I came out of the cafe? You should have seen him. You said you'd be watching. God, he almost killed me!"

"Annie, I know I can never make it up to you. But try to understand. This was the biggest story of my life. I . . . I had to call it in to the paper. I did some writing in the parking lot, jotting down notes, pulling it all together. That's when he must have grabbed you. One second you were standing on the doorstep of The Irish Rose, then you were gone. I couldn't believe it at first, then when I realized what had happened, it was too late. So I called the cops . . . Rhodes burned my butt." He drew a long breath. "All's well that ends well, anyway. And this will make everyone sit up and take notice." His eyes gleamed, and he smiled. "The big time . . . all of it, the whole damn ball of wax . . . it's coming my way, baby."

She closed her eyes, fighting the sick feeling in the pit of her stomach. He'd almost got her killed. Bob and his goddamn ambition, his obsession with fame and fortune. *Damn him.*

A few days later, when things had more or less returned to normal, Uncle Ira drove Annie back out to the desert. They went back to the place where the UFO had crashed on church land. He wanted to show her the piece of metal that had cost three people their lives.

It was a beautiful day, Annie conceded as they got out of the car. She made sure Claudius's leash was snapped tight and followed her uncle down the barely discernible path.

An early morning mist had burned off a few hours ago. Purple mountains in the far distance soared to the blue bowl of the sky. Starkly beautiful. She watched three hawks soaring in circles. "That was some meteor shower the other night. Which one was it? The Perseid?"

"That's in August. As far as I know there's nothing for the rest of the month except the odd shooting star. Was it bright?"

"Spectacular."

"Hmm, must have missed it. I take it that you're not planning on seeing Bob Colfax before you go back East."

"He's busy, anyway. Interviews. He's in line for some big job in Chicago."

"Oh, another newspaper?"

"No, TV."

He shot a quick look at her. "Well, it's probably for the best."

She shrugged. "We didn't have all that much in common."

There didn't seem to be much to say after that, so they walked on in silence. Finally, they reached the place where Uncle Ira had found Jan Stalker's body. No trace of it remained, of course. Jan was buried in the churchyard, and her killer, John Barnard, was locked up in the county jail, awaiting trial.

Scorch marks still darkened the arroyo wall, burned there fifty odd years ago by an alien spacecraft. Uncle Ira reached up to run his hand along the marks. Then he turned and took something from his backpack. A silvery piece of metal.

"This is what I found. It belongs to the church." Shrugging, he put it in her hand. "I don't believe it belongs to anyone, really. I wanted you to see it out here where I first saw it."

She held the piece of metal wonderingly. It felt light, almost as if when she touched it, it reflected heaviness and gravity. If she threw it up in the air, would it float away? It was flexible, John Barnard had been right about that. When she tried scratching it, it remained pristine and shining. Deep down she knew it had not come from earth.

She was so ashamed. All this time she thought her aunt and uncle were a pair of gullible fools, drawn in by the hoary tale of alien spacecraft landing outside Roswell.

"Can I throw it up in the air?"

"Go ahead. That's what I did, first time I held it."

She looked up at a strip of high cirrus clouds and threw it high. The silvery metal floated light and free, flashing in the sunlight.

Claudius stood and watched intently, straining on the leash. And somehow, she was never quite sure how it happened, the dog broke free, tearing the leash from her grasp. He raced after the piece of metal, which was at last coming down to earth. "Claudius, heel!"

He disappeared over the ridge.

"He'll be back soon," said Uncle Ira. "Don't worry. There's no place to go. There's nothing over that hill but a dry creek bed and miles of more desert."

She nodded, furious with Claudius and with herself for not holding the leash tighter. It was inexcusable. "Sorry."

"What's to be sorry about?" Putting his arm around her, he kissed the top of her head. "The dog's just having a little fun. Now turn around and look at that view. Isn't that something?"

The mountains shimmered like a dream. Waves of heat rose from the valley floor, and the sun beat down. Uncle Ira sighed. "We should have figured out Barnard was the murderer days ago. Remember that red clay in the potting shed?"

"What about it?"

"Old-timers will tell you that the only place you'll find red clay around here is the old graveyard behind the church. As the caretaker, John Barnard was in there a couple of times a week, clipping shrubs, mowing the lawn, and keeping it tidy. Clay's hard to get off. Makes a real mess. Once you get that stuff on your boots, you have a devil of a time cleaning them up."

"Well, it wouldn't have made much difference in the end."

"You're wrong. For one thing, you wouldn't have gone through that ordeal in the desert if we'd realized what the clay meant."

Annie gave him a rueful look. "I wonder why the police didn't pick up on it."

"Gardens and sheds are dirty places, and there wasn't much clay to see, just a small clump or two of dried mud. It didn't stand out. The police were more interested in the scarecrow—they expected to find dirt on the floor. My boots were right there by the bench, muddy as all get out. Dried top soil and compost, though. Not red clay. Still, it's no wonder they missed it."

"True," she agreed.

"Photographs taken at the party showed that John changed his shirt late in the evening. That was a dead giveaway, too. I didn't notice, and neither did your aunt."

But Jan and Elvira had and paid with their lives.

A silence fell after that. Annie and her uncle savored the mountain view and watched a buzzard wheeling high in the sky for a few more minutes. Then Claudius came back, trotting over the ridge. His paws and muzzle were caked with dirt.

A terrible suspicion gripped her heart. "Oh, no! He's buried it somewhere over the ridge! We've got to find it!"

But Uncle Ira held her still as the dog ran up, eyes gleaming with uncanny intelligence, wagging his tail. He caught the leash and wound it around his hand. "That piece of metal cost three lives. Maybe the dog is right. Mankind isn't ready for the stars just yet."

Annie was at a loss for words, but her uncle seemed to have made up his mind that it was all for the best. Just as the events of that July day in 1947 had happened so long ago, almost like a dream, so the piece of silvery metal seemed destined to be part of a myth.

At least for now.

* * *

Four weeks later, all the loose ends had been tied up. Elvira had been buried in the church graveyard after a dignified funeral. Claudius had completed his obedience training, but Pam Hardaway refused to give him a certificate, saying he was a hard case and needed a refresher course.

Enough was enough. Somebody else could pick up the slack as far as Claudius was concerned, Annie thought as she drove away from her uncle's for the last time. Her vacation over, she was going back home to New Hampshire, and Lydia-the-bitch could take him to obedience class for all she cared.

Claudius curled up beside her in the Escort's passenger seat, chewing on a rawhide bone. Every few minutes he got up and stuck his nose out the window and sniffed the air with little snorts of glee. He knew where they were headed.

"That's right, we're going home."

He eyed her, tail wagging. He could hardly wait.

"It may take a few days to find Lydia, but I'll do my damnedest. You miss her. That's the way it should be. She's your master."

His tail thumped.

"She's also a no-good bitch who abandoned you without a second thought. She's a liar and a cheat, but you love her, so that doesn't matter."

His black eyes gleamed excitedly, and he flashed his teeth in a happy smile.

She drove past the alien museum and the dancing chicken sign, turning east on the highway, wondering why she felt hollow inside. Lydia was as trustworthy as a snake. She'd never take him back. Her life was a laundry list of abandoned people, places, things . . . even this damn dog. If he ended up at the pound, no one in his right mind would adopt him. People wanted cute little puppies . . . cocker spaniels, retrievers. Not a huge, black wolflike creature with jaws like a shark and a mind to match. Who ate books and bossed her around.

He'd be put down.

Annie had fallen silent. He swung his head around and stared, his tail stilled.

"What the hell's wrong with you? After what I've been through, three murders and almost getting killed, I have a right to be happy." She glared at him and turned on the radio. "You'll be back with Lydia before you know it, then we'll both be happy."

He eyed her warily. She turned the volume up. As the alien museum and the dancing chicken dwindled in the distance, the plaintive strains of an old Patsy Cline song floated away on the hot desert air.